Touched by

LOVE

The Remingtons

Love in Bloom Series

Melissa Foster

ISBN-13: 9781941480410
ISBN-10: 1941480411

TOUCHED BY LOVE

Cover Design: Elizabeth Mackey Designs

WORLD LITERARY PRESS
PRINTED IN THE UNITED STATES OF AMERICA

A Note to Readers

From the moment I met Janie and Boyd (in my very crowded head), I knew I had to bring their love story to life. I fell hard for both fiercely independent Janie and our huge-hearted hero, Boyd, and I hope you love them, and our Remington world, just as much as I do. If you're a fan of the Remingtons, please note that this book was written two years after the rest of the Remington series. As with all Love in Bloom stories, the Remingtons' lives have been updated in other Love in Bloom books. If you are just starting the series, don't worry, all Love in Bloom books are written to stand alone, so dive right in and enjoy the fun, sexy ride.

Sign up for my newsletter to keep up to date and to receive a free short story.
www.melissafoster.com/NL

About the Love in Bloom Big-Family Romance Collection

The Remingtons is just one of the series in the Love in Bloom big-family romance collection. Each Love in Bloom book is written to be enjoyed as a stand-alone novel or as part of the larger series. There are no cliffhangers and no unresolved issues. Characters from each series make appearances in future books, so you never miss an engagement, wedding, or birth. A complete list of all series titles is included at the end of this book. You might enjoy reading the entire Love in Bloom collection in the order in which they were published. You can find that list here: https://melissafoster.com/LIBPubOrder

Visit the Love in Bloom Reader Goodies page for free first-in-series ebooks, checklists, family trees, and more! www.MelissaFoster.com/RG

Love in Bloom Subseries Order

Snow Sisters – Book 1 FREE

The Bradens – Book 1 FREE

The Remingtons – Book 1 FREE

Seaside Summers – Book 1 FREE

The Ryders

Bayside Summers

Tru Blue & The Whiskeys

Wild Boys After Dark – Book 1 FREE

Bad Boys After Dark

Harborside Nights

For Mel Finefrock, one of the kindest, bravest,
most inspiring women I know

Chapter One

BLAINE'S MOUTH BLAZED a path up her inner thigh. His hot breath teased over her wet flesh. Kenya fisted her hands in the sheets, dug her heels into the mattress, and rocked her hips, aching for his talented tongue in the place she needed him most. Blaine lifted smoldering dark eyes, a hint of wickedness shining through, as his tongue slicked over his lips. He was a master at seduction, but Kenya didn't give a shit about seduction. She wanted to be fucked hard. Now. She needed his—

A large hand landed on Janie Jansen's desk beside her braille device. She nearly jumped out of her skin and nervously yanked out her earbuds. *Holy shit.* She was supposed to be finishing a technical editing assignment, not listening to the latest hot romance audiobook.

"Nice article in the newsletter this week, Jansen. 'The Oxford Comma Revolution.' Catchy." Her boss, Clay Bishop, was slightly less arid than a desert, but Janie didn't mind. He'd hired her to work at Tech Ed Co., or TEC, on a trial basis, and four years later her respect for him had only grown. He was a fair and equitable boss and was currently considering her for a promotion.

It was difficult to spice up a weekly column geared toward

grammar and editing, but Janie tried. It was just one more step toward the promotion of technical writer she'd been vying for, a nice step up from editor.

"You're here late. Trouble with the ARKENS handbook?"

"I'm just catching up on a few things. The handbook is almost done." Well, technically not *almost* done, but she'd meet the deadline. She had yet to miss one. She loved editing, but she hadn't set out to be an editor after college. She'd wanted to be a journalist, but that door had closed and she'd tabled her dream and settled for editing. Usually the intensity of her job didn't get to her, but after weeks of grueling revisions on this particular medical equipment handbook, she'd needed a short mental break. But Clay would never think to take a break. He was all business all the time, even hours after their workday officially ended.

"Perfect. Don't forget, Monday afternoon we have the peer review of your writing sample. If that goes well, your promotion will be in the hands of the management team. I'm not worried—you're always on top of your game."

"Yeah, she is." Boyd Hudson's amused voice brought a smile to Janie's lips.

Boyd consulted at TEC only a few days a month, and though Janie didn't know him well, he was quippy and flirtatious, bringing a spark of amusement into her otherwise quiet days.

"Hudson," Clay said dryly. "Okay, well, it's late, so…"

"See you Monday, Clay." Janie listened to his retreating footsteps and let out a relieved sigh.

"He almost caught you again, didn't he?"

She heard the smirk in Boyd's voice. "He didn't *catch* me last time. I was on my lunch break last week. And besides, I was just studying the nuances of the romance genre.'"

"If by 'study' you mean 'getting swept away in the sexy fantasy life of some fictional, ridiculously unattainable hero,' then yeah, I'd buy that."

"Why do you trash the genre when you know it's my favorite escape?" She began gathering her things to leave for the day.

"Because it's fun. You're too smart to be a cliché, Janie. You know that, right? Girl who's blind whiles away hours of her youth reading romances because her parents are too controlling. Grows up wanting a fictional life that can never exist. Break free from it." His voice rose with excitement. "Let it go. Romance isn't real. It's crap writing about fake people."

She never should have revealed that tidbit about her parents in the break room last month. They'd been talking about their childhoods, and while others had fun stories of hanging out at the mall, or going on spur-of-the-moment outings with groups of friends, Janie had very few spur-of-the-moment anything to share. Her parents worried about every step she made, questioning her safety and whether this or that location would be difficult for her to navigate without them to hold her hand. They'd been a noose around her neck, and it had often been easier to escape into fictional worlds than to battle for the chance to go out.

"And your sci-fi adventures are more real than romance? Ha!" She hefted her bag over her shoulder. "I bet you've never even read a romance."

"Don't need to. It's crap."

"It's not crap. I bet I could write a romance that you'd not only read, but love." Janie turned off her computer and braille device.

"Not unless it's got a heroine who likes sci-fi, is smarter

than me, *and* is into kinky sex."

"God, you're a pig. Fine, sci-fi and kinky sex. It shouldn't be hard to make her smarter than you." She lifted her brows with the tease. "But if I write it, you not only have to read every single page of it, but you also have to go to the Romance Writers Festival with me in October and stay all day. Plus," she added, getting excited about the bet, "you have to buy me every romance book I want for a month."

He placed Janie's cane in her hand. "A little greedy, aren't you?"

"Hey, if I'm writing a whole novel, it's got to be worth it."

"Fine, but I'm not buying you romance books for a month."

"Whatever. Torturing you with the festival for an entire day will be worth it. It's Friday night. What are you doing here so late?" It was after nine o'clock, and a group of people from work had gone down to NightCaps, a local bar where they often hung out.

"Had a busy day before coming here," Boyd answered.

"Are you going to NightCaps, or are you going to *while away the hours* with your nose in outer space?" Janie loved the constant vibration of laughter, hushed whispers, and the hum of sexual tension at NightCaps, but her best friend, Kiki Vernon, was out of town, and she didn't like to go to bars without her. She'd planned to spend a quiet weekend at home, but she assumed Boyd would want to go.

"I've got a date, so I'm pretty sure my nose won't be any-where near space, but I'll walk with you. I'm headed that way anyway. But first, shake on our bet."

"Game on, dude," she said as she shook his hand. "And you're *so* gonna owe me, but I'm not going to NightCaps. I was going to read, but now I think I'll start plotting my romance.

Hm. What should I call it? *Sci-Fi Sexiness?*" She couldn't wait to tell Kiki about the bet. She loved the genre as much as Janie did, and she'd get a kick out of Janie actually trying to write a sexy story.

"That doesn't even sound romantic," Boyd said. "I'm going to win the bet, and when I do, you have to attend Comic-Con with me. You'll make a hot Catwoman."

Janie laughed. "Yeah, that's *so* not going to happen. I'm writing this book and you're going to spend an entire day meeting romance authors and male cover models."

Boyd hooked his arm in hers as she touched the tip of her cane to the ground.

"You know what that cane does to me," he said in a seductively low voice.

"I know what it's going to do *to* you if you don't stop teasing me."

As they left the office, the crisp night air rolled over Janie's skin. The sounds of people walking by, cars moving along the road, and horns honking were familiar and comforting. The smell of exhaust tangled with what Janie had come to know as the dark scents of the city. Tension was thicker at night in New York City, as if everyone was shrouded with awareness. Janie felt that awareness prickling her skin.

"Want me to flag down a cab?" Boyd asked.

"No thanks. I hate riding in cabs here. The drivers petrify me. I like the subway better." She'd ridden in cabs with Kiki when they'd first moved to the city after college, and the constant stopping and starting and traveling alone when someone else was in complete control of her end destination made her feel unsafe. Navigating the city alone presented enough of a challenge. She didn't need to end up in some back alley with a cab-driving killer.

"The subway? To each their own, I guess."

Janie's phone rang as they made their way down the sidewalk.

She stopped to dig it out of her bag. "Sorry. We can keep walking as long as you can guide me. It's a little distracting to use my cane and talk on the phone."

Boyd placed a hand on her arm. "Sneaky way to get me to touch you."

Janie shook her head and answered the phone, immediately greeted by Kiki's excited voice.

"Hey, just wanted you to know that since you blew off coming home with me this weekend, I'm not going to tell you about the date I had last night." Kiki had been her best friend since the third grade, when Kiki had put a boy in his place for teasing Janie about using a specially lighted magnifying device to read large-print books. Not that Janie needed protecting. Even back then she'd known some people were just too self-centered to care about other people's lives. Not Kiki, though. As soon as she'd finished with the bully, she'd wanted to know everything about Janie's eye condition: cone-rod dystrophy, a degenerative eye disease. The disease had varying degrees of severity, from mild to complete loss of vision. So far Janie was lucky. She still had some light perception. If there were very bright lights, large planes of bright colors, or if the contrast was just right and she looked out of her peripheral vision and got up super close, she could still sometimes make out shapes.

"Was it your headboard I heard banging the wall at three in the morning?" She loved teasing Kiki about her sexual proclivities.

"I wish. Anyway, when I come back, we're having a girls'

night for sure," Kiki said. "I need to touch up your roots, so we'll do margaritas and hair dye. A great combination." Ever since they were little, Kiki had insisted on helping Janie with all things girly, which included not only hair and makeup, but also clothing and manicures and anything else Kiki put into the *girls must do* category. Kiki was the only person who had ever *not* been afraid to jump into those personal aspects of Janie's life, and Janie loved her even more for it because Kiki accepted and pushed and made sure that Janie missed out on nothing.

"Last time we did drinks and dye you blonded me out, which is why I *have* roots."

"You're a hot blonde," Kiki said.

"You also said I was a hot brunette. I gotta run. Have fun." She ended the call.

Boyd chuckled and said, "You'd be hot no matter what color your hair was. Careful stepping off the curb."

Janie was used to his flirty comments and knew better than to take them seriously. He doled them out in the office like she dotted her i's and crossed her t's, adding a touch of humor to their otherwise stoic workplace.

"Curb, careful," he said as she stepped back onto the sidewalk.

She liked that he knew enough to warn her to the change in her footing. Not everyone did, which was why she continued to use her cane, especially if guided by someone she didn't know very well. She knew they were nearing the subway and shifted her bag to her other shoulder, dropping her phone in the process.

"I've got it." Boyd stopped to pick it up. "So, you're really going to try to write that novel?"

"Darn right I am." She resituated her cane and bag, and

they continued walking.

"You sure you want to take the subway?" Boyd asked again. "I'll even pay for a cab if you're worried about the money."

"It's not the money. It's the freakishly fast driving and then slamming on the brakes thing that New York cabbies do. I'm fine, really. Have fun on your date. I'll see you the next time you're at TEC."

Janie made her way down the steps to the subway, mentally playing with ideas for her romance story. At twenty-seven, she had only a few sexual experiences to draw from, although they'd never fully lived up to the sexual exploits of the heroes and heroines in the novels she'd read. She also knew absolutely nothing about sci-fi, or for that matter, kinky sex, other than what she'd read about. She might not have experience, but she was a master at research.

The subway platform was eerily quiet. She tried to focus on the bet instead of the fact that every *tap* of her cane echoed in what she assumed was an empty station. She'd boarded trains alone plenty of times, but as much as other people feared strangers, in the subway, she relied on auditory cues from them. Tingles of anxiety prickled through her chest as the heels of her shoes echoed chillingly.

She tapped her way to the bumpy strip along the edge of the platform, which was designed to let people who were visually impaired know they were nearing the edge. Her bag slid down her arm. She twisted sideways, trying to catch it. Her toe caught on a bump, sending her sprawling forward. In the space of a breath, her cane dropped through the air, and suddenly she was falling. Fear gripped her seconds before she landed on her right side with a painful *thud*. She sucked in air as pain spiraled through her. Something sharp dug into her cheek. *Rocks?* The pungent smell of grease and gasoline permeated the cold, dank air, and she realized she'd fallen off the platform.

Her heart thundered in her chest, battling with the blood rushing through her ears as she frantically searched for her cane while listening for a train. Tears streamed from her eyes as fear consumed her. *Get up. Get away from the tracks. Move. Move. Move.* Finding her cane, she clutched it to her aching chest and pushed up to her knees. A blood-curdling pain shot through her ankle. Fighting light-headedness, she clenched her teeth together and forced herself upright, bending her right knee to keep from putting pressure on her ankle. She gripped the cold, hard edge of the platform and tried to pull herself up.

"Help!" Her voice echoed in the empty station, magnifying her fear.

Her ankle rolled on the rocks, sending her tumbling down to the ground again. *Get up. Get up.* Pushing past the pain, she rose again, determined to get to safety. Her fingers moved over the platform's bumpy ridges, which had tripped her up. Her fingertips grazed the smoother concrete just beyond. She used her left, uninjured foot for leverage as she pulled, pushed, and climbed her way onto the platform. Vibrations rumbled beneath her, and the sound of the train squealed in the distance. On the platform, she rolled onto her back, gasping for air and clutching her cane to her chest. The concrete vibrated as the train approached. Sobs wrenched from her lungs, and miraculously, she felt herself smile, because *goddamn it*, she wasn't going to get run over by the stupid train.

BOYD HUDSON RAN a hand through his thick hair as he

descended the steps toward the subway, hurrying at the sound of the approaching train. He'd had a hell of a shift at the firehouse, followed by a few hours at TEC, and his brain must have been too tired to realize he'd walked away with Janie's phone. He stepped onto the empty platform, wondering why it felt like a ghost town. He rounded the stairwell and his heart caught in his throat. Janie lay on her back, treacherously near the edge.

"Don't move!" He raced toward her and knelt between Janie and the edge of the platform, doing a quick visual inspection. She clutched her cane with a white-knuckled grip. She had a nasty gash above her eye. Her cheek was already beginning to bruise. His gut clenched with empathy and anger as he scanned the empty platform.

"Who the hell did this to you?"

"Boyd?" She sat up, and when she opened her mouth to speak, sobs burst out.

Christ, he was ready to kill someone. Boyd gathered her trembling body in his arms. "Try not to move. It's okay, Janie. I've got you. What happened?"

He held her until her breathing calmed, reassuring her and trying to restrain his mounting anger. Once she calmed, he drew back and did another quick visual assessment of her limbs and the angry abrasions on her face.

"I know you're scared, but can you tell me what happened?"

"I tripped and fell off the platform. My ankle..." She tried to lift her knee and sucked in a breath between her clenched teeth. A flood of fresh tears tumbled down her cheeks, and she began searching beside her with her hands.

Off the platform? His gut ached knowing how terrified she must have been. He looked at the steep drop as a train rolled into the station, wondering how in the hell she'd managed to climb back out.

"My bag. Do you see my leather bag anywhere?" She whipped her head around and cried out again when it jerked her ankle.

"Try not to move, Janie. I'll find your bag in a minute. I'm just going to take a look at your ankle. Did you lose consciousness at all?"

"No, please. Don't touch it." She held out her palm, staving him off.

A few people stepped off the train, and Boyd asked one of them to call 911. Luckily, other than a few curious glances, no one stopped to gawk.

"I just wanted to assess your injuries." He reached for Janie's hand. "I'm not going to hurt you. But I really need to take a look. The more you move, the more it will hurt, so if you just let me take a quick look and stabilize your ankle, it'll help."

She squeezed his hand, and more tears came. Boyd embraced her again, careful not to jostle her ankle. The train pulled out of the station, and he glanced over his shoulder again at the drop where she'd fallen.

"It's okay, Janie. I won't let anything happen to you now."

She nodded against his shoulder. "Th-thank you. You smell good."

It took a moment for him to process what she'd said, and relief swept through him. If she could joke, she probably wasn't in too much pain.

"If that's a pickup line, I have to warn you, I'm an expensive date."

When he pulled back enough to study her face and wipe her tears, he was struck, not for the first time, by how beautiful she was, despite the cuts and bruises. He'd been attracted to Janie since the first time he'd seen her. She had delicate, graceful features. A slender, upturned nose, high cheekbones, and almond-shaped eyes. Her brows were darker than her blond hair, and her painted lips were full and small. *Cupid's lips.* He had no idea where *that* thought came from.

"It wasn't a pickup line. It was just an observation." Miraculously, a smile lifted her cheeks. "I'm a romance writer now. I notice those things."

"You do, huh?" Boyd was blown away. She'd just taken a fall that would have sent anyone into a full-on panic, and Janie was joking?

She drew her shoulders back and sniffled, clearly working hard to regain control of her emotions. Her blouse was torn, revealing her bra. Boyd shrugged off his button-down shirt and draped it over her shoulders.

She leaned away. "What are you doing?"

"Your shirt is torn. I'm giving you mine so you're covered up." He helped her put her arms into the sleeves, then rolled them up.

"Thank you for not letting me flash anyone else."

"My pleasure."

"I bet." She scoffed.

"I wasn't look—" As he said it, she smirked. Janie Jansen was very different from the women he knew. They would be in tears, and rightly so, but they'd also add a layer of drama to the already horrible situation by shrieking and gasping for the attention of others just because they could *and* would be worrying about their hair and makeup. "Is there someone I can call for you? Family? A boyfriend?"

She shook her head. "No, but that was a sneaky way to see if

I'm single."

"Hey, *you* used a pickup line, so…" Smart, funny, and beautiful was a rare combination, and Boyd couldn't deny the attraction he'd felt toward Janie for months was growing stronger, but he pushed those feelings away to take a look at her ankle.

"I'm a trained paramedic. Do you hurt anywhere besides your ankle? Your back? Chest? Head?"

She shook her head.

"There must be someone I should call for you."

"I don't need to bother anyone because of a twisted ankle."

His mind turned to his brother and sister. They'd lost their parents when they were young, and if this had happened to either of them, he'd definitely want to be there for them. And he knew they'd want to be there for him. It bothered him that Janie felt she should shoulder this alone. "You're pretty banged up. You really need to be checked out, and since you won't let me check out your ankle, we don't know if it's twisted, sprained, or broken." He wiped a tear from her cheek.

She shook her head. "I'll be fine. Oh, my bag." She tried to push to her feet.

"Janie, don—"

The second she put weight on her foot, she collapsed into his arms.

"I see you're as stubborn as you are beautiful." He helped her back down to the floor.

"Sweet talk will get you nowhere," she quipped through another flinch.

"Just giving you fodder for your romance. Are you okay here for a minute? You won't try to sprint away?"

"Ha-ha."

He held her delicate hand between both of his, glad she was no longer shaking but needing to know she would stay put and not further injure herself. "I want to see if your bag fell off the platform. Please don't try to stand."

She nodded, and he quickly went to the edge of the platform, spotted her bag, and jumped down to retrieve it. He pulled himself up, wondering again how the hell she had pulled herself onto the platform with an ankle she couldn't stand on. He knelt beside her and placed her bag in her lap.

"Somehow your bag fell against the wall and not on the tracks. I'm going to call an ambulance again. They should be here by now."

"An ambulance? I..." Her eyes filled with fresh tears, and he wrapped his arms around her again.

"I'll be right there with you. The ambulance needs to take you to the hospital."

She bit her lower lip and turned away.

"Talk to me, Janie. Does something else hurt?"

"No. Yes. My right side aches, but that's not it. I...I told you that I don't like to ride in vehicles in the city."

He curled a finger beneath her chin and turned her face toward him, again struck by her beauty, her strength, and now this sudden flash of vulnerability.

"I'll go with you. I won't leave your side, but we have to get you checked out."

He called for the ambulance, just in case the person he'd asked hadn't, and tried again to assess her ankle. Each time she moved, she cringed. Finally, she allowed him to take a look. Her ankle didn't appear to be broken. Though he wasn't a doctor, he was on his way—two weeks earlier he had interviewed with the University of Washington School of Medicine, and he was hoping to be invited to interview with at least a few of the other schools he'd applied to.

"I'm going to stabilize your ankle with my hands to keep it from moving."

"Okay."

"How did you manage to get back onto the platform from the tracks?"

"I pulled myself up. I was so afraid a train would come that I just made myself move."

"That's incredible. You're a brave woman, Janie."

She lifted her eyes to him then, as if she could see him, or was mentally assessing his face the way people did when they were weighing whether someone was being honest. Boyd tried not to notice the sparks that look sent through him, but it was impossible.

"I don't know if I'd say I was brave as much as I was driven by not wanting to die a painful death in a New York City subway station."

Her modesty made her even more attractive. The ambulance crew arrived a few minutes later. As they moved her into the ambulance, she gripped the sides of the gurney, and her entire body began trembling again. Boyd climbed into the ambulance and held her hand.

"I'm right here. I won't leave your side."

"I...I hate vehicles here. I'm okay anywhere else, but drivers here petrify me. I know it's weird, but it's my only quirk." She squeezed his hand so tightly her fingernails dug into his skin. "Seriously, other than that I'm totally normal."

She'd just fallen off a subway platform and managed to pull herself to safety, and she was worried he might think she was strange to be scared to ride in an ambulance?

"Well, Janie. You've one-upped me, because I have way more than just one quirk."

"You don't have to stay with me," she said in a shaky voice.

He wondered if she was aware that the death grip she had on his hand was telling him a lot more than her words did.

"Don't you have a date?" she asked with that snarky voice he was quickly learning was her defense mechanism.

"That's a sneaky way to see if I'm single."

"You said you had a date."

"Right. It got canceled." He didn't tell her that his *date* was really his way of not sounding like a loser who was going to go home and study for the medical school interviews he hoped to have. Or that he'd been attracted to her since the first time he'd seen her in the reception area of TEC. But even back then he'd hoped to be heading off to medical school soon, and there was no room in his life for a girlfriend, which was why he kept up the playboy act. More to ward off his own attraction than hers, but every bit helped.

"I do have a date," he answered. "With a sassy blonde at the hospital, and I can't think of anyplace I'd rather be."

Chapter Two

BOYD TALKED TO Janie the whole way to the hospital, and she couldn't have been more thankful. Not only did he have the most soothing voice she'd ever heard, but it was deep and sexy, and every word made her brain turn to mush. He'd even coerced her into letting him take a picture of her so she could laugh about it later. Did he suddenly forget she was blind? She doubted she'd laugh if someone described the picture to her, but he had an easy way about him, and she gave in. He told her a story about when he was little and fell out of a tree and broke his ankle. By the time he finished his story, they'd arrived at the hospital and she'd completely forgotten about her fear of riding in the ambulance.

Things moved quickly after that. If it weren't for Boyd narrating everything going on around her, she'd have been even more frightened. *You're in triage so they can assess your injuries. The emergency room isn't too crowded.* The hospital staff addressed Boyd by name.

"How do they all know you?" she asked.

"I was a paramedic, moved up to firefighter. I still work part-time as a paramedic here at the hospital. Just a shift every now and then," he explained, then went right back to explaining what was going on, like he hadn't just thrown her for a loop. "They're taking you back into a private room now."

He held her hand as they wheeled her toward the private room. He was a fireman, a paramedic, *and* worked at TEC? She'd had him pegged as a bit of a flirtatious slacker, since he only worked at TEC a few days each month.

A nurse tended to Janie's cuts and Dr. Blankenship, *Dr. B*, checked her out and explained that they were going to take X-rays.

Boyd brushed her hair off her forehead and leaned in so close it was impossible not to notice his now familiar musky, manly scent. "You're okay. I'll be right here when you come back."

True to his promise, Boyd was waiting for her when they brought her back into the room a while later.

"Doing okay?" he asked.

She nodded, although her heart was going crazy from everything she'd been through. The room was so bright, she wished she could bring her face right up to Boyd's and find that perfect angle where she could make out his coloring, or the shape of his head. Something to get a better sense of him. But she was getting carried away. She shouldn't be fantasizing that sexy-sounding Boyd Hudson could be anything more than a coworker helping her through a hard time.

"I don't want to be a burden. You really can leave." She hoped he wouldn't, but surely he had better things to do than hang around a hospital on a Friday night.

He squeezed her hand. "No chance. But don't worry. I'm only staying out of some sort of sick curiosity. I want to know what happened to your ankle."

Disappointment washed through her, despite the lightness

of his tone.

He leaned in, warming the air and sending a ripple of awareness through her. "I'm kidding. I want to be here."

A relieved sigh escaped before she could stop it. Luckily, he either pretended not to notice, or was kind enough to let it go.

"Want me to tell you about the lovely curtained-off room we're in?"

She wanted him to talk all night. She would have been scared shitless without him there, and not just because she couldn't see. She'd fallen off a frigging subway platform! She could have been struck by a train and killed. Her ankle was injured, and she was being helped by a handful of strangers. All of that was unsettling, but even though she didn't know Boyd well, just having someone with her whom she was at least familiar with helped ease her fears. But she didn't need a pity party, and she didn't want him to think she was some sort of damsel in distress.

Look at that. I'm already thinking like a romance writer.

"Boyd, why *are* you staying? I might be blind, but I'm perfectly self-sufficient." She confidently lifted her chin. "Well, other than falling off the stupid platform, but that was hardly my fault. I tripped."

"Is that why you think I'm staying? Out of pity?"

The hurt in his voice brought a lump of guilt to her throat. "I don't know."

The mattress sank with his weight as he sat beside her, sending another jolt of adrenaline through her.

"Will it bother you if I sit here? I had a long shift at the firehouse before working at TEC this afternoon and I'm beat."

"No, it's fine. But that's even more of a reason for you to go home and get some sleep."

"Janie, I am most definitely *not* staying out of pity." He stroked his thumb over her hand, and it felt intimate and somehow made his words seem even more sincere. "You won't let me call anyone for you. You just had a traumatic fall that would send the strongest of men into a tailspin, and you said you don't like to ride in cars in the city. How will you get home once they dress your ankle?"

She hadn't thought that far ahead. Maybe she should call Kiki after all, but it would take Kiki hours to get back from Maryland. Kiki rented the apartment next door to Janie, and they were at each other's apartments so much they probably should be roommates. But they each valued their privacy too much for that.

Before she could answer, the doctor's voice pulled her back to the present.

"Hi, again. Janie, it's Dr. B and nurse Kelly. I've got your X-ray results."

"Thanks, Doc," Boyd said. "Hi, Kelly. How are you?"

Janie felt the mattress shift and assumed Boyd was standing to greet them, but he remained beside her, one hand still on hers, comforting her.

"Great, Boyd," the nurse said. "You're not on duty, are you?"

"No. I was returning Janie's phone and found her after she'd battled the tracks. Figured it was destiny."

Janie's jaw slackened with his declaration.

"She's lucky you found her," Dr. B said.

"She sure was," Kelly said. "Janie, Boyd is the best. Not only a great paramedic and fireman, but he's also one of the good guys."

"Great, Kelly, you blew my cover," Boyd teased. "I was

trying to convince her that I was a jerk."

Yeah, right.

"Like you could convince anyone of that." Kelly patted Janie's shoulder. "He's a sweetie. He hates it when I say that, though, because you know guys. They love to be called rough or rugged. But Boyd's sweet as chocolate."

"Great," Boyd mumbled.

Janie laughed.

"Okay, now that we've reduced Boyd's masculinity to *sweet*," Dr. B said with a chuckle, "let's focus on our patient. Janie, it looks like you have a sprained ankle."

"I think the toe of my shoe caught on the bumps near the edge of the platform and my ankle twisted and tripped me up."

"Well, you're a lucky young lady," Dr. B said. "A fall like that could have been far worse. Your sprain is mild, and probably more from that twist you described than from the fall. But since you landed heavily on your right side, you'll probably be bruised and sore for a while."

She'd expected as much, but ever since Boyd had asked her about how she was going to get home, she'd worried about a lot of other things. Like how she'd get around in her apartment and to and from work if she couldn't walk.

"How long will it be before I can walk on it?" she asked.

"Well, that's hard to say," the doctor said. "It's a mild sprain, and it should take only a day or two for the swelling to go down, but you'll need to stay off of it during that time, until your ankle can bear partial weight. Boyd is familiar with the treatment—"

Boyd gave her hand another reassuring squeeze.

"You'll follow what we call the 'rice' method," Dr. B explained. "Rest, ice, compression, and elevate. Rest your ankle.

Ice it a few times over the course of the next day or so to keep down the swelling. Compression helps control swelling and stabilizes your ankle to reduce the chance of further injury. We've got a brace for that, and while you're off your feet, elevate your foot."

"So, are you talking days? Weeks?" Her pulse quickened with the realization that she might not be able to walk for a while.

"Every injury is different, but yours is mild, so probably not long. You should be able to bear partial weight within a week. But like I said, it's hard to tell for sure, and if you're not careful, it could take as long as four to six weeks before you're fully recovered."

"Four to six weeks?" She fisted her hands in the sheets. "I'll have to learn to use a crutch and my cane. How will I get around until I can use crutches?"

"I'll help you," Boyd offered with that sincere, sexy tone of his that made her stomach flutter and her brain turn to mush.

She couldn't afford to have mush brain at the moment. Her independence was on the line. "That's nice of you, but I'm serious."

"So am I," Boyd said.

"Dr. B, what are my options?" She felt the energy in the room shift, the space between her and Boyd growing slightly colder. She was surprised at the flash of sadness she felt, but she pushed it away to focus on the doctor's answer.

"The options are a bit limited from a mobility standpoint. Once the swelling is down and you can stand putting a little weight on your ankle, wearing the brace, of course, you can try a walker in your home and a crutch with your cane outside. I would want you to practice using the crutch in your home first, so you don't fall and further injure yourself. But until the swelling is down, over the next forty-eight hours, I suggest a wheelchair for getting around outside so there's no chance of pressure on your ankle. I realize this is going to be an inconvenience—"

As Dr. B explained about inconveniences and risks associated with walking too early on a sprained ankle, Janie fought back tears. She'd spent her life becoming independent, and she'd done a damn good job of it. Now she had to rely on someone else to push her around in a *wheelchair*? She tried to listen to the instructions for the brace they were fitting around her ankle, but her mind was a million miles away.

"Janie? Honey? Are you all right?"

The worry in Boyd's voice pulled her back to the moment, and the endearment he used took her by surprise. It sounded so natural. He brushed her tears away with the pad of his thumb, another intimate gesture.

"Yeah," she managed, but the tears continued to fall.

"You zoned out for a few minutes. Dr. B and Kelly have gone. It's just you and me, and I can't sit by and watch you cry. So I'm going to hold you, but not if you don't want m—"

She reached for him before he even finished speaking.

"I'm sorry this happened to you." He stroked her back as she cried.

She clutched the back of his shirt as she soaked the front with her tears. "I'm not a crier," she said vehemently between sobs.

"I know. Anyone can see that these tears are just frustration and not weakness."

Despite herself, she smiled against his soft T-shirt. "Why are you so nice to me? You don't even know me."

He drew away, and her arms slid from his back to his firm biceps. She sensed him studying her face. His finger moved over her cheek as he tucked her hair behind her ear. She'd never longed to see a man's face before, but more than anything she wished she could see Boyd's. His thoughtful tone made her wonder about his expression and what he saw when he looked at her. Did he see only a blind, injured girl? Or did he see, as she hoped he might, the woman he'd been getting to know? The woman who wasn't as weak as she felt in that moment.

"I know you're a really nice, beautiful, and fiercely independent person who took a hell of a fall and now needs a little help. And I know I'm a guy with a few days off and not much else on my plate besides the desire to get to know you better."

Did guys really talk like that? "You sound like you walked out of one of my romance novels, which means you're a real smooth talker. I'm blind. Not dumb. How do I know you're not just trying to get laid?"

He laughed. "Did you *seriously* just ask me that?"

She swiped at her tears and gave him what she hoped was a *damn right I did* look.

"Number one, no, I'm not trying to get laid. There are easier ways to do that. Number two, I have a sister, and she's had it pretty rough with the guys in her life, so I know how *not* to treat a woman. And three, I still can't believe you asked me that. What if I was a liar and getting laid *was* my goal? Do you think I'd tell you?"

BOYD'S PULSE RACED as he waited for Janie to say something. Anything. Her brow furrowed, as if she were weighing his answer.

Her right hand slid from his arm to his chest. "May I touch you?" she asked, completely ignoring his question.

"Janie." He pressed his hand over hers, keeping it against his chest. What was it about her that made him want to see her smile and take away all her worries?

"Of course you can touch me. But if your goal is to get laid, I'm not an easy mark. I like to get to know the women I sleep with. A little wining and dining is always nice, and maybe you could bring me flowers."

She playfully swatted him and, finally, her lips curved up in a smile. Boy did he love her smile.

"I just want to see what you look like," she explained.

"Go ahead, honey. Touch me, but don't get too frisky. I'm not sure Dr. B would like that."

"Oh, I think Dr. B *would* like it, actually. At least the doctors in the story I'm going to write would." Her hands moved over his chest. "Your heart is beating fast. Are you nervous?"

"A little." Boyd tried not to focus on how gentle her touch was, or the way she licked her lips as her fingers trailed over his pecs. But it was impossible to ignore the way he felt when she wasn't making witty remarks, but concentrating so hard he could practically see her creating a mental image of his body.

What was she thinking as her hands moved up the thick column of his neck and lingered over his Adam's apple? Her luscious lips were barely parted, and as her fingers climbed over the underside of his jaw, across his unshaven cheeks, she swallowed hard. Was that a good sign? Could she feel how attracted to her he was? As her fingers grazed his cheekbones and slid up beside his eyes, could she sense that he wanted to tell her he wasn't anything like most guys? That he was good, and honest, and that he lived his life in an honorable way? If she could see him, would she have seen that in his eyes? He kept those things about himself private, opting to give off a not-interested vibe, but with Janie he was pretty sure she'd have seen right through that.

She exhaled loudly as she touched his dark brows.

"May I..." She licked her lips again, pausing just long enough to cause a stir low in his gut. "I want to touch your hair."

"Yes. Anything." He sounded breathless, unrecognizable to himself. *Jesus.* What was she doing to him?

She pushed her fingers through the short cropped sides of his hair, then into the long, tousled top that he'd barely had time to towel dry that morning before the alarm sounded at the firehouse and they'd raced out to a fire.

When she moved her fingers from his hair, she was trembling, and so was he. Her touch left him aching for more of her. Not just in a physical way, but to know what made her so strong that she could face this crazy city on her own instead of living in a quiet town where subways and crowds weren't part of the equation. He watched her gaze drop, and he wondered how all that internal strength could be wrapped up in such delicate beauty.

She sighed. "Yes."

"Yes?" Had he missed something? Spoken without knowing it?

"I think if getting laid was your only goal you'd tell me." She lifted her gaze, and though he knew she couldn't see him, he swore she could not only see his physical being, but right through to his soul.

He cleared his throat, trying to get his brain to cooperate

and his body to settle down. "You can tell all that from touching me? You must have Spidey senses."

"My senses are the same as yours, but you use sight before everything else. I use my hearing first, sometimes my sense of smell. You can tell a lot about a person without ever seeing them." She said this all as a matter of fact, but when she continued speaking, her tone became warmer, more intense. "Touching you was more for me to get a sense of your physical being than to determine if I could trust you. I wouldn't have left work with you if I didn't trust you."

"How did you know you could trust me? We've only spoken in passing." He really wanted to know. He assessed people by what he saw in their eyes, how they carried themselves. But Janie couldn't see any of that.

"I can't explain it. The few times we'd talked at the office you were always nice. Flirty, but never inappropriate. And when you found me at the subway, it was everything you said and did." She fidgeted with the seam of her pants.

Boyd wasn't very good at keeping secrets from people he cared about, and he wanted to be honest with Janie. "I didn't really have a date tonight," he confessed.

"Oh. Maybe I shouldn't trust you. Why did you tell me you did? So you wouldn't have to go to the bar if I was going?" She drew back, and he gave her that space willingly, feeling like a heel for lying to her, even though it wasn't meant maliciously.

"No. Definitely not. You're gorgeous, and sweet, and smart, and a wiseass, but hey, I happen to like that. I was embarrassed that it was Friday night and I was going home to read."

"Seriously? That's what I had planned before we made our bet. So does that make me a loser?"

He smiled and couldn't resist touching her cheek, because

when he did, she smiled, and he wanted to see that smile awfully bad.

"Not at all. It makes you even more attractive. There's something else."

"Oh great, you're gay, and now you want me to write a gay romance?"

"If only it were that easy. No." He drew in a deep breath and let the truth flow. "I'd be lying if I said I wasn't attracted to you. So if that's a problem, you should probably tell me now."

"Do you want to change your earlier answer about your goal?"

A laugh slipped out before he could stop it. "No. I can assure you that getting laid is never a goal of mine."

"Oh." Her smile faded and her lower lip came out in that impressively sexy pout women probably practiced to perfection. "There goes my idea of making you a romance hero in my book."

"Really? Romance heroes' goals are to get laid? That seems pretty shallow. I told you those books were crap. I'm going to introduce you to real writing."

"Um, no thanks to the sci-fi. And sex isn't their only goal, but it's on their mind when they're with the women they're attracted to."

He scrubbed a hand down his face, completely baffled. "Is this a test? Because I feel like I'm failing miserably."

"No test," she said with a slight lift of her chin. "Just sharing information. Can you please hand me my cane?"

He handed her the cane, wondering what he'd said that made her go from teasing to serious so quickly. Did she think it was okay if he was having sexual thoughts about her? Was she disappointed that he hadn't admitted to them?

Kelly pushed a wheelchair through the curtains. "All right, Janie. Your ride has arrived, and I assume you'll have Boyd as your chauffer tonight?"

Janie barely stifled a groan. "I have to leave in a *wheelchair*?"

"Come on. It'll be fun," Boyd urged. "Besides, it's either that or a piggyback."

"Damn," Kelly said. "I'd take that offer. Strong man like Boyd?" She waggled her eyebrows and handed him Janie's discharge papers.

"Okay, okay. Enough, Kel. Janie, I'll put your discharge papers in your bag."

"Believe it or not," Janie said, "I'd much prefer the piggyback to the wheelchair."

"If we didn't have rules about those things, I'd help you mount him, but…" Kelly's blue eyes lit up with the innuendo.

"Christ, Kel. Get outta here, will you?"

"Aw, sugar. Did I embarrass you?" She bumped him with her shoulder. "You should be proud, but you're such a prude. See, Janie? Sweet 'n' sexy. Great combo."

"Get outta here, will you?" Boyd gave Kelly a friendly shove through the curtains, glad to see Janie smiling again. "Christ, you'd think she was a dating service."

Janie shifted to the edge of the bed. "She really likes you."

"I've worked part-time at the hospital for years. She's a good friend and an excellent nurse, when she's not giving me a hard time." He sat beside Janie and took her hand again. He liked holding her hand. After months of fighting his feelings for her, he was finding it hard to keep his distance.

"Janie, I'm a nice guy. I want to help you get home safely, but if it makes you uncomfortable, I can call my buddy Cash, and I'm sure his wife would be happy to come by and take you home."

Frustration crossed her face and filled her voice. "Do you have any idea how much it sucks to have to rely on someone else to get to my apartment? Any idea how long and hard I worked to be able to navigate this city alone?"

"I can only imagine, which is why I don't want to be another thing that makes you uncomfortable. Do you want me to call Cash?"

She was quiet for a long moment. Boyd hoped to hell she wouldn't send him packing.

"No. There's no need to bother your friend or his wife. Besides, Kelly saw me with you. If I end up dead, she'll know you were the last one with me."

"Wow, you're a real confidence builder."

"I'm kidding. I'm just frustrated by all of this. If you sprain your ankle, you whip out crutches and go about your life. It's a little more complicated for me."

"I know. I get it, and I'm sorry. But let's make the best of it. Want to lean on me to get into the chair, or do you want me to lift you into it?"

"Can you please lift me? My balance will be off without using my foot."

He wrapped one arm behind her back and the other beneath her knees, lifting her easily into his arms. Her arms circled his neck, and he saw her struggling not to smile.

"It's a good thing you can't see me right now," he said, "because I'm grinning like a fool."

"You are brutally honest, aren't you?" She ran her fingers down his arm, sending waves of heat through him. "And strong."

"Honest, yeah. Strong?" He shrugged as he placed her carefully in the wheelchair. He helped her lift the footplate and situate her ankle. Then he knelt beside her and held her hand again. "Close your eyes."

"Kinda silly, don't you think?" she asked.

"Just do it for me, please? Even if it's silly."

She sighed, but the edges of her lips curved up. "No one ever asks me to close my eyes."

"You're obviously not hanging out with the right people." The bruise on her cheek sent a shock of pain to his chest, heightening his desire to help her feel more comfortable. "Closing your eyes is like letting everything else go. Even if you can't see when they're open, doesn't it feel like you're blocking things out more purposely?"

"I swear Kiki must have hired you to watch over me this weekend, right? Because only she would have the guts to say something like that to me."

"Kiki?"

"My best friend since third grade. She's the one who called earlier. We live next door to each other."

"I like her already. Okay, ready?" When she nodded, eyes still closed, he said, "Imagine this chair is your chariot. You're a queen, and I'm a fat, sloppy guy you can boss around."

She laughed. "Do you have to be sloppy? Can't I picture you the way you are and still boss you around?"

"Well, yeah. But I didn't want to distract you from your chariot ride."

"I like the distraction," she said.

Good to know. "Then you'll love how I keep you distracted during the cab ride home."

Her mouth dropped open and embarrassment flushed her cheeks.

"Do all romance writers have dirty minds?" he teased. "Because I meant by talking to you."

"I wasn't...I..."

He chuckled, folded her cane, and set it in her lap. "Do you want to hold your bag or would you like me to carry it?"

She reached a hand up for the bag. "You're a brat." She put her cane inside the bag.

"Hey, at least I took your mind off of the cab ride."

As he pushed the wheelchair toward the exit, she said, "I really don't want to ride in a cab."

He settled his hand on her shoulder, and when they reached the exit, he knelt beside her again, struck by the worry lines that had formed on her forehead.

"I was kidding, Janie. I'm not going to try anything."

"I know that. I just..." She clutched her bag tighter. "I wasn't kidding about the cabs here making me *really* uncomfortable."

He pulled out his cell phone. "You know what? They make me uncomfortable, too. Hang tight. Let me see what I can arrange." Boyd made a few calls, and after pulling a few strings, he arranged to borrow the wheelchair for forty-eight hours.

Chapter Three

BOYD PUSHED THE wheelchair through the hospital doors and kept on going.

"Please tell me we're not stealing the wheelchair." Janie white-knuckled the arms of the wheelchair.

"Shh. Don't tell anyone."

"*Ohmygoodness.*"

"I'm kidding. I got permission to borrow it. Give me directions to your place and we'll be all set."

"What if I live twenty blocks away?"

"Then it's a good thing I'm in shape."

She'd felt his muscular chest and arms and knew he could probably push the wheelchair for miles.

"I'm just a few minutes from here." She gave him her address.

"You live that close? I really could have given you a piggyback."

"Yup. Thank you for making arrangements to borrow the wheelchair. I can't believe you did that."

"No worries. Are you warm enough?"

It was a chilly evening, and she realized she still had on Boyd's shirt. She casually lifted her arm to her nose and breathed in his masculine scent, hoping he wouldn't notice.

"I'm warm enough," she answered. "Are you?"

"I'm fine, thanks for asking. But you're the injured one, remember?"

"Yes, but you make me forget I'm hurt. I feel like we're breaking the rules, and I never break rules." She liked the feeling more than she probably should. "Kiki will be so happy."

"Your friend likes to break rules?" Each time Boyd came to a bump in the sidewalk, he slowed and carefully maneuvered over it.

"She just skates around them sometimes. Oh gosh, my phone. I need to text her, actually."

"I've got it right here. Just think, if it weren't for your phone, you wouldn't have the best chauffeur around tonight."

"Thank you for taking the time to bring it back. It was my lucky night."

"Honey, I hate to say this when you've had such a terrible fall, but I think tonight was my lucky night, not yours."

Excitement tiptoed through her. He'd called her *honey* again. She swore he said it like he'd been calling her that forever. She wondered if he called all women *honey*, but then again, he said he and Kelly had known each other for years, and he didn't call her *honey*. That made her feel sort of special.

She really needed to stop qualifying the things he did, but she was drawn to him more and more with every minute they spent together.

"I should probably listen to my messages first, in case Kiki called." She dug in her bag for her earbuds, but came up empty. She held up her phone and said, "I hope it won't bother you if I use the voice program to listen to my messages and to send texts. I have earbuds, but they must have gotten lost when I fell."

He stopped the wheelchair and touched her shoulder again. "I think you left them at your desk."

"No, I keep some at the office, too. But it doesn't matter. I can get more."

"Why don't I give you privacy? I'll walk a few feet away while you check your messages."

"You don't have to, but thank you." She turned the volume down on the phone as he walked away, and checked her messages.

Hey, Janie, where are you? I'm home, and Sinny's already a big pain. She heard Kiki's older brother Sinclair's voice cut Kiki off. *Yup! Miss you, baby girl! When you're free, give me a ring. We'll catch up.* She heard them wrestling for the phone. Kiki's laughter filled the airwaves and then suddenly burst loudly through the phone. *Text me, and pleeease tell me you're not answering your phone because you've met a hot guy.*

She heard Boyd pacing—*Speak of the devil*—and quickly texted Kiki.

I had a little fall. Sprained my ankle, but I'm in good hands. I'll call you tomorrow. She shoved her phone in her purse and listened to Boyd, who must have been on the phone.

"Hi, Haylie." He paused. "Good. And my little buddy? I miss you guys."

Haylie? Little buddy?

"What guy? What does he do for a living?" He paused again. Janie couldn't even pretend not to listen. He sounded annoyed. "Uh-huh. Have Chet meet him." He paused again. "Fine. Okay, love you. Bye."

She heard his footsteps approaching and dug around in her bag, pretending to look for something. Boyd touched her shoulder again.

"Everything cool? Did you reach Kiki?"

"I texted her." She tried to figure out who he might refer to as his *little buddy*, but the only answer she came up with was a son.

"I know it's late and you've had a rough night, but there's a café on the way to your place where we can grab some hot chocolate if you'd like."

"I'm in a wheelchair," she said sarcastically. She tried to put together the image of a married man and the flirtatious Boyd she knew from work but couldn't reconcile the two. Besides, if he was married, why would he want to go anywhere with her? She wasn't exactly a quick hookup, and he'd said he wasn't that type of guy anyway, but still. He said he *loved* someone.

"Oh, right. People in wheelchairs can't have hot chocolate," he teased as he started pushing her along the sidewalk again. "I really need to review the wheelchair rules."

"It's a little embarrassing." She felt stupid saying it aloud, but she hated not being independent, and he took it all in stride.

"Hey, you don't have to be so harsh," he said teasingly. "I might have come off a long day's work, but I don't look *that* bad."

She laughed, realizing she'd laughed more in the last few hours than she had in the last week, despite the fact that she'd had an awful accident and had ridden in an ambulance. It should have been her worst night ever. Only it wasn't. The fall was awful, and the injury sucked, but being with Boyd wasn't horrible at all. He'd made her feel like everything was going to be okay from the moment he'd knelt beside her. And now he was asking her out for hot chocolate?

But…he loved someone. Someone with a *little buddy*.

"It's okay if it's too late," he offered. "Or if you're too tired."

"Boyd, before I answer…Are you married?"

"Married?" He sounded exasperated.

"I heard you on the phone. I didn't mean to eavesdrop—"

He touched her arm again, gently, without any tension, which put her at ease. If he were a scumbag, surely she'd feel some kind of tension in his touch.

"Janie, I'm not married. I was talking to my sister, Haylie. She's a single mom, and I worry about her and my three-year-old nephew, Scotty. We touch base every week."

"Your sister? I'm sorry. I feel so stupid. I thought…"

"You thought I was a douche bag cheater? I get it. You don't know me well enough to realize that I am anything but that kind of guy. One day I hope you will."

He began pushing the wheelchair again. "What do you say? Want to grab that hot chocolate, or are you too tired?"

"Even though I just totally misjudged you?" He wasn't even offended?

"I don't blame you. We live in a crazy world. You've got to be careful. So, what do you say?"

"I'd like that, but only if you're sure you don't mind. I feel like I've taken up enough of your time already."

"Honey, you haven't taken up nearly enough of my time."

"I'M GOING TO tilt the front wheels up to get your chariot into the café, so hold on." Boyd angled the wheelchair, causing Janie to lean back.

"Every guy in the place is checking you out," he whispered in her ear. "I might get a little possessive."

She laughed as he pushed the wheelchair over the threshold.

"All right, let's see. There are a few couples sitting whispering and talking, but the guys keep checking you out, so the women are probably going to give you the stink-eye in a minute. Maybe we should have had the doc put a few stitches in your face to make you a little less attractive."

Janie knew she was grinning like a fool, but she couldn't stop. Boyd had a way of making her discomfort disappear, and the relief that came with that was immense.

"Kiki will definitely love you," she said as Boyd brought the wheelchair to a stop.

"Yeah? Why?" He pulled out a chair, and Janie heard him moving it closer to her.

"Because you don't focus on my disability."

"Holy shit. You have a disability?"

"Ohmygod. Boyd, you're really too much." She shook her head.

"Why would I focus on the fact that you can't see? There's plenty of stuff I can't do, and I don't think I'd want you focusing on those things."

"Name one," she challenged.

"Well, you're great at editing, and it sounds like you think you'll be great at writing, which I don't doubt, but I can't write creatively at all. I seriously suck at it."

"That's not the same, and how do you consult at TEC if you can't write?"

"I consult on the viability of the descriptions used in certain types of manuals, mostly medical. Technically, I'm fine, but creatively? Nope. Not for me. And now that I'm hanging out with you, I realize that there are two more things I can't do: read braille or use a cane without whacking someone in the knees. I also can't play tennis worth shit, and I'm not very good at relationships."

"Really? You suck at a lot of things." She laughed softly. "I'm kidding, but I can't believe you're bad at relationships. You're so warm and friendly, but even if you aren't great at relationships, that's not the same as being blind."

"I know it's not, but I do understand what you mean. Some people's disabilities are worn on the inside."

The sadness in his voice tugged at her heart, making her wonder what he wasn't telling her. Just as quickly as that sadness appeared, his tone became happy again.

"I hope you don't mind that I'm not sitting across from you. It's too far away with all these dudes around. I moved my chair next to you so I can do this." He covered her hand with his. "Okay?"

"Um…" *Yes? No?* She had no idea if it was okay or not to let him hold her hand now that the whirlwind of events surrounding her accident had passed, but she really liked him. So many people acted weird around her because she was blind. They spoke loudly, as if she were hearing impaired, or they didn't speak to her at all, and gave her a wide berth that she could sense rather than see, making her feel like an outcast. Boyd treated her like she imagined he'd treat anyone, only he definitely seemed interested in her. But then again, he'd already confessed that.

He moved his hand away, and she fought the urge to reach for it again. He made it so easy to like him. Where was the guy who seemed wrapped up in flirting and dated a different girl every month? The flirt was still there, but he was awfully attentive for a guy who she'd assumed didn't have a serious bone in his body.

"Sorry, that was the Neanderthal in me," he said. "Funny, I've never been a jealous guy, but here I've only just gotten to know you and it bothers me to see these guys checking you out."

"I'm sure you're reading them wrong. They're probably wondering how bad of a driver you are to have left me blind and casted."

"You are a smart-ass, aren't you?" He leaned in close again. She loved when he did that, like his words were meant only for her ears. "I'm going to walk up to the counter and get our hot chocolate while you figure out how to accept a compliment."

Ouch. Her phone rang with Kiki's ringtone, and she dug it out of her purse as Boyd went for their drinks.

"Hi."

"I'm gone for a few hours and you sprain your ankle? What the heck, Janie? Are you okay? Do you want me to come home? How did you get to the doctor? Oh God, did you have to take a cab? I'm coming home." Kiki spoke so fast Janie couldn't get a word in until she finally stopped to take a breath.

"Calm down. I'm fine." She rubbed her sore hip. "Well, for the most part."

"Spill it, Janie. I'm a nervous wreck over here."

"The toe of my shoe got caught and I twisted my ankle and fell"—a spear of pain sliced through her with the memory—"off the subway platform."

"Ohmygod," Kiki said in a painful whisper. "Off the platform? What the fuck? I'm sorry but...what the *fuck*? Janie, are you sure you're okay? I knew I should have made you come home with me. You must have been so scared. How did that happen? You've been taking the subway for years."

Tears filled Janie's eyes. Not from the memory of the fall, but from the sound of Kiki blaming herself and sniffling through tears on the other end of the phone. She swallowed hard, willing the tears away. That's all she needed, to cry in the middle of the café.

"It was a fluke. There was no one around, and I must have been distracted. I made a bet with this guy from work that I could write a romance novel, and I was thinking about that one second, and then I realized I was alone and I got nervous. My bag slid down my arm and I lost my balance. I tripped and fell ass over teakettle. But I'm okay, Kiki. I got lucky. Boyd came back to return my phone, and he rode with me in the ambulance, stayed with me in the hospital—"

"I hate that I'm in Maryland," Kiki interrupted, and Janie had a feeling she hadn't taken in what she'd said. "Are you home? Did you do okay in the ambulance?"

"Surprisingly, yes, I did okay. Boyd has been wonderful. He—"

"Boyd?"

"The guy who helped me. He totally distracted me in the ambulance, and he's like you, Kiki. He lets me know what's going on without making me feel like a burden."

"That's great. We'll send him a big thank-you when I get back, but where are you now?"

"I'm actually out at a café with him."

"With *Boyd?*" The surprise in Kiki's voice told Janie her best friend's protective claws were coming out.

"Yes."

"Can I talk to him?"

"Kiki…" She knew this wasn't a battle she'd win, because

Kiki would always be her protector, no matter how much Janie might try to deny her that right. At least she didn't smother her like her parents used to. Kiki picked and chose her protective moments.

"How do you know he is who he says he is?"

"He consults at my office, and the people at the hospital knew him. I like him. He's nice."

"Ohmygod," Kiki said, exasperated. "A strange guy is bringing you to your apartment and you're not worried? *Please* can I talk to him?"

"You go to strange guys' apartments all the time," she reminded her.

"Not without texting you their name, address, and phone number first!"

She had a point. Kiki might sleep with plenty of guys, but she always put safety first.

Boyd's hand landed on Janie's shoulder, and he whispered, "The cup is hot." She heard him sit beside her. He took her hand and guided it to the cup.

"Thank you," Janie said, loving the way he knew to show her where the cup was so she didn't spill hot chocolate all over herself.

"Is that him?" Kiki asked.

"Uh-huh."

"Please put him on the phone."

Janie sighed. "Boyd, my overprotective best friend would like to harass you."

"Cool," he said eagerly. Their fingers brushed as he took the phone, sending an electric current straight to her core.

"I'm sorry," Janie whispered. Boyd squeezed Janie's hand reassuringly and leaned in closer with the phone between them, so she could hear their conversation.

"I'm not," Kiki said in his ear.

"Hi. This is Boyd Hudson."

"Hi. This is Janie's friend Kiki. Thank you for helping her tonight."

"No worries. Janie's doing great, and it's my pleasure to help her."

"That's great," Kiki said sarcastically. "Tell me, *Boyd*, where do you live? And you need to know that even though I'm not there, if you do anything to hurt her, I'll sic my brother Sin on you."

He cleared his throat, masking a chuckle. "Really, that won't be necessary." He told her which firehouse he was with and gave her his home address, his phone number, and his chief's phone number, too.

Janie was mortified, but once again Boyd acted like this happened every day, as if answering Kiki's questions were no big deal. Kiki asked him a few more annoyingly intimate questions, and then she said, "Great. I'm going to Google you and call your firehouse. If you're not who you say you are, a policeman will be at her apartment when you get there."

"Kiki!" Janie snapped. She took the phone from Boyd's hands. "Okay, enough. I want to enjoy my hot chocolate. I'm fine. I promise."

"He does sound nice," Kiki said. "But I'm still checking him out."

"Would you stop? I love you, but I'm really fine, and I'm going to hang up now because you sound a little too much like my mother."

"I can't believe I'm not there. Just be careful. Love you."

Janie ended the call and exhaled loudly. "I'm sorry."

"Stop apologizing. She sounds like a great friend. And she's right to worry. We're in a big city with lots of crime, and we don't know each other that well. How about tomorrow I take you over to the firehouse to meet the guys I work with?"

"You want to see me tomorrow?" Her pulse quickened.

"Yes, I do. What do you say? You'll get out in the smoggy air for a nice chariot ride, and I'll get to show you that I am who I say I am."

"I believe you are who you say you are, and you must have something better to do than hanging out with me."

"Why don't you pretend like you believe me when I say we haven't spent enough time together yet, and go with it? What's the worst that can happen? You'll meet a bunch of great guys and spend the afternoon with me. What could be better?"

"You're doing that thing you do, where you make everything feel like it's going to be okay."

He took her hand in his and leaned in closer, bringing a heat wave that made her head spin.

"Honey, you're doing that thing you do, when you make me remember how much better than *okay* things can be."

Chapter Four

AS BOYD CLOSED Janie's apartment door behind them, she felt her tension fall away. She always breathed a little easier at home, and tonight that relief was magnified. It had been a long night, but she was glad Boyd had taken her to the café. For a while he'd taken her mind off of how scary the night had been. She imagined him now, taking in her narrow kitchen and cozy living room. She didn't have much space, but she was able to fit her grandfather's antique writing desk beside the window, which was her favorite piece of furniture.

"You didn't tell me you had a dog," he said.

It took Janie a minute to realize he meant Romeo, the knee-high cardboard dog she'd gotten when she'd moved in. He sat beside her writing desk, and just knowing he was there made her happy.

"I've always wanted a guide dog, but it seems like it would be too hard in the city, so I got Romeo."

"Romeo. Why does that name not surprise me?" He inhaled deeply. "It smells incredible in here."

Nearly every surface had a vase of fresh flowers or leafy plants.

"I'm a flower hoarder. A few times each week I walk down

to the corner florist and buy fresh flowers. I love the smell of them, and just being near them makes me happy."

He knelt beside her. "Janie, I don't think there's room for your wheelchair to maneuver around the furniture, into the bathroom, the bedrooms…"

"Oh." She wrinkled her brow. "I hadn't thought of that. How will I shower? I feel so dirty."

She gripped her bag tightly again. Boyd uncurled her tense fingers and gently stroked the back of them with his thumb.

"Honey, you can't put any pressure on your ankle. We need to ice and elevate it. Once the swelling is down, in a day or two, you'll be able to use a crutch. Until then, I'm afraid you can't put any weight on that foot. What I'd like to do is get you settled. I can fill a bath for you, then wait outside the bathroom door in case you need me."

"I didn't think…" Could she trust him if she were naked behind the door? Did she have a choice? It had been so long since she'd relied on anyone in such a major way that she didn't know if she was angry, frustrated, or sad about having to do so now.

"This is going to be a major change for you, and I can't even begin to imagine what it must feel like. But I'm here, and you can use me however you need me."

"Oh, I can tell you exactly what it feels like—a bad joke. Like when I was younger and could still see and I knew that eventually that ability would be diminished. I had no control over it, and I scrambled to memorize everything I possibly could so I would have some idea of what the world looked like and so I wouldn't have to rely on someone else for every little thing."

Anger tightened like a vise in her stomach, and she couldn't stop the frustration from bubbling out. "I got over that, so please don't think I'm bitter over my blindness, because I'm not. In some ways I'm glad I don't have to see some random guy's face on the subway as he treats his wife badly, or the look of pity or warped fear in people's eyes when I walk by with my cane. That would suck even more." Tears burned down her cheeks. "And now I'm getting to know you, and you're so nice, and you don't treat me different from other people. And you're offering to be my *caretaker*? As nice as that is, no one likes to need a nursemaid."

Boyd's arms gathered her against him, surprising her. Shouldn't he be running from her apartment? Telling her to get a grip or something? She couldn't stand to hear the frustration streaming from her lungs. How could he?

With one hand on the back of her head, the other holding her around her shoulders, and his scruffy cheek pricking her face, he said. "According to Kelly, I'd make a pretty hot nursemaid."

She laughed despite her frustration.

"But I prefer the term houseboy to nursemaid, because you're not sick. You're just someone who needs a lift every now and again. Besides, when your hip feels better and your aches and pains heal up, you can scoot around on your knees and you won't need me at all. For now, I have a few days off, and all I had planned to do was read during that time, so I'm pretty much at your disposal."

He pressed a kiss to her cheek, and the tenderness of his touch and the sincerity of his words made her cry even harder, because if by any stretch of God's good imagination he really did like her for her, how could he ever see her as strong and independent if she relied on him to carry her around?

BOYD'S HEART FELT like it was being torn to pieces. How he'd come to care so much for Janie in a few short hours was beyond him. But for the first time since he'd lost his parents and had his world turned upside down, he wasn't walking through life with blinders on. He wasn't solely focused on his career and making it to medical school. He wanted to slow down and get to know Janie. Everything about her. Figuring out how she'd get around the next few days barely scratched the surface.

He drew back from her just far enough to wipe her tears. "Even when you're sad, you're incredibly beautiful."

She smiled through her sadness. "Sweet talker."

"I'm being honest." He framed her face with his hands. "And it's not just your looks, Janie. I'm in awe of your strength and tenacity. I've had to rely on others, too, and I know how much it sucks."

"It's not the same. What could possibly be the same as this?"

He rubbed an ache in the back of his neck. He wanted to ease her pain of feeling like she'd somehow become weak, because he knew all about feeling weak. There was only one way to gain her trust and help her understand that it was okay to need a little help. To need *his* help.

He struggled with the idea of revealing such a private part of himself, but one look at the sadness in Janie's eyes and he was powerless to do anything but ease her pain.

"I want to show you something. It's not something I've shown many people, but I want to share it with you."

"Are you going to get kinky?" she asked with a sniffle. "Because now isn't the best time."

"You are a sassy girl, and I sure do like that, but no kink here, sorry." His hands left her face, and he instantly missed the contact.

"But you said the heroine in my romance had to like kinky sex." Confusion riddled her brow.

"She does." He wasn't about to go down that path with her, unless he wanted to contend with a hard-on. It was difficult enough trying to ignore how incredible she felt in his arms every time he carried her. All her soft curves against him, warm and…

He pushed those thoughts away and said, "I'm going to carry you to the couch—is that okay?" He didn't wait for her to answer before scooping her into his arms.

"I have to admit," she said with a playful tone, "I don't hate it when you carry me, even though I probably should."

"Why should you hate it when I carry you?" He settled her on the couch and elevated her ankle with a pillow.

"Because, I don't know. It's not like we're dating, and I've been in your arms all night."

"You don't see me complaining. I'm going to get a bag of ice for your ankle, and then I'll show you what I wanted to share with you, okay?"

He quickly gathered the ice and turned to ask her where to find a plastic bag. She must have sensed his question, because she said, "Bags are in the drawer to the right of the fridge."

"Thanks." Boyd's stomach churned nervously as he filled the bag. He glanced over the microwave, noticing clear plastic stick-on buttons on top of each of the numbers on the control panel. The oven had the same type of stick-ons on the dial, marking *off, medium heat*, and *high*. He'd never thought about how people who were blind used flat-faced appliances. *Clever.*

"Do you have a clean dish towel we can use?"

"The drawer beneath where you found the bags," she said, plumping the cushions behind her and settling in. "Thank you again for taking care of me."

He took off her brace, and she sucked in a sharp breath.

"Oh, honey, I hate that this happened to you." He checked the time on his phone and laid it on the coffee table. "Are you okay? You can't take more pain meds for a while."

"Sure." She clutched a pillow to her chest as he laid the towel over her ankle.

"This will be cold, but not too bad with the towel. Tell me if it's too much, okay?"

She nodded as he gently situated the ice over her ankle.

"Okay?"

"Yes, thank you."

"May I sit beside you?" When she nodded, he sat beside her. "Where else do you hurt?"

"My right shoulder and hip are achy."

He leaned over and kissed her shoulder. "Sorry. I couldn't resist." A smile lifted her lips. "Do you want to try to ice it?"

She shook her head. "It's not that bad."

"A bath will help." He was procrastinating, terrified of the emotions revealing his most private thing would unearth inside him. But his fears didn't matter after everything Janie had been through. All that mattered was letting her know that he really did understand the way she felt.

"Are you okay? You're breathing fast." She reached for his hand. "And your hand is hot."

"I could say it's because of who's holding it, but that's only a partial truth. I'm a little nervous."

"Why? You've been so confident this whole time, except when I was touching you. You got a little revved up then, but I assumed, you know, it was because I was touching you." She lowered her gaze, and he lifted her chin so he could see her face.

"It *was* because you were touching me. And right now it's that, too, but it's also because..." This was so much harder than he'd thought it would be. "I need to take my shirt off, but don't worry, it's not for anything sexual."

"You don't need to warn me. Just rip that shirt off already."

She had no idea how much he wished he could warn her about what was coming, but he wasn't sure he could find the words to explain. He reached over his shoulder, pulled his shirt off, and set it on the coffee table. She was right; he was breathing really hard. Holy shit. Why was this so difficult? Women had seen him naked before.

But I've never explained.

"Boyd?" she asked, reaching her hand out, searching for his.

"I'm here." His voice cracked, and he cleared his throat. "Sorry."

"You don't have to show me whatever it is if this is hard for you."

He cupped her cheek and brushed his thumb just below her lip. He'd never wanted to open himself up to anyone as much as he did with Janie.

"Thank you. But I want to."

He took her hand in his and turned away, placing her hand on the back of his shoulder. Closing his eyes, he pressed his hands firmly to his thighs.

Her fingers trailed over the patches of uneven skin across his upper back. Boyd remained silent in hopes of staving off the painful memories of how he'd earned the scars that had changed his life. He expected Janie to recoil, like most women did. But her touch was featherlight, almost sensual, and she traced every single scar, from his shoulders, over his shoulder blades, to the few inches of unmarred skin. Her fingers lingered there, moving over and back between the grafted skin and the unmarred area. She placed her hands flat across the divide, as if she might soak in the feel of him.

Boyd held his breath. The memory of his father's strong arm pressing tightly against his back as he carried him out of the burning house under one arm, his younger brother, Chet, under the other, crushed his chest anew. The smell of burnt skin and hair, the explosion—*the fucking explosion*—and his brother's and sister's shrieks, came rushing back, fracturing his thoughts. He drew in a few jagged breaths, but it was impossible to calm his anxiety.

He waited for the questions to come, but Janie remained silent and began tracing the map of the worst night of his life with careful precision. She followed that history around the sides of his body and found the lines that divided his hurtful past from the branded areas of his donor skin sites. He focused on her touch, and when her hands returned to his back, moving over the angled line of unmarred skin to the ridges and grooves below, his head dropped between his shoulders. Emotions warred inside him—love for those he'd lost, gratitude for his father's strength to save him and his siblings, and the over-whelming despair that morphed into nightmares and threatened to slay him. Then Janie's cheek was resting, warm and comfort-ing, against his back, causing unexpected and powerful emotions to bloom inside his chest.

She flattened both hands on his lower back, just above the waist of his jeans, and she moved her fingers along his flanks, up his back again to his shoulders. A second later he felt her lips touch his back. He blinked against the sting of tears and tried to swallow past the emotions lodged in his throat.

Janie wrapped her arms around him from behind and held

him. He crossed his arms over hers, soaking in her comfort. He felt wetness on the path of skin where his father's arm had protected him and knew she was crying, and that drew his tears, which had vied for release.

He turned and framed her face with his hands, feeling her tears beneath his thumbs. She was so sweet, so beautiful, so trusting. He wanted to press his lips to hers, to feel all the emotions coursing through them in a deeper way, but he resisted the urge, wanting so much more than one kiss would ever provide.

"I'm sorry I doubted you," she said.

"You couldn't have known." His voice was rough with emotion, gravelly and pained.

She placed one hand over his on her cheek and then placed the other on his cheek. "I like when you touch me like this. Does it feel good to you?"

She was so caring, so careful, and he was learning that verbalizing and clarity were important to her. She couldn't see a smile reach his eyes, or the quirk of a brow, or the way he felt his insides go soft when she touched him, which he knew had to resonate on his face—because there was no way something so potent could go unnoticed.

"Yes," he finally managed. "I like the way it feels when you touch me very much."

Still holding his cheek, she turned serious. He could smell the faint scent of hot chocolate on her breath, feel a kiss on her lips, waiting for him, welcoming him. Usually, a woman's eyes told Boyd if she wanted to kiss him; with Janie, it was written in the softness of her smile, the slight knitting of her brows, in her tongue as it slid slowly across her lower lip. Boyd knew that once they kissed, once he had a taste of her, it would open a door he couldn't easily close. He already felt too close to her to walk away. Not that he wanted to. No, for the first time in his life, he wanted to stay exactly where he was.

"Are those burn scars?" she asked.

"Yes." He swallowed hard. "Mostly skin grafts."

Her eyes filled with sadness again, bringing a lump to his throat.

"That must have been so painful," she said softly. "You must have been terrified. I can't imagine..."

Her hands moved up his face and he closed his eyes, not wanting her to feel his tears. It was a futile effort. Her delicate fingers found them quickly, and then her lips followed. Soft pillows of tenderness touched the skin just beneath each of his eyes. When she drew back, Boyd took her hands in his, and for a long moment they remained like that, his secret laid bare between them and their emotions intertwining.

She lowered her hand to his jaw, and he couldn't have kept the truth from spilling out if he had wanted to.

"It's all a little foggy. It was physically and emotionally painful. Janie, I understand the feeling of not wanting to rely on others. I was in the hospital for a long time, and I had to rely on other people for everything. I guess I was lucky they grafted my skin, because if they hadn't, I wouldn't have been able to become a firefighter. But that wasn't the worst part of that time in my life."

"Boyd," she whispered, and that one word pulled more of his past from his heart.

"I was nine, and so scared—not just for myself. For my brother, Chet, who was eight, and my sister, Haylie, who was six. For my parents. My father carried me and Chet to safety. One kid under each arm, which is why you felt that patch of skin that hadn't been burned. That area was protected by my father's arm. Luckily, Chet didn't suffer burns as badly as I did. After my father got us outside safely, he went back for my sister." He paused to try to calm the internal turmoil that followed the memories. He rarely let himself revisit that awful night or the painful weeks that followed.

"There was so much smoke. I can still smell it, thick and ashy, black as night. I can still feel my eyes and throat burning. My father was a big lumberjack of a man. Plumes of smoke swallowed him the second he went back inside for Haylie. There were flames shooting out the second-story windows. I'll never forget the sounds of glass shattering. My mother managed to use her body to shield Haylie completely, except for one small burn on Haylie's foot. My father got Haylie out safely and raced back in for my mother."

"You're shaking." She ran her hands up his forearms. "Boyd, you don't have to tell me anymore."

"I want you to know what I went through, so you can see that I understand why you value your independence, why you don't want to be treated differently than anyone else. So you know the real me." He inhaled a long breath and blew it out slowly. "We lived in an old farmhouse in Meadowside, Virginia. Balloon-frame construction is what they call it. Old wiring caught fire, climbed up the walls to the attic, engulfing the house, weakening the walls. It was a terribly windy night. The kind of wind that howled through the trees. They called it the perfect storm—crazy name for a tragedy. There was no actual storm, just wind—but all the ingredients were there. A propane tank with a faulty valve next to the house, flames spreading with the wind from the house to the yard, snaking under and around the tank. I remember watching the flames consume the tank, and I don't know if it was in my head or if I was screaming, but I remember thinking my dad needed to hurry. Seconds after my father disappeared into the smoke to save my mother, the roof collapsed and then there was an explosion that blew us back. I must have passed out. When I woke up, I was in the hospital and my parents were gone."

Chapter Five

JANIE AND BOYD talked for almost two hours about his parents. He opened himself up in ways she never imagined. He also took care of her, giving her more pain medication and changing her ice pack. As he revealed details about the awful weeks that followed his parents' deaths, his lengthy hospital stay, and what it was like to be raised by his grandparents, the depth of his pain and sadness crept inside Janie and made her want to be equally as open with him.

"When I was younger, I mourned the loss of my eyesight. I'd always equated it to how others might mourn the loss of a loved one. Now I know how wrong I was. I have a full life, and not only did your parents lose theirs, but you lost the people who loved you most."

"You had a right to mourn your loss, too. There's no right or wrong way to handle these things."

"Is that why you became a paramedic and a firefighter? Because of what happened to your family?"

"Yes. We lost so much. I wanted to keep others from experiencing the same.

My brother, Chet, is also a paramedic and a fireman."

"I'm sorry that I doubted your ability to understand what I

was feeling." She realized she'd been touching him the whole time they were talking, touching his cheeks, his chest, running her hands up and down his arms. She'd felt his pulse quicken, heard the longing in his voice deepen, and each emotion brought them closer together.

"You couldn't have known," Boyd said. "Like I said, I haven't really shared this with many people. Thank you for not freaking out at the feel of my scars."

"Do people? *Freak out*, I mean? Do your girlfriends?" She nibbled on her lower lip, hoping he didn't have girlfriends.

"I think most people are pretty PC about things like scars. They try to hide their reactions, but I'm sure you know how it is. I can feel their reactions when they touch the scars and stop cold, or avoid touching them once they know they're there."

"Oh." *So you do have girlfriends. Well, I did ask.* She wanted to know more, but she was too embarrassed to ask, because the jealousy slicing into her wasn't warranted, or appropriate, as he was sharing himself with her in such a meaningful way. She wasn't one of Boyd's girlfriends, after all.

"How about if I run that bath for you now? I'll sit outside the bathroom door in case you need me. After you're dressed, I'll get you settled for the night. Or, rather, *morning*. It's late."

He moved easily from the past to the present. She assumed that he was well practiced at burying the hurt when the past became overwhelming.

"Okay. I need to get clothes to sleep in. Can you take me into my bedroom?"

"Now who's getting frisky?" He lifted her into his arms, and she touched his face, glad to feel a smile there.

She was surprised at how comfortable she felt with him. He was playful and kind, and there was no denying the hot bod she felt against her, but he was nothing like the slacker flirt she'd pegged him as. They'd only begun to get to know each other, and she could already tell that there was more depth, more realness, to Boyd than any man she'd ever dated.

"Well, well, well. What do we have here?" he said with her still in his arms. "White tulips next to the bed and on the dresser? I have a feeling you have a large floral budget. Are white tulips your favorite?"

"Yes." She hadn't had a man in her bedroom before, and now that they were there, and she was in Boyd's arms, her pulse went a little wild.

He brushed his lips over her cheek and whispered, "Want to know one reason I'm sure we were destined to meet?"

"Uh-huh," was all she could manage. His mouth was warm and soft against her skin, and she desperately wanted to turn toward him. To taste the man who was giving her his full attention and making her feel so good all over.

"White tulips were my mom's favorite flower."

"Are you making that up?"

"No. I promise. She had beautiful gardens when we were growing up, and she planted white tulips everywhere. We still own the land where our house burned down, and although the land was cleared, my grandmother kept up her gardens. I expect one day Chet or Haylie will rebuild there."

"Why not you? Didn't you like the area?" she asked.

"The area's beautiful, very rural. Horse pastures are more prevalent than baseball fields." He paused, and she could feel his heart hammering again. "But that night is still so vivid in my nightmares. I don't want to relive it."

"You have nightmares?" She'd had nightmares about going blind when she was younger and hadn't yet lost so much of her sight. In the nightmares she was running from darkness. The fear stayed with her, terrifying her, until she'd finally accepted her fate and found ways to embrace the change instead of trying to escape it.

"Sometimes."

She hated the thought of him suffering. It didn't matter that he was a virile man who fought fires and saved lives. Nightmares were like cancer, silent villains with the power to cripple even the strongest of people.

"Are they bad?" she asked.

"Sometimes, but it's not a big deal."

His voice told her otherwise.

"How did you end up here?"

"I came to New York for college," he explained, his heart calming a tad. "I met some of the guys from the firehouse before I finished college, liked them, and became a paramedic, then moved on to being a firefighter. I've been saving for medical school, and I actually had an interview in Washington State a few weeks ago."

"Medical school? Wow." Her heart sank as she processed the rest of what he'd said. "So, you might be moving away from the area?"

"I've applied to several schools, so I'm not sure where I'll end up. I'm going to set you down on your good foot, okay?"

"Okay." She was still thinking about him moving away. She'd only just found him, and as silly as it might be, she hated the idea of him not being around.

"Keep your arm around me, and *not* because I like how it feels." He chuckled as he lowered her until her left foot touched the ground.

"You make a good crutch, even if this is just your way of

making me lean against you."

"Honey, I'll be your crutch anytime you need it." He lifted her hand to his lips and kissed it. "I'm happy to service all your needs."

She bit her lip at the innuendo as he wrapped an arm around her waist and pulled her in closer. His lips brushed against her cheek again, sending heat from her head to her toes.

"Did you mean that to sound dirty?" she asked.

"Maybe. But the word *service* has no place in my vocabulary when it comes to those types of needs." He moved his mouth to her ear and said in a husky voice, "If I'm ever lucky enough to be your boyfriend, I'll take great pleasure in satisfying your every desire. But it'll be driven by emotions, not servicing. I can already see that whatever this is between us"—he gently brought her flush against his hard, hot body—"it's nothing like anything I've ever felt before."

He touched his lips just beneath her ear, and she let out a breath she hadn't realized she was holding. Her knees weakened and she tightened her hold on him.

"You okay, honey?"

She nodded, and he kissed her again in that sensitive spot just below her ear. With one gentle touch, he turned her face toward his. Her pulse raced, and desire burned outward from her core.

"I want—" *To kiss you so badly.*

"What, Janie?" His voice was seductively low, like night air rolling off the sea, beckoning her. "What do you want? Want to get your pajamas? We're right in front of your dresser."

She nodded, not wanting that at all, but trying to distract herself from how badly she wanted his lips on hers. *What do you want?* His question awakened her darkest desires, and the feel of their bodies touching from chest to thigh was all consuming. One of his hands curled around her hip, and the other hand lay possessively on her belly.

Thankfully, her hands didn't need her brain to move. She retrieved a pair of sleeping shorts and shirt from the drawer and clutched them to her chest so he wouldn't notice her trembling hands. She felt his gaze on her, intent, sexual. She wondered what he was thinking. She *knew* what he was feeling. He was sporting an impressive erection, which was burning its shape into her thigh, but while he'd said all those sexy things, he didn't make a move toward kissing her. She was confused, and turned on, and she almost wished she could text Kiki to get her take on him. But even though Kiki always said she wanted Janie to find a hot guy, having one in her bedroom might freak Kiki out—and that was the last thing Janie wanted. She wasn't at all freaked out. Boyd was tender and considerate, and...

"Want to try to use me as a crutch, or should I carry you?"

His voice pulled her from her reverie. "Carry me." There was no way her legs would work with all that heat consuming her, *and* she really liked being in his arms. He didn't make her feel like she was any less independent. He made her feel good, and whole, and hot all over.

He lifted her into his arms, and she draped one arm around his neck, resting the other over her chest as he carried her into the bathroom. Curiosity was killing her. She had to know what he was thinking, so she let her hand drift up to his jaw, which she found clenched, in contrast to the tenderness his voice exuded.

"You're tense. Am I too heavy?" She was five five, curvy, and he'd carried her a lot. He'd also said he'd worked a long shift before consulting at TEC. He was probably dead on his feet.

"No, honey. You're the sweetest woman I've ever met, sexy as hell, smart, funny, and it's all I can do to keep my emotions in check."

"Do you call all your female friends 'honey'?"

"No. It just comes naturally with you."

She was desperate to see more of him, but she couldn't ask to get in her weird, too-close-for-comfort position and try to see him out of her peripheral vision. She could feel his face, but she wanted to *see* him. In the hospital she'd wanted to see him to get a better sense of him. But now she had a better sense of him. And this? This desperate need to get closer to him, to see more of him? She hadn't felt all these wants in so long. They felt tangible and dangerously alluring.

"I like your lips. I want to taste them." *Ohmygod.* She couldn't believe that slipped out. She snapped her mouth shut before anything else came out to mortify her.

"Janie," he warned in a gravelly voice, and touched his forehead to hers. "Can I set you on the sink so we can talk?"

She nodded, and her stomach plummeted as he set her on the counter. She'd crossed a line. Was there a line? After everything he said? How could there be? There wasn't a line. Was there?

He gently parted her knees and stood between them. *Okay, maybe there isn't a line.* She'd obviously erased it. Her pulse quickened. She just wanted to kiss him.

He framed her face with his hands again, sending goose bumps along her flesh. It was another intimate gesture. He was full of them.

"Janie, a few hours ago I had to convince you that I didn't have ulterior motives for helping you, and I was honest. I didn't. And I don't now. But you need to know that I am very attracted to you, and I desperately want to kiss you, and—"

Screw the line. She pulled his face toward her and kissed him. She didn't think, didn't worry, didn't do anything but melt into the most glorious lips, the warmest, most wonderful kiss, of her life. She pushed her fingers into his hair as he deepened the kiss. God, she loved his hair. It felt untamed, just like he made her feel. The first touch of their tongues was urgent and reckless. He tasted decadent, like sex and sin wrapped in heat and sweetness, and she wanted to devour him. One strong hand clutched her hip, holding her steady. The other held the back of her head. He groaned into her mouth, setting her entire body aflame. Her hands were on a mission, running through his hair, over his arms, up his neck. The need to feel him was overwhelming, the tangling of their tongues sensual and possessive, and the combination was electric. His hand moved from the back of her head to the nape of her neck—and oh, that felt good! He kissed like he spoke, confident and full of truth, warmth, and promise.

BOYD WAS IN heaven and hell at once. Janie's mouth was satiny soft, hot, and delicious. Her tongue swept hungrily, passionately, over his. He felt shudders race through her, so much like the thrum of desire moving through him, he was afraid to stop kissing her. He didn't want those sensual feelings to ever stop, or her hands to stop caressing, groping, taking him. He could only imagine what they'd be like tangled up in her sheets—and that was the problem. She was injured, and he'd made her a promise. But hell if his mind wasn't already thinking ahead to how her bare breasts would feel in his hands, how her skin, flushed and heated with desire, would feel as their bodies came together. He fought for control, and he wanted to lose the battle. Wanted to give in.

He used all his focus and reluctantly pulled away. A sigh of longing escaped her, and that sweet, sexy, needy sound was too much for him to bear. He had to go back for more. He gazed into her unseeing eyes.

"What have you done to me?" he whispered before taking her in a slow, seductive kiss that turned his body to liquid fire. He kissed the corners of her mouth, traced her lower lip with his tongue, wanting more, more, *more.*

They were both breathing hard as he stroked his thumb beneath a bruise on her cheek, wishing he could magically take it away. Wishing he'd followed her down to the subway. He never should have left her in the first place. But he knew that wasn't right, either, because she hadn't been his to care for, and she was so independent she wouldn't have wanted him to.

"Sorry," she whispered. Her fingers found his mouth, and he sucked the tips onto his tongue. "Boyd…"

Her heady whisper ricocheted through him as he laced their fingers together and kissed the back of her hand.

"What are we doing, Janie?" He struggled to keep his head on straight, for Janie's sake—and for his own.

She shrugged in response, her sweet cupid lips curled up at the edges in a sensual smile he was too weak to resist. He took her in a tender kiss, craving so much more.

"I don't know either," he admitted. "But I'm putting on the brakes. I made you a promise, and as much as I want to kiss you until neither of us remembers what that promise was, you've already become too important to me for that."

"I'm…" She absently licked her lips again, as if she was processing what he'd said. "I didn't mean to be so forward. I mean, I did, but I'm not usually like this."

He couldn't resist kissing her again. "I'm not sorry at all. I like you being forward. I've been fighting the urge to kiss you for the past two hours. But, Janie, this isn't a goal. I have no endgame. I'm not like most guys. I've probably slept with fewer women than you have men."

"No way. I've—"

He placed his finger over her lips. "Don't say anything, because the idea of you with another guy weirds me out."

She kissed his finger.

"You have no idea how sexy you are. Everything you do is so…" He groaned and gripped her thighs to keep from taking her in another greedy kiss. "Let's get you cleaned up and into bed."

She smiled, and he added, "Alone."

"I'm blind, not asexual," she teased.

"Honey, there's nothing asexual about you. But I want to get to know you—all of you. And unless you're looking for a quick hookup, then I hope you want to get to know me, too."

"Damn it. You figured me out. I'm all about hookups, and you seemed like an easy mark. Now my night is shot to hell."

"Christ, you're going to be the death of me." He couldn't resist taking her beautiful face in his hands and kissing her again. And again. And one more time to hold him over.

Boyd ran a bath for Janie and laid fresh towels and her pajamas within easy reach.

"Can you leave the door open a little without peeking in?" she asked. "I want to be able to talk to you."

"Sure, and I'll try not to think about you being totally naked." He cleared his throat, and she laughed.

He sat outside the bathroom door, thinking about their mind-blowing kisses and listening to the water splash over her. It was pure torture.

"Boyd?" she called out.

"Right here." He rested his head against the wall. "You okay?"

"Yes. Tell me about the girlfriends you've had."

"Janie…"

"Please?" She paused just long enough for him to accept the fact that he'd tell her anything she wanted to know. "I'm curious."

"You sure? Because I'm not sure how much I want to know about your previous boyfriends."

"Yes. It's for research. I'm a romance writer now."

He closed his eyes, picturing how cute she'd look as she teased him. "Okay, honey. But stop me if it weirds you out, okay?"

"I will."

"I haven't had many girlfriends. When I was younger I was insecure about my scars, but I'm not sure that was all it was. I think a big part of it was also that I was still messed up from losing my parents. I was nervous about getting close to anyone."

"That's understandable," she said sweetly.

"I guess. When I went to college, I was able to shake some of that off, and I focused on my grades and goals, which kept me busy. I've always wanted three things in my life: to fight fires, become a paramedic, and go to medical school. I knew I had to work extra hard to achieve those things."

"You've accomplished two-thirds of your dreams." He heard the smile in her voice.

"Getting there. Have you always wanted to be a technical editor?"

"I'm a technical editor slash romance writer as of tonight, and we aren't talking about me right now. Tell me more about you."

"About me, or the women in my past?"

"Both. Knowing about the girls will tell me about you."

"You're good at this inquisition stuff," he teased.

"It's the writer in me."

"It's the woman in you." He knew this because guys did just about all they could to avoid hearing about their girlfriend's previous relationships, but women seemed to want all the details.

"You might be disappointed. There's not much to tell. In college I dated a girl for about two years. Holly. She was my first…" He wasn't sure if he was giving her too much information, but once again he found himself not wanting to keep anything from her. "I was young and naive, and I put my schoolwork ahead of her. She didn't like coming second on my agenda."

"Were you good to her?"

"Yes and no, I think. I mean, I was good to her in that I treated her well when we were together, but I didn't give her the attention she deserved. While her friends were out at parties with their boyfriends, I was studying. I was the nerdy guy who went out only on the weekends."

"And she didn't like that?"

"Would you?" He cocked his head, interested in her answer.

"When I was in college? I don't know. I hung out with friends all the time, but I've never been a big drinker, so I wasn't a party girl. We went to parties, but mostly on the weekends."

"I wish I knew you when you were in college."

"Why?"

"Because I want to know you so much better than I do. I want to know how you became the strong woman you are. I don't even know how old you are. I'm twenty-nine."

"Twenty-seven. Now, back to the girls, Mr. Subject Changer."

"You're a tough one." He smiled, knowing she was smiling, too. "There are only a few other women I've been intimate with. I dated, but like I said, I was never the kind of guy to sleep around."

"Because of your scars?"

"I used to think so. But as I got older I realized it was more than that. I know how quickly a life can end and how precious time is. I guess after Holly, I didn't want to hurt another woman. I learned not to make promises I couldn't keep, and the other girls I dated knew up front that I was focusing on my schoolwork and, later, my firefighting career. They thought they could handle it, but in the end I wasn't enough for them."

He knew his weaknesses—they'd plagued him his whole life—but admitting them aloud stung. He was glad he'd put the brakes on going further with Janie, because she was the last person on earth he'd ever want to hurt and chances were he'd end up leaving for medical school at some point.

"Did you love any of them?" she asked tentatively.

"You don't ask easy questions, do you? Aren't you getting chilly in that water? Maybe it's time to get out."

"I struck a nerve, huh?"

He scrubbed a hand down his face. "I thought I was in love with Holly, and maybe I was on some level. But I obviously wasn't in love enough to change who I was for her. Yeah, it's a sore spot. I don't like knowing I hurt her."

"But you were up front with her about your lifestyle and your goals?"

"Yes, but she believed I'd change."

"Then that's on her," she said emphatically.

He heard the water draining from the tub and imagined Janie lying naked as the water disappeared: her nipples tight from the cool air, droplets of water begging to be licked off her body. His hands twitched with the desire for her hips to fill them again.

"People don't change," she said, her voice strained.

"Do you need help?"

"No, Mr. Peeper. I can do this."

"Don't try to stand. And I didn't peep." He laughed under his breath, because he'd like to peep, and touch, and suck, and lick, and…Great, he was hard again. *Sweet Jesus.* He changed the subject in an effort to keep his mind off of touching her.

"People do change, Janie. That's just it. I made a choice not to. I wasn't going to let anything stand between me and my future. It wasn't fair to her. She did the right thing by breaking up with me. They all did."

"Um. I think I need your help."

He froze. No way would he be able to resist her if she was naked. He pushed to his feet. "Are you covered?"

"No. I'm buck naked and asking you to come in here and help me because I want to torture myself when you put on the brakes."

"That was cruel," he said as he pushed the door open. His voice caught in his throat at the sight of Janie wearing a shirt that barely touched the tops of her thighs, her nipples poking against the thin material. Her right knee was bent, suspending her hurt ankle. She leaned one hand on the counter, and the other hand clutched her shorts. Her face was devoid of the makeup she'd had on earlier—and she looked even prettier.

"You're barely covered, honey."

She ran her hand down the front of her shirt. "I'm covered, unless you're going to bend down and peek under my shirt. Now stop making me nervous and come here, please. I can't figure out how to get my shorts on without using my bad ankle for leverage."

"Huh?" He was busy trying not to think about her naked beneath her shirt.

"Such a man." She giggled, and reached for him.

He tugged her shirt down. "Christ. Don't move."

She laughed softly.

"Don't laugh. Don't make a sound. This is like another awful test or cruel joke." She smelled fresh and clean, and as she gripped his arm, he wanted to drop to his knees and taste the rest of her. It had been a long time since he'd been with a woman, and he'd spent the last few months trying not to fantasize about Janie—and failing miserably. Her hand stroked his arm and her mouth was dangerously close to his. He was on fire.

She poked his chest. "You're bossy all of a sudden."

"Hold on to the sink with both hands and I'll help you."

She held on to the sink and her shirt lifted, revealing the curve of her ass. *Perfect. Fucking perfect.* He tried not to focus on how those sweet ass cheeks would feel filling his palms, or how inviting it would be to take her from behind. *Holy shit. That isn't helpful.* Not thinking about it made him think about it even more. How incredible would it feel to sink into her sweet heat? *Great.* Now he was hornier than a teenager with a *Playboy* magazine.

Only she was a zillion times sexier than those girls, and she was standing right there and at the moment giggling as she said, "Boyd, hello?"

"Maybe you shouldn't talk either," he growled. "You're standing here nearly naked, and I...Aw, hell. I'm going to close my eyes and help you step into your shorts. But please do it fast. I'm only so strong." He huffed out a breath.

With his eyes closed like a good boy—or a fool—he knelt and guided her right leg into her shorts. "Hold your shorts and I'll hold you up by the waist while you put your other leg through." What was he thinking? He should have just brought a chair into the bathroom, or had her sit on the edge of the toilet lid. But no, instead he was putting himself through hell, because he wasn't exactly thinking clearly.

"Okay, all dressed," she said happily. "You can open your eyes."

Boyd tried to think of something to tame his mounting desire, but he had a one-track mind. *Janie.*

"I'm not sure I should," he said honestly.

She removed his hands from around her waist and slid them down to her hips.

"See? All covered." She wound her hands around his neck. "Will you carry me into my room?"

He scooped her into his arms, trying desperately not to think about how incredible she felt, and settled her into bed, wrapped and elevated her ankle, set the bottles of pain medication and a glass of water on the bedside table, then put his contact information into her phone.

"Are we on for tomorrow?" he asked.

72

"Tomorrow?" She yawned and snuggled beneath the blankets.

He wanted to climb in beside her and wrap her in his arms. "Our date to the firehouse?"

"I'd really like that." She reached a hand up, and when he took it, she pulled him down beside her and placed her palm on his cheek. "I like you, Boyd Hudson." When he smiled, she added, "And I can tell you like me, too."

"Ya think?"

She play smacked his cheek. "Shut up. I'm a verbal person. Let me say my piece before you leave and realize you don't need to be strapped down to a girl who's gimpy and blind."

"If you were a guy, I'd deck you for saying that about the girl I'm totally into."

"Ooh. So now you're into me." She yawned. "Sorry."

"Don't be, honey. It's late. You should get some sleep and dream about how I'll be into you tomorrow, too. Your phone is on the nightstand, and I put my contact info in with the speed-dial number seven."

"Why seven?"

"Because it's a lucky number, and I got lucky when I met you."

"Cheesy." She poked his chest. "But I like it anyway. Thank you for everything. You're an amazing guy, and if you change your mind about tomorrow, I'll understand."

"I'm not going to change my mind, so get some sleep. I don't want to hear that you're too tired to go out tomorrow. Call me if you need anything. I don't care if it's ten minutes or an hour from now, okay?"

"Okay, bossy."

"Don't try to walk, okay? In fact, call or text when you wake up and I'll come right over so you don't need to take any chances."

She yawned again, and when he kissed her forehead, she reached up and pressed a kiss to the bottom of his jaw.

"You're going to test all of my willpower, aren't you?"

"I'm not worried. You don't sleep around, remember? I trust you."

For the first time ever, Boyd wondered if he could trust himself.

Chapter Six

BOYD BOLTED UPRIGHT and ran from his bedroom, searching for the source of the noise that woke him. Flames chased him down the halls, down the stairs, into the basement—and then he was scooped up from behind. His father was crushing him. Black smoke filled his lungs, and tears burned down his cheeks. Chet's tortured face flashed through the smoke against his father's other side as he cried, "Haylie! Mom!"

Boyd inhaled a jagged, tortured breath, torn from his nightmare by the sound of his phone ringing. *Fuck.* He didn't have nightmares often, but when they hit, they consumed him. Sweat beaded his forehead as he blinked away the horrific images. The pungent smell of smoke still hung around him. His phone rang again, and his surroundings came into focus. *Janie.* Last night he couldn't imagine going home and being even ten minutes away in case she needed him.

He yanked his phone from his pocket, and Cash's name showed on the screen. He'd texted Cash and another friend, Heath Wild, an orthopedic doctor, and asked them both for major favors. He'd owe them for this, but it wasn't like he minded.

"Hey," Boyd said, trying to calm his internal panic.

"Hey, man, you okay?"

"Yeah. Bad dream, you know." Boyd had known Cash for years. Cash's family and the other guys at the firehouse were the only people around who knew about his family's history. He trusted his team with his life, and Cash's family had taken Boyd in as one of their own from the moment he'd met them. "I'm sorry to bother you with all this, but I really didn't want to leave Janie alone."

Boyd ran a hand through his hair, his pulse finally beginning to calm.

"No worries on my end. You sure you're okay? That was some text to wake up to. Is Janie okay? You must be beat."

"She's doing great, and I'll be fine. Just a little tired, no biggie."

"I got a text from Heath, and he's arranged everything just as you asked."

Cash knew better than to dwell on Boyd's nightmares, and Boyd was glad for it.

"He's going to meet me and Siena in half an hour so we can pick up the stuff. He had early rounds at the hospital, so the timing worked out well. We'll swing by the address you gave me afterward. Will that work?"

"Yeah, man. Thanks. Can you bring two coffees with you?"

"Hey, you've never asked me for a thing in all the years I've known you," Cash said. "I'll bring the damn barista if you want me to."

After they ended the call, Boyd rose to his feet and stretched. He sent a text to Heath thanking him for his help, then dropped to the floor and did fifty push-ups and fifty sit-ups to wake himself up.

His phone *dinged* with a text about forty minutes later. He smiled as he read it, glad it was from Janie.

Hi, bossy Boyd. I'm awake, but don't feel like you have to rush over. I can crawl to the bathroom.

He was glad she was in good spirits, but he knew how much her ankle probably hurt. He sent off a quick reply. *Is your ankle throbbing with pain?*

Her answer came immediately. *Maybe.*

He typed quickly. *Don't move. Is it okay if I come in?*

He read her response as he opened the apartment door, his nightmare long forgotten. *Of course. Let me know when you're here.* The floral scent embraced him as he called out, "Honey, I'm home."

"Boyd? You're *here*?" Janie called from the bedroom. "How did you get in?"

He crossed the hardwood to her bedroom doorway and hesitated before walking in, not wanting to overstep his bounds, but realizing he already had.

She was lying in nearly the same position she'd been in when he'd left. His gaze rolled over her face, taking in the angry purple bruises on her right cheek and the scabs that had formed over the abrasions. His gut clenched tight. He would give anything to take her pain away.

"I can't believe you came back," she said, holding a hand out toward him.

"I never left. I knew you couldn't get to the door to let me in this morning, so I left it unlocked and hung out in the hall. Are you doing okay?"

Her mouth dropped open. "All night? In the hallway? You're lucky a neighbor didn't beat you up."

"Nah. They looked at me a little funny, but I could take 'em if I had to."

She patted the bed beside her. "I can't believe you slept in the hall."

He noticed she wasn't moving her right arm very much, which told him that her shoulder was hurting even more than it had yesterday.

"I didn't want to take a chance of you needing something and not being able to get to you. Sorry. I probably should have told you that I left your door unlocked, but I stayed right outside all night so no one else could get in."

She reached for his cheek, and he leaned in to her touch. "If you would have told me you weren't going home, I would have told you to sleep on the couch."

"I didn't want to make you uncomfortable. It's really early. You didn't sleep well?"

She pointed to her ankle and wrinkled her nose.

"Let's get some medicine in you." He handed her the pain medication and a glass of water. "Do you want me to carry you to the bathroom?"

"Yes, please."

"Okay. Then we'll need to ice your ankle. It's important to keep the swelling down." He lifted her easily. She was warm from sleep, and as she slipped her hands around his neck, he realized he'd missed her in the few hours they'd been apart.

"Okay, Doc."

He kissed the tip of her nose, wanting to kiss her lips but not wanting to move too quickly. He was hoping she didn't have any regrets after their kisses last night.

"I'm not a doc yet, but maybe someday. How do you want to do this? I'll set you on the floor beside the sink, and you can hold on while you brush your teeth, and whatever it is girls do."

"That would be pretty much the same thing guys do."

He set her down beside the sink. "Really? You shave your face? Because it feels pretty darn soft to me."

She smiled, and it cut straight to his heart again. *Yup.* She'd gotten to him, all right.

"You don't shave," she said, reaching for his face again. "You're all scruffy."

"Speaking of that, Cash is bringing me a few things, including a razor. Once you're settled, I can go home and shower, or I can stick around and shower here. I wasn't sure what you'd be most comfortable with."

"Wait until Kiki hears I have a new roommate."

Boy, that sounded good to him. "She'll love me. I cook and do laundry. And apparently I make a pretty good chariot driver. I'll be right outside the bathroom door if you need me."

They spent the next hour getting Janie bathed and dressed, in much the same fashion as they had the night before, with Boyd doing all he could to not peek as he helped her dress and Janie taking great pleasure in teasing him about it. She wore a pair of black leggings, a black spaghetti-strap top, and a rust and cream-colored striped shirt that hung sexily off one shoulder. She pinned her hair back with a clip, leaving sexy blond tendrils framing her face, and she couldn't have looked prettier, despite the bruises.

"You're so different from the other women I know," he said as he settled her on the couch with an ice pack on her ankle.

"I bet you don't know many blind women with sprained ankles."

"I sure don't, but if I did, I have a feeling they'd be a lot whinier than you. You haven't complained once about the pain in your ankle, or your hip, shoulder, or arm. I know you have to be in pain. And you only took a little while to get ready, but you look like you spent hours."

"Stop it. You're embarrassing me."

"Honey, you need to learn to accept compliments, because I pretty much say what comes into my head most of the time, and holding it in around you doesn't seem likely."

"I'm not used to compliments. I mean, Kiki compliments me all the time, but usually when people say something like what you just said, it's because they don't know what else to say. And I know you're not doing that, but I'm not used to it. I keep wondering if I'm going to wake up and find out it was all a dream."

"I hope you don't dream about falling off subway platforms. This is as real as it gets, Janie, and I hope you'll let it take its course. See where we end up."

She rolled her lower lip between her teeth. "And you really don't feel trapped because you were the one who found me?"

"I'm a firefighter. I find injured people all the time, and not one other time have I spent the night in someone's hallway. And I think we have to nip this worry in the bud. You've mentioned this type of thing a few times, and I don't want you to be concerned about something that isn't going on, okay?"

"Okay. Got it," she said too confidently for him to believe.

He brushed his fingers over her unmarred cheek. "I'm serious. This is scary for me, too. You could decide you really don't want me hanging around, or that I'm a pain in your ass, or…"

"Or that we're both worried about things that we shouldn't be?"

He slid his hand to the nape of her neck and drew her in closer. "Yeah, pretty much. I want to kiss you so badly, but I haven't brushed my teeth."

"Shut up and kiss me."

Their mouths came together in a smoldering kiss, filling Boyd with desire. He wanted more than this moment, this kiss. He needed to settle her worries, to show her just how much he wanted to be with her. He took the kiss deeper, tasted more of her, explored the recesses of her mouth.

"So sweet. I love kissing you." He kissed the corner of her mouth, her cheek, her chin, and finally claimed her panting breaths as his own as he took her in another possessive kiss. She kissed him wildly, arching against his chest and grabbing ahold of his arms. His hand slid over her rib cage, around the small of her back, drawing her closer.

"Feels so good," she whispered as her head fell back, exposing the creamy expanse of her neck.

Boyd licked, sucked, and kissed her soft skin as she pushed her hand beneath his shirt and stroked his back. Feeling her hands on his scars, without as much as a second's hesitation, made their connection even sweeter. He ignored a knock at the door, not wanting to break their incredible connection. Being this close to Janie, hearing her ragged breaths, feeling desire pulse through her body, was sheer ecstasy, and he wanted to stay right there, kissing her, touching her, all day long.

Another knock sounded, and they both stilled.

"Your friends," she said breathlessly.

"Sorry." He kissed her one more time, needing one last taste. He was hard as steel and his heart was going crazy. What was it about her that had him so hot? He pulled his shirt down to hide his erection and rose from beside her. She licked her lips, and even though he knew she couldn't see him and probably wasn't trying to send a sensual message, lust coursed through him.

"I have to remember that kiss," she said with a serious tone.

"I want to write the first kiss in my book just like that."

CARRIED AWAY BY the intensity of her desires, Janie tried to calm herself down as Boyd answered the door. She felt a flush on every inch of her skin, and she was certain that if she felt it that strongly, Boyd would surely see it. His kisses were better than her fantasies. They were real, possessive, dark and sweet at the same time. And the things he said and did—*slept in the hallway, like a sentinel standing watch over her?* She loved that way too much. Or maybe not *too* much. Maybe she loved it exactly as much as she should, because it felt good to know that Boyd liked her enough to do that. And the fact that he hadn't told her and hadn't asked to stay over made his gentlemanly intentions even clearer.

She had the urge to call Kiki and gloat, since it was usually Kiki doing the gloating. This feeling of being on a cloud, so happy despite the aches harboring along her right side, or the pulsing pain in her ankle, was so new, so wonderful, she could burst with it.

"Come in," Boyd said as two sets of footsteps sounded on the floor. "Thanks, Cash."

Janie heard the warm sounds of an embrace, followed by a single loud pat on the back, the way men in her family greeted each other.

"Siena," Boyd said. "Thank you for letting me drag you guys out this early."

"Don't be silly." Her friendly voice spoke of strong familiarity, like Janie sounded when she spoke to Sin, she supposed. More like family than friends. "We'd do anything for you." The click of heels sounded on the hardwood, and she touched Janie's hand. "Hi. You must be Janie. I'm Siena, Cash's wife. I'm so sorry about your fall, but at least you're in good hands."

Janie touched her bruised cheek, wondering how bad she looked. "Thanks so much. Boyd has been wonderful."

"That bruise isn't too bad, and it's perfectly placed to highlight your cheekbone. I have friends who would kill to look as pretty as you do even with that bruise." Without missing a beat, Siena said, "Can I sit with you while they carry the stuff in?"

Relief swept through her with Siena's compliment. "Sure. Stuff?"

"Didn't Boyd tell you? He said you hated the idea of using a wheelchair, so he made arrangements for us to pick up a crutch and a walker, and I think Cash brought a bag of clothes and stuff for Boyd since he slept in the hall. Oh, I almost forgot." She opened Janie's hand and set a small package in it. "Earbuds. He said you needed them."

Janie gazed in the direction of Boyd's voice. "He did all that? This morning?" She couldn't believe he'd gone to so much trouble.

"He texted Cash around three in the morning, and I guess he must have texted his friend Heath, too, because he had it all ready when Cash called him."

He inconvenienced three people for her? "I'm sorry he bothered you guys for me." She hated troubling his friends, but she was overjoyed that he'd taken her independence so seriously. The only other person who would have gone to those lengths was Kiki.

"Don't give it another thought. We're happy to help. Boyd never asks for a darn thing. It worries me. He's always working so hard, or studying." She leaned in closer, bringing with her the scent of expensive perfume. "When Cash said Boyd was with you, I was elated. He's not a big dater, and he's got such a huge heart. I've been begging Cash to let me set Boyd up, but Boyd wanted no part of it, and it seems like you two were meant to meet. Did he tell you how Cash and I met?"

Siena was so easy to talk to. She told Janie all about the awful winter storm that sent her car careening over a mountainside, and how Cash had rescued her.

"I thought he was arrogant and pushy, and he thought I was a big pain, too. But we've been together ever since, and we couldn't be happier."

"Are you spreading rumors about us?" Cash's deep voice swooped down toward Siena, and Janie heard them kiss. "Hi, Janie. I'm Cash. I work with Boyd at the firehouse. I'm really sorry about your fall."

"Hi. Thank you, and thanks for bringing all that stuff over."

She felt Boyd's familiar touch as he placed his hand on her shoulder.

"Yeah, thanks, you guys. Janie, let me get the ice off your ankle, and—"

The apartment door opened again and Kiki's voice rang out. "Janie, I'm ba—"

"Hey, Kiki." Janie imagined Kiki's surprise at seeing her normally empty apartment bustling with people and medical supplies. "You guys, this is my friend Kiki. She lives next door. Kiki, this is Boyd, and these are his friends Cash and Siena."

"Oh, hi. Looks like I missed the party." The wary smile in Kiki's voice told Janie that Kiki was trying to figure out why they were all there.

"You didn't have to come back early," Janie said.

"I was worried about you. Oh my God, look at your beautiful face. I can hide that bruise with a little makeup."

"No, thank you." She didn't want anything touching her cheek, except maybe Boyd's lips.

Kiki sighed. "You're right. You're gorgeous as is, but your apartment looks like a medical supply ward. Are you sure you just hurt your ankle?"

"Boyd borrowed the wheelchair from the hospital last night so I wouldn't have to take a cab, and he asked Cash and Siena to bring the other things over this morning," Janie explained.

"Really?" Kiki said with surprise in her voice. "Thanks, you guys. I guess Janie didn't need me to come home early after all."

"She's in good hands with Boyd," Siena said. "He stood watch outside the apartment door all night."

"Outside the apartment?" Kiki asked as she sat by Janie's feet on the couch.

"I didn't want to be too far away in case she needed anything," Boyd explained.

"And he didn't want to make me uncomfortable by staying on the couch." Janie knew Kiki would love that. She imagined her giving Boyd a long, assessing look.

"I did call your chief last night," Kiki said in a kinder tone, which Janie appreciated. "He basically said you were a trustworthy guy."

"You called our chief?" Cash asked. "Weber must have gotten a kick out of that."

"Hey, she did the right thing," Siena defended her. "She was worried about Janie, and she doesn't know Boyd. He *is* trustworthy, Kiki. He's like a brother to Cash."

"While you guys talk about me as if I'm not in the room," Boyd teased as he took the bag of melting ice from Janie's ankle, "how about I whip up some breakfast?"

"You cook?" Kiki asked.

"And do laundry and push wheelchairs around," Boyd said. "Janie, Cash and Siena brought you coffee, too. Would you like it?"

"I actually drink tea in the mornings, but thank you for thinking of me."

"Tea. I'll remember that. Any special type?"

"Earl Grey is her favorite," Kiki said. "I'll get it for her."

"Thanks," Boyd said. "Honey, what's your pleasure? For breakfast, I mean."

Janie bit back the urge to say, *You.* "Anything."

Cash offered to help Boyd cook, and minutes later they were clanking around in the kitchen and Kiki was explaining to them that the buttons they'd put on the appliances helped Janie to use the controls.

A few minutes later Kiki joined her and Siena. "Here's your tea, Janie. It's hot; be careful. Siena, would you like some?"

"No, thanks. But, Janie, if you're not going to drink the coffee, I'll gladly take it off your hands."

"Sure."

"You're a lifesaver," Siena said. "I forgot to get some for myself."

Janie's cell phone rang with her parents' ringtone. She groaned.

"Let it go to voice mail," Kiki said.

Janie sipped her tea, relieved that Kiki silenced her phone. The last thing she needed was for her parents to find out she'd had an accident. They'd be all over her about moving back home.

"Tell me again how you fell," Kiki asked.

Janie went over her accident and the trip to the hospital.

But she didn't want to dwell on what happened. She was ready to move past it and think about happier things, like writing romance.

"Boyd and I made a bet."

"A sexy bet?" Kiki teased.

Everything with Boyd is sexy. "Sort of. I bet him that I could write a romance novel he'd love, and if I win, he's going with me to the Romance Writers Festival."

"Boyd?" Siena asked. "At a romance festival? That'll be the day."

"And if he wins," Janie said. "I have to go to Comic-Con."

Kiki laughed. "Now, that I would pay to see. You can totally nail this, Janie. You're a ravenous romance reader, and you're always making me describe things in vivid detail, so I know you can write a great story."

"Yup." She lowered her voice. "And Boyd doesn't know it yet, but he's my new research partner."

"Do I need to buy earplugs?" Kiki teased.

"I'm sure he won't mind," Siena added.

Janie's cheeks heated. She and Kiki had roomed together in college, and Janie had heard more of Kiki's trysts than she cared to admit, which was one reason they'd decided not to continue rooming together after college. They'd been lucky to find apartments they could afford next door to each other.

Great, now she was thinking about trysts and having sex with Boyd. She tried to push those ideas away and tune in to Siena and Kiki's conversation about sex scenes and romantic dates in books, but it was a struggle. Instead of pushing Boyd from her mind completely, she focused on their bet.

"The heroine I write has to be smarter than Boyd, like kinky sex, *and* like science fiction." Janie lowered her voice. "I know nothing about science fiction." She wasn't about to admit her lack of experience in the kinky sex department.

"We'll read a little dinosaur porn," Kiki joked.

"Oh my God! Is that a thing?" Siena laughed. "Dinosaur porn?"

They joked about scenes Janie should write and tossed around heroes' names and settings for the story, but every time Boyd's voice came into focus, Janie's mind drifted back to him. To their perfect kisses. To the sweet things he'd said and done. It was nearly impossible for her to focus on the girls, but she tried.

Kiki told them about her brief trip to see her family, and when the conversation circled back to Janie's fall, she finally forced herself to take part in the conversation, which led to more discussion about the night Cash and Siena met and, finally, their recent wedding, which sounded beautiful.

Boyd and Cash cooked a delicious breakfast of pancakes and eggs, and they ate around the coffee table, since her kitchen table was too small, and talked like old friends. Janie couldn't remember the last time she'd had such a fun morning.

After Cash and Boyd cleaned up from breakfast, they made plans to get together as a group later in the week. Siena swore she'd find a hot guy to hook Kiki up with, though she said she doubted Kiki needing setting up at all, because she had an *exotic appeal* with her dark hair, blue eyes, and incredible figure. Kiki soaked in the compliment, assuring Siena that dates weren't an issue. It was finding men who were *worth* dating that was difficult.

Now, alone in the quiet of the apartment, Boyd insisted on Janie icing her ankle one more time. She reveled in his touch and attention.

"What are you thinking about?" he asked as he sat beside her on the couch.

She didn't try to temper her words or cushion the intensity of them. She had a feeling Boyd was right. This was as real as it got.

"I was thinking that you're a man worth dating, and I'm really glad we met."

"Now, there's the confident girl I like so much." He lowered his lips to hers again in a series of slow, intoxicating kisses.

The front door flew open again. "I forgot my purse!" Kiki let out an exasperated sigh. "Oh, sorry! Should I expect to see a make-out show every time you're here?"

"Kiki..." Janie cringed.

"Sorry, Kiki. We'll behave," Boyd offered.

"No. *Please* don't behave. I was kidding. This is good," Kiki said. "No guy could fake the way you turn all googly-eyed around Janie. He does, Janie. I wish you could see this big sexy man getting all, 'Oh my God, you're so amazing I just want to love you up.'" She laughed, and Janie felt her cheeks heat up.

"Guilty as charged," Boyd said, giving Janie's hand a squeeze. "Well, except maybe the sexy part."

"No, you're definitely sexy, and Janie loves descriptors. She'd kill me if I just said, 'Some big guy,' right, Janie?"

"Ohmygod." *Googly-eyed?* Happiness danced through her. "She's right. I love descriptors. Besides, I already know you're sexy. I felt your body, remember?"

"Okay, stopstopstop," Kiki said. "Sharing naughty secrets about Boyd, in front of him, is just wrong."

"I can see this is going to be fun," Boyd teased. "Do you mind if I take a quick shower? Then I'll water whatever plants and flowers need it so we can go out for a walk. Or a wheel. Or a hop."

"Or a piggyback ride?" Janie suggested, marveling at the fact that he remembered her flowers.

"Whatever you want, honey." He gave her another quick kiss, and she heard him go into the bathroom and shut the door.

Kiki was beside her in two seconds flat. "That guy is seriously hot."

"I know."

"If he hurts you, I'll kill him, and then I'll probably go to jail and you'll be stuck without a BFF."

"I know." Janie laughed.

"He totally digs you. And he called you 'honey' like he's been calling you that forever."

"I know."

"Did you guys...*you know?*"

"Kiki!" Janie swatted her. "No. We kissed."

Kiki sighed. "Was it wonderful? He has great lips."

"Stop checking him out!" Janie knew exactly how great his lips were, how kissable and pillowy soft they were, even when the kisses turned hard and demanding.

"Okay, but spill, woman. I tell you everything. How was the kiss?"

"You know that feeling you get the very first day the heat of summer eases and fall is in the air? The way everything feels lighter? Brighter? Happier?"

"Mm. Yes. I love that feeling. It's crisp and electrifying."

"Exactly. It's like that at first, but then it turns sinful and addicting. I never want it to stop. My stomach gets all quivery, and my entire body just liquefies, like molten lava. *God, Kiki.* When we kiss, I just want *more.* And when he touches me, or talks to me in that voice that drips with sex and need, and—"

Janie couldn't finish her sentence, because things with Boyd felt different, more important, more private, more special. Not only did she not want to share every last detail, but she never wanted any of it to end.

Chapter Seven

BOYD QUICKLY LEARNED how intent Janie was on maintaining her independence. She wanted no part of the wheelchair, even if it meant that the swelling in her ankle might not go down as quickly if her leg wasn't elevated. And she was just as adamant about getting out of the apartment, so staying in and elevating her foot wasn't an option. As much as he wanted her to enjoy the freedom of using the crutch, her ankle hadn't healed enough to bear even a little weight. She still had another day or two before the swelling would reduce enough for that to happen. He also worried about the soreness in her shoulder and arm, which she wasn't complaining about but he continued to notice when she moved in certain ways. After a long debate, including several unfairly used coaxing kisses, which Boyd soaked up like a starving man, he reluctantly agreed she could *try* using the crutch.

He moved the coffee table to the side of the room so Janie could practice safely. Boyd held on to her left arm, unwilling to take a chance that she'd fall and hurt herself even worse, despite her insistence that she could do it on her own.

"I don't have to be able to see to feel the worry rolling off of you. Have faith in me," Janie said as she stood with the crutch beneath her right arm, holding on to Boyd with her left hand.

"I have total faith in you. It's your sprained and swollen ankle that worries me," Boyd said.

"I'm fine, really." Janie put the crutch ahead of her right leg, then carefully placed her right foot on the floor. "See?" She tried to step forward and sucked in air between gritted teeth, immediately lifting her ankle off the ground.

"Oh my God! How can that still hurt so badly?"

Boyd lifted her into his arms. "Because you fell off the subway platform. Have you always been this stubborn? Your determination is kind of a turn-on."

He kissed Janie's cheek as he set her on the couch.

"So now what? The awful wheelchair?" Janie asked.

"Only if you want to see the light of day," Boyd answered. "Besides, you just finished telling me that you wanted to start plotting out your kinky-sex, sci-fi romance novel."

"I'm going to write a kick-ass story, and you're going to spend all day at the romance festival. I've been reading romance practically since I was in the womb."

"When we made the bet, I didn't exactly think you'd take it seriously."

"Don't even try to get out of this, Boyd Hudson," Janie warned.

"I'd never dream of it. Seeing you all dolled up in a Catwoman suit at Comic-Con is going to be awesome." Boyd slid a pillow beneath her ankle. "If you elevate and ice your ankle for one more day, you'll probably be able to bear at least partial weight soon. Staying in and writing is the perfect way to heal."

She leaned her head back and groaned. "If I stay inside I'll just think about how frustrated I am that I can't walk."

"Then we have two options. We can wheelchair it for today,

or I can give you a piggyback and do the walking for you."

"You're a fireman. You're probably used to lugging people around. But you've carried me enough. I'm excited to actually start writing. It will totally distract me from my evil injury."

"Can you write anywhere?" Boyd asked.

She nodded and pointed toward her desk. "I can bring my braille device or my laptop anywhere, or just use my recorder. But if I use my recorder, I can't have a bunch of noise around me, because it'll throw it off."

"Then let's forget the trip to the firehouse and pack a picnic lunch, your laptop, and any accessories you need, and take the wheelchair to the park. I'd like to get some reading done anyway. We can find a quiet spot. That way if you want to dictate, you can do it without interruption. I can bring an ice pack, and you can elevate your foot while we're there."

"You know how you said that romance is crap writing about fictional heroes that don't exist? Well, Mr. Hudson, I think you've proved yourself wrong."

He scoffed. "Get over yourself. I'm not romantic or heroic. I'm just a guy trying to make a beautiful woman's day a little brighter." He kissed her forehead and added, "That's my story, and I'm sticking with it."

An hour later they found a quiet spot at the park, and other than the sounds of cars in the distance and birds overhead, it was blissfully peaceful. Janie had opted to bring her braille device with her new earbuds and her voice recorder. Boyd bundled up his sweatshirt and draped it over the small cooler, using both to elevate Janie's ankle.

Her fingers moved rapidly over the keyboard on her braille device.

"You can't possibly be writing the romance already." He

pulled her back against his chest.

"Yes, I am."

"Seriously? But we just made the bet."

"What can I say? You've unleashed the sexy beast in me. Only…" She stopped typing and sighed. "I have to admit, I'm going to need to do a lot more research. And you, my friend, are going to have to help."

"I am *not* reading romance novels to help you win the bet."

"Wow. For a guy, you have no imagination."

"Oh." He gathered her hair over one shoulder and kissed her neck. "You mean…" He slicked his tongue along the shell of her ear, and she shuddered against him.

"Now you're getting the idea."

He sucked her earlobe into his mouth.

"Stop." She laughed softly. "You're too distracting."

"Research," he whispered before forcing himself to pull back. "Fine. I'll let you write, but I get to take a picture of us to fantasize over later."

She stuck her tongue out as he snapped the picture. "Oh, good. I get a picture of that sexy tongue."

"How is that sexy?"

"Now I can dream of all the things I want that tongue to do."

"Maybe you were right about romance after all," she teased, bringing her attention back to her braille device.

"This might be a naive question, but I've seen you at work typing on that thing, but how does it work with your computer? I don't really understand it."

"That's not a naive question. I'm glad you want to know. There's so much technology out there, with smartphones, voice-recognition software, and screen-reading software, that there's almost nothing I can't do."

She ran her fingers along his forearm as she spoke, and he loved that she seemed to crave the contact as much as he did.

"My braille device takes everything you see online and translates it to braille, so I can surf the Internet, research, write. It doesn't translate the pictures unless they have captions, but beyond that, I'm pretty much reading what you see on the screen, through my device. Anything I write can be transferred from it to my laptop with a flash drive. But when I'm editing at work, I prefer to have the audio on so it reads back to me what I write."

"You mean so you can sneak in listening to your romance novels."

"Sometimes," she admitted. "But I don't do that often. It was really nice of you to have your friends bring me the crutch and walker this morning. I couldn't believe you remembered the earbuds. They're such a little thing."

"I figured you'd want privacy to listen to your phone messages, and privacy isn't a little thing." He kissed the top of her head. "Sounds like they're pretty important for your work, too."

"If I'm with other people and I use audio they are. But you also remembered to water my plants. Are you always so attentive to the little things?" she asked.

"I guess I don't think those are little things either. The plants and flowers are obviously important to you, and they're living things. That's like remembering to feed a baby."

She laughed. "I hope not, because when I visit my parents Kiki almost always forgets to water the plants."

"I like her, by the way," Boyd said. "She really cares about you."

"I care about her, too. We grew up together in Peaceful

Harbor."

"Maryland?"

"Yeah. You've heard of it?"

"Sure. It's not far from Meadowside." He couldn't believe they'd grown up only an hour and a half or so apart. "We visited a few times with my parents."

"Good memories, I hope?"

"Yeah." He had fond memories of the little town, although his memories were fleeting. Flashes of his family on the beach. "So you and Kiki grew up at the Harbor, went to college together, and moved here together, too? That's an awesome friendship."

"I never would have had the guts to come to New York without her. But Kiki will lash out if she thinks I'm being dissed. It's embarrassing sometimes, but not smothering, like my parents were."

"Your parents were overprotective?"

"*Beyond.* They were oppressive, trying to make every decision for me, calling ahead to prepare parents of other kids that I was blind to make sure I'd have special attention. Even when I was a teenager they wanted to do that, and they hemmed and hawed over every decision I made, which only made me want to be even more independent."

Boyd placed his hand over hers. "Any kid would have rebelled against that."

"Right? If I could see, I probably would have snuck out every night and gotten into trouble just to be able to have some amount of control over my life. Since that wasn't an option, I holed up in my room and read. I couldn't wait to get to college, which was another bone of contention. If they had it their way, I'd have lived with them forever. When I finally went to college they called *all* the time, and when Kiki and I decided to move here, it was partially to show them that I was totally fine on my own. It took forever for them to back off."

He hated knowing she didn't have a wonderful relationship with her family, but it was also a little hard to hear, because he'd give his left arm to have his parents hovering, smothering, or doing just about anything.

"How's your relationship with them now?"

"Sort of distant. I only go home twice a year, which I feel a little guilty about, but when I'm home they still hover over me."

"Maybe one day they'll see that you don't need to be smothered, just loved. Either way, I like knowing someone's watching out for my girl." As soon as the words left his lungs he held his breath. It was a big assumption to make, and it just slipped out like it wasn't an assumption at all.

"*Your girl?*" Her lips curved up.

"Will you be my girl, Janie?"

"You want me to be your girl?" She turned to face him and gazed at him in that way that made him feel like she could see him.

"More than you could know."

"Yes, I'll be your—" She squinted, grabbed his shirt, and tugged him closer. "Stop. Right there. The sun is behind your head, and I can see a little bit of you. Don't move. Okay? Please. Don't move at all."

"You can *see* me?" His heart accelerated as she moved up onto her left knee and turned her head, as if she were looking away. Then she peered out of the corner of her eyes at him. He held her by the waist to keep her from putting any pressure on her right leg.

"I can only see shapes when the contrast is just right. And I can't see any details, but…*Oh my God.*"

Her face was so close to his, he didn't know how she could see anything at all.

She ran her right hand over his head. "Thank God you have dark hair. I can't see blonds. Stay still. Please don't move." She ran her fingers over his cheekbones to his nose.

"You *see* me?" Tears dampened his eyes. "Janie, I had no idea you could see anything."

"I'm always afraid I'll forget what people and things look like, what I look like. I can't see your eyes or any details, but if the contrast is just right, sometimes I can catch a glimpse of the shadow cast by a nose or eye sockets. Not everyone with cone-rod dystrophy loses their sight completely, but I have a stronger strain of it. Right now I just see kind of a dark shape." She pressed her lips to his, and her whole face lit up. "A shape of my man is better than nothing."

The way she said *my man*, full of elation and possession, brought a rush of emotions.

"I wish I could see your eyes," she said as her fingers traveled over them. "I bet they're really expressive."

Boyd knew they were full of emotions. "Especially around you."

THE MORNING SPUN away, and afternoon crept in. A dog barked somewhere in the distance, and the din of passersby came and went. Boyd was just as attentive to Janie at the park as he had been in the apartment. They ate their picnic lunch and talked about what it had been like for Janie when she had first come to the city, and she was surprised to hear that he'd found it overwhelming, too.

As she typed up her story ideas, the characters began coming to life. This was going to take a lot more work than she'd imagined. The more she fleshed out the hero, the more she was describing Boyd. She made a mental note to spend more time researching personalities, looks, and other ways she could differentiate the hero in her book from him. She'd already figured out her hero's profession: comic book store owner. That was sci-fi, wasn't it?

She never realized her imagination was so limited. She tried to change it up, to draw from the other guys she'd dated, but she didn't have much to draw from in the romance department. The guys she'd dated would never have been happy sitting in a park for hours, while Boyd seemed quite content. Every so often he stroked her back or he'd lean over and kiss her cheek. No wonder she drew inspiration from him.

It had been a while since he'd moved, and she sensed the intensity of his concentration. Removing her earbuds, she asked, "What are you reading?"

"Just reviewing my applications to med schools and notes on each of the schools I applied to so I'll be prepared if I get invited for an interview."

She'd known he was applying to medical schools and that he might leave the area, but that didn't stop the uneasy feeling from washing over her anew. How could she care so much about him so quickly? She didn't want to think about him leaving, not when they were having such a nice afternoon. She put her earbuds back in and tried to focus on writing, but her mind got tangled in worries of Boyd going away.

By midafternoon the night of no sleep caught up to Janie, and she was having a hard time staving off her yawns. They packed up their things and headed back to her apartment. She didn't mind the wheelchair as much as she'd anticipated, but she had a feeling that was because she was with Boyd and he could make anything feel good.

Boyd carried her into the bedroom to rest.

She patted the mattress beside her. "Close the door and lie with me?"

"Anything you want, baby." The mattress sank with his weight, and he gathered her in his arms, carefully moved her right thigh over his, and tucked a pillow beneath her ankle.

He smelled like sunshine and man. Janie never realized how incredibly sensual the two were when they blended together.

"Sorry I conked out today." She tugged his shirt up and slid her hand beneath. His skin was warm and intoxicating. She followed the dusting of hair up to his chest. His nipples pebbled beneath her palms, sending tingles of excitement through her.

He placed his hand over hers. "Honey, if you keep touching me like that, you're not going to get any rest."

Good, because she wanted to continue her provocative exploration. She pressed a kiss to his chest, feeling the steady beat of his heart. "I just want to feel you."

He groaned, and the sound was so full of restraint that it awakened all her senses. He leaned up and pulled his shirt over his head, and she felt his heated gaze searing into her.

"I'll never deny you anything. Not a kiss." He pressed his lips to hers. "Not a single touch." He kissed her hand and placed it on his chest again. "Not anything your beautiful heart desires."

She felt him leaning in for another kiss and rose up to meet him. Their mouths crashed together in an eager, hungry kiss. Lust and desire spiraled through her chest, down her belly, and all the way to her toes. She rocked against him, clutching at his chest and arm, wherever she could find purchase. He was careful as he rolled toward her, one hand beneath her right knee, guiding her leg carefully to the bed as he came down over her left side without ever breaking their connection. His hard length sank into her thigh as he laced their fingers together and pinned her hands beside her head. When he dragged his tongue along her lower lip, desire radiated down her spine.

"I want to touch you," she pleaded.

"And I want to touch you."

He sucked her lower lip into his mouth and stroked his tongue over it again, taking her in another savagely intense kiss. He framed her cheeks with his hands.

"Janie," he said breathlessly. "Tell me what you want, baby."

She considered the question for only half a second. "You. On your back."

As Boyd rolled onto his back, he was extra careful of her ankle again. He was so attentive, so good to her. Her need to touch him went beyond sexual exploration. She wanted to know his body intimately, to feel his strength, his heat, and his caution all at once.

Resting on her left side, she caressed his cheeks. She loved his face; he had strong cheekbones and a chiseled jawline. Her fingers traveled upward and she felt his eyelashes as he blinked.

"Close your eyes," she whispered, and touched her lips to his as his lashes touched her fingertips. "I want you to feel how nice it is to be touched when you don't have visual stimulus."

His hand pressed firmly against her back. "Anything you want, baby."

The muscles in his jaw jumped beneath her fingers as they

moved over them and down the tight muscles in his neck and along his shoulder. She wanted to feel that strength as he held her, wanted to feel the release of all that knotted-up restraint as their passion ignited. She shifted her weight further onto his body and kissed his chin, his neck, and when he swallowed, she licked over the sharp edge of his Adam's apple, surprised by how much it turned her on to touch him in this way.

When he moaned, his chest and neck vibrated deliciously. She took her time, as she had when he'd allowed her to touch his back. She wanted to soak in all of what he was offering. She followed her hand with her mouth, placing kisses across his shoulder, then lower. His hand touched her cheek as she kissed his chest. She turned to his palm and placed a kiss there, before running her fingers over his nipple again. His hand returned to her cheek as she laved her tongue over the hard nub and sucked it into her mouth. His hips bucked up, and he groaned again, sending heat to her core. She loved feeling and hearing the effect she had on him.

She sucked his other nipple into her mouth.

"Baby, baby, baby," he whispered. "You're killing me."

"Should I stop?" she asked, praying he'd say no.

"Never." His fingers touched her mouth, and she sucked them in and swirled her tongue around them. "I'm trying to lie still, but seriously. You're driving me crazy."

She touched her hand to his ribs and inched lower, the heat of his skin burning into her cheek. "Why do you keep touching my face?"

"I like how it feels when you're kissing me. You asked me to keep my eyes shut, and it makes me feel closer to you. Does it bother you? I'm not trying to guide you."

Could he possibly know how much she loved hearing that?

That he liked experiencing their intimacy through the veils of senses other than sight.

"No. I like your hands on me."

A low laugh escaped his lips. "You haven't even begun to feel my hands on you."

"Promise?" She wondered where her confidence was coming from, but she wasn't about to stifle it.

"Promise."

She kissed a path down the center of his body, over the dips and planes of his abs, all the way to his waist. Running her hands along his sides, memorizing the serrated scars that separated his painful past from his unmarred front. A facade, she knew. He still had nightmares. The unscarred skin wasn't really unmarred. He'd been honest when he'd said that some people wore their differences on the inside. She wondered about *those* scars. The ones she couldn't feel with her hands but sensed just as strongly. And the physical scars? Could he feel every-thing, or were there parts with no feeling? Were they like her eyes? Certain parts offering nothing, but if touched the right way, could she reach some undiscovered nerve and give a sensation as powerful as it had been for her to see him this afternoon?

She showered those scarred edges with kisses, explored the skin with her tongue, wondering how anyone could freak out over any part of this incredible man. The more time they spent together, the more she touched him, the more she adored him.

Even through his jeans she could feel his powerful thighs, his formidable erection. He was solid, manly. She imagined his legs pressing against her inner thighs, his thick shaft buried deep inside her. She resisted the urge to touch his arousal, not sure she wanted go that far yet, although her stomach and chest had already brushed over that big treasure.

Kissing her way up his stomach, she brought her fingers back to his lips, tracing them as he panted out hot, sensual breaths. When she lowered her mouth to his, he met her in a greedy kiss that made her ability to think rationally spin away. Shocked by her own insatiable need, her hand fell back to his stomach, then lower, grazing over his thick, hard length.

She moaned, and he swallowed it down.

"Janie," he warned.

She smiled against his mouth as he wrapped her in his strong arms and moved her gently onto her back.

"My turn."

Chapter Eight

BOYD HAD NEARLY come undone the moment Janie brushed over his erection. She had him so tightly wound his entire body was shaking. As she lay beneath him, trusting and open, a smile curving her beautiful lips, he wanted to bring her the same titillating pleasures she'd given him.

He cradled her face in his hands and kissed her deeply, feeling her body quiver against him as he drank in her sweetness. Between all the blood in his head rushing south and his thundering heart, he could barely concentrate. He moved carefully, gently parting her legs as he settled himself in between them. She was fully clothed, and he still had on his jeans, *thank God*, because he'd definitely have lost it if she'd touched his bare cock. He wanted to feel her legs touching him and see her from this angle, even if they weren't making love. He wanted her to feel what it would eventually be like for them to come together.

"Okay, baby?" He brushed the sexy tendrils from her eyes.

"Yeah." She licked her lips, and he couldn't resist kissing her again.

"Am I too heavy?"

"No. You feel good."

"Don't worry. I'm not going to do anything you don't want

me to."

"Boyd..." She stroked his face, and he closed his eyes, soaking in her touch. "Don't treat me like I'm blind, okay? Treat me like I'm any other girl."

His chest constricted and he opened his eyes. "Janie, I'll never treat you like you're 'any other girl.' Please don't ask me to, because you're not just any other girl to me. Can't you see that? Can't you feel it?" He kissed her again, a long, languid kiss that he hoped conveyed everything he felt.

"Your blindness doesn't factor into how I touch you. When I look at you, I see *all* of you. The sweet, sexy woman, the fearless editor who's going to blow me away writing romance, and the beautiful person who's weaseling her way into my heart like no one ever has. I know you're blind, and that's part of you, too. Just like my scars are part of me. But it doesn't define you, at least not to me."

She nodded with damp eyes. He kissed away her salty tears.

"When I touch you, I touch you how I *want* to touch you. In ways that I hope turn you on, or comfort you, or make you feel safe, depending on what we're doing. But in bed, when we're intimate, I'm not thinking about if you can see me, because what I feel for you, I know you'll feel in my touch."

She reached up and drew him into a kiss, as she had when they'd shared their very first kiss, and he couldn't disguise his body's reaction. Every time she initiated their intimacy, it revved him up. He rocked against her center, and she moved with him, turning him on even more.

"Can I take your shirt off?" he asked, knowing she had the spaghetti-strap top underneath. She sat up, allowing him to lift it over her head. His heart ached at the sight of the purple bruises on her right shoulder.

"Oh, honey," he whispered. "How can you possibly not complain? This has to hurt."

"I'm fine," she said.

His inclination was to stop touching her and hold her, pamper her, and let her know she could trust him enough to admit that she was in pain. But she'd just trusted him with something equally personal. *Don't treat me like I'm blind, okay? Treat me like I'm any other girl.*

"Are you sure you don't want to stop?"

Her face flushed as she said, "I want you to touch me. I'll tell you if it hurts."

He'd never been more careful in his life as he kissed along her arm, carefully avoiding her bruises and wishing he could magically sweep the pain away. He moved slowly, kissing her collarbone, her neck, and paying special attention to the sensitive skin just below her jaw, earning a whole-body shiver with each slick of his tongue. If he couldn't erase her pain, he would bring her enough pleasure to make up for it.

She felt so good, smelled so feminine, and as he kissed his way down the center of her body, *she* pulled up the bottom of her clingy top. He took the hint, and the invitation, and rolled her shirt up further, pressing a kiss to her belly. Her skin was soft as satin. He slid his hands beneath her shirt, moving it up and over her ribs, feeling each of her breaths in the rising and falling of her skin against his tongue. She clutched his wrists and he lifted his eyes, gauging her reaction.

"Want me to stop?" he asked.

She pulled her shirt higher. "Help me."

He lifted her shirt over her head, revealing her beautiful, full breasts. Air left his lungs in a rush as he tried to rein in the urge to devour her. But his hands had a mind of their own, and apparently his mouth did, too, because as he filled his palms, he sucked one erect nipple against the roof of his mouth, and she cried out.

"Too hard?" he asked quickly.

"No. So good. Don't stop." She pushed his head down, and he chuckled as he did it again, loving her sweet, sexy cry of delight as she guided his mouth to her other breast.

He sucked and teased and caressed her breasts as she moaned and arched beneath him. Her fingers dug into his arms. His skin prickled with heat. He kissed the underside of her breasts. As he kissed his way south, he rolled her nipples between his fingers and thumbs.

"Boyd." Her plea was loud and clear.

When he reached her hips, he rained kisses over each one, then licked his way to her belly button, where his mouth lingered. She rocked her hips, sending another clear message. His hands skimmed over her waist, carefully gripping her hips as he used his teeth to lower the waistband of her leggings to just above her pubic bone. His hands splayed over her creamy skin. He placed openmouthed kisses on every inch of her exposed flesh, sensing the thrill of her arousal.

"More," she begged.

Hell, he wanted more, too, but he needed to know she wasn't just lost in the moment. "Janie, you're sure, honey?"

"Ohmygod. Do you need to ask?"

She pushed at her leggings, and he helped her draw them down and off her left leg, leaving her black panties in place. The leggings got stuck on her ankle brace.

"Leave it," she pleaded, guiding his hands back to her body.

"No, baby." He carefully maneuvered her leggings over the brace. "I want you to be comfortable."

Her right hip and thigh were darkly bruised, and he lavished them with tender kisses, gently brushing his fingers around the harsh reminders of her fall. He ran his hands up her legs while he slicked his tongue along her inner thighs. Goose bumps rose beneath his tongue. The scent of her arousal was too tempting to ignore. He slid one finger inside her panties and moaned at the feel of her slick heat. She arched to meet his touch, clutching the sheet in her fists.

He moved her panties to the side, exposing her damp curls and glistening sex, and dragged his tongue over her wetness. She tasted so fucking sweet and so exquisitely hot.

"Oh God, yes. Don't stop."

She didn't have to ask again. He took her panties off and tossed them to the floor, nearly coming at the sight of her, naked and trusting. He hadn't intended to go this far, but there was no going back now. He needed her, she needed him, and as he lowered his mouth to her velvety heat, she fisted her hands in his hair. He devoured her, thrusting his tongue deep inside her, sucking her clit into his mouth, then going back for more of her sweetness. This became his rhythm. With every slick of his tongue, she cried out, and with every suck of her sensitive nerves, she moaned. He felt her thighs flex, felt her orgasm building as she clawed at his shoulders. He slid his fingers in deep and used his mouth to take her over the edge.

Her hips bucked as she cried out his name—

"Boyd—"

She writhed and panted, another breathy, needy plea sailing from her lips like a secret, and as she came down from the high, he took her right back up again.

"Ohmygod," she cried as another climax claimed her. Her head thrashed, her nails carved moons into his skin, and as he eased his efforts, she cried out one last time before falling limply to the sheets.

A fine sheen of sweat coated their chests as he rolled her nipples between his fingers and brought his mouth to her for a third time. Then he gathered her sated body in his arms, kissing her as aftershocks quaked through her.

They stayed like that for a long time, and when Janie drifted off to sleep, he pulled the sheets over her and went to use the bathroom. The man he saw in the mirror wasn't the man he'd known for all these years. He saw open, caring eyes, not the cautioned look of someone who had suffered so much loss they couldn't help but wait for the next shoe to drop. It had been a long time since he'd seen or felt that way himself. There was no mistaking the changes in his reflection.

When he returned to the bedroom, Janie came into focus, and his heart bloomed inside his chest. She was lying on her left side with the blanket pulled over her side, barely covering her breasts. Her right knee was bent, favoring her injured ankle.

She lifted her head and smiled groggily. With his heart in his throat, he helped her put on clean panties and a shirt so she wouldn't feel self-conscious, then stripped off his shirt and jeans and curled behind her warm body. He held her as she drifted off to sleep again, wondering how he would go away to medical school if he already couldn't bear leaving her for even a few minutes.

Chapter Nine

JANIE AWOKE HOURS later nestled against Boyd. His arm circled her waist, and as she turned toward him, she touched his face, loving the scratchy whiskers that had appeared since the morning.

"Are you okay?" he asked.

"Yes. Not too achy, but starved."

He laced his fingers with hers, and she couldn't think of a nicer way to wake up, unless, of course, her ankle would miraculously heal.

They ordered pizza, and Janie iced her ankle again. Thankfully, the swelling was going down. Kiki texted to check on Janie, and they invited her to join them.

"Did you get any writing done?" Kiki asked as they ate. "I can't wait to read what you write."

"I started, but I have a long way to go. I think I'll have to write a short story instead of a whole novel. A whole novel seems really *big*," Janie said.

"Copping out already?" Boyd teased. "You will make a hot Princess Leia at Comic-Con."

"Ohmygod. I'm so not *princess* anything. I'll write it, you'll read it, and it won't matter how long it is. I'm going to rock the heck out of *Sinful Fantasies*, and you'll be eating crow instead of pizza, my friend."

"Sinful Fantasies?" Boyd asked.

"Yeah, that's the title."

"Watch out, Boyd. If she writes romance the way she reads it, you don't have a chance of winning this bet."

"We'll see." Boyd put his arm around Janie and kissed her temple. "I know Clay raves about you, but what I can't figure out is how someone as vivacious as you ended up doing technical editing instead of something more fun."

"I'm afraid it's not a very exciting story." Janie took a bite of her pizza.

"So you went to college for…" Boyd asked.

"English lit. I wanted to be a journalist, but when I got out into the real world, it wasn't meant to be."

Boyd wiped her cheek with a napkin. "Pizza sauce. I'd lick it off, but I don't think Kiki would appreciate that."

"Smart man," Kiki teased.

"Why wasn't it meant to be?" Boyd asked. "You'd make a great journalist."

"Ugh. I hate talking about that time of my life. It was so frustrating. I had a college degree, experience working for our college newspaper, and I couldn't find a job to save my life. I started looking at publishing houses, tried to find work as a freelance proofreader, but…"

Boyd's hand tightened around hers.

"But people are assholes," Kiki said. "They think because she's blind, she's stupid or deaf, or unreliable, or whatever."

"Jesus, really?" The anger in Boyd's voice was palpable. "You were discriminated against?"

"Don't get all tied up in knots over it. It is what it is, and probably none of those people thought they were discriminating. You'd be surprised how people rationalize things in their own minds. I tried to get jobs at call centers, thinking that at least there no one would worry about me not being able to see. But I couldn't even get that." She remembered how it had felt to go on interviews across town, filled with hope, only to be let down several hours later. Some interviewers even told her on the spot that the position had been filled, which she knew couldn't have been true, because she'd always confirmed her appointments in the mornings before venturing out. Kiki had been right there cheering her on, telling her, *Fuck them. When you find the right job, you're going to blow everyone away.*

She pushed those hurtful memories aside, moving on to happier ones. "Then one afternoon I met Clay on the train, and we got to talking. He gave me a shot as a temp for a week, and I've been there ever since. I'm up for a promotion to technical writer, which is like a dream come true. It might not be journalism, but hey, it's writing."

"I hate that you went through such a hard time." Boyd's tone was empathetic and frustrated at once.

"Why don't I clean up from the pizza," Kiki offered. "Then I have to take off. I figured I'd make the most of being back in town. I'm meeting Arty down at NightCaps." Arty was one of Kiki's friends from the clothing store where she worked.

"Thanks, Kiki. I'm glad you came over. Have fun tonight."

Kiki threw away their trash and cleaned the dishes. She hugged them both and thanked them for dinner.

After Kiki left, Boyd said, "I can't see anything holding you back. You're too driven. Look at how you handled your accident. I still can't believe you got yourself up from the tracks."

"It was either that or get run over by a train, and besides, you're just as driven. You knew you wanted to be a paramedic and a fireman and then go to medical school, and you're doing it all. So what I did wasn't so remarkable. I just got lucky."

"That's not true. I didn't run up against the same type of adversity as you did."

"But you had other obstacles." She lowered her voice. "You said you have nightmares, and still you put yourself back into situations that must bring up memories of that night."

He squeezed her hand again but didn't say anything, and she could tell it wasn't something he wanted to talk about. She hoped one day he would, because she knew from experience that until he really dealt with that awful night, his nightmares would probably continue.

Wanting to ease away from the uncomfortable subject, she brought the conversation back to her work.

"I am glad Clay gave me a chance. I like my job, but I have to admit, lately I've wanted more of a creative outlet. That's why I started writing the column in TEC's newsletter. It's not much, but it allows me to write instead of edit, and I can inject some of my personality. And this bet we've made? You know, the one I'm going to win," she said with a smirk. "It's got me totally juiced! It's like, what I do at work is playing it safe, but trying to write this story, even just the little time I've put in so far, makes me feel *alive*. It's been years since college, but this bet has me thinking about how much I love writing. Thank you."

"Don't thank me, because as much as I'm happy about what you've said, this is still a bet, and I still hope to win."

She smacked his arm.

"I'm teasing…sort of." He hugged her and planted a wet kiss on her lips, making her laugh. "Life is too short to do anything you aren't passionate about."

Janie's heart ached for how well he knew that.

"There's this little thing about needing to make a living," Janie reminded him.

"I think you've proven that there's nothing you can't do." Boyd's tone was so serious it took her by surprise. "If you want to write, you'll find a way."

Thinking of his nightmares, she wondered why it was so easy for him to encourage her to take risks and face her fears when he couldn't even talk about his.

JANIE AND BOYD talked until eleven, and then Janie asked him to read to her. They'd gone back and forth about what he should read and finally settled on a Nora Roberts novel. Janie had promised him it wouldn't be too fluffy, and she was right. It wasn't science fiction, but he could stomach a story about a guy renovating an old inn. Every time he considered stopping, Janie's appreciative smile pushed him to read more. But now it was nearly midnight, and between Janie's yawns and heavy eyelids, Boyd couldn't deny her need for sleep much longer.

She'd taken the clasp out of her hair, and blond waves framed her beautiful face as they lay together on the couch. He'd spent the last few minutes trying to rationalize a way to stay with her, but she had Kiki next door now, and she didn't need him as she had before. By now she was probably craving a little alone time, but that didn't mean he wasn't aching to stay.

"I should go," he said, hoping she'd ask him to stay.

"It's going to feel weird without you here." She tightened her hand on his waist.

Weird didn't begin to describe how empty he'd feel without her by his side, but he didn't want to chance her feeling smothered. He kissed her luscious lips, tugging their bodies closer together. "You've got Kiki next door, and I don't want to overstay my welcome. Can I see you tomorrow? The flowers in your bedroom are starting to wilt. We could walk down to the florist together."

"You mean wheel down." She snuggled in closer, making it even harder for him to find the resolve to leave.

"How about we piggyback it?"

"You think I'm kidding about that. I really do love piggyback rides. Whenever Sin comes to visit us, he gives me at least one piggyback."

Her smirk told him that she'd intended to send the spear of jealousy that was currently piercing his chest.

"Then piggyback it is." He pulled back as a thought tripped him up. "Sin? *Sinful Fantasies.* Any connection?"

"Maybe." She giggled. "Sin is Kiki's older brother."

"Christ. You're doing this to torture me, aren't you?" He brushed his lips over hers.

"Every time you get jealous, your muscles tense, and I like the way it feels."

"My muscles get tense for lots of reasons. When you were touching me in the bedroom…" The memory of her mouth and hands on his body made him aroused all over again.

"I loved touching you." She kissed him softly. "I don't have a thing for Sinny."

He breathed a relieved sigh. "Well, that's one man on this crowded earth I don't have to worry about."

"Because I've had so many," she said, laden with sarcasm.

"I wouldn't care if you'd been with a hundred men. Well,

maybe that's not true. That's a lot of men."

"Stop." She kissed him again. "I've only been intimate with two other guys."

"It's still weirding me out to think about you and other guys, baby."

"I just thought you'd want to know."

"I do, but I don't." This was a double-edged sword for sure. He was curious about her old boyfriends, mostly because he couldn't imagine anyone being with her and ever wanting to be anywhere else.

"My first real boyfriend was in college, and he was blind. We dated for a few months. He was my first…"

Boyd's hand spread possessively across her lower back, and he asked her the same question she'd asked him about Holly. "Was he good to you?"

She touched his cheek, and he knew she was gauging his mood. There was no hiding the tension gripping him while he waited for her answer.

"Yeah, he was good to me. We were friends before we were intimate, and that helped me feel safe when we did the deed. But we realized that while we'd become physical, our relationship hadn't really progressed past friendship. We were comfortable, and I wanted more than comfort. We remained friends after we broke up, but you know how that goes."

He pressed a kiss to her forehead, relieved that she hadn't been taken advantage of by some asshole.

"And the other guy?"

"He was a sightie, like you." She ran her finger down the center of his chest, leaving a trail of heat behind.

"A 'sightie'?"

"Mm-hm. He could see. We went out during my senior

year of college and dated for a few months. We always went out with friends, so if we went to a party together and he got busy talking to other people, there was always someone around to help me find the bathroom or get a drink. But right before graduation, we spent less time with friends. You know, as we figured out what came next. And we drifted apart. Or he did, anyway. I was slow to realize what Kiki had figured out weeks before. He hadn't just gotten busy at parties; he'd been bored with me."

Thinking of Janie left alone at parties made Boyd want to track down that guy and teach him some respect. How could anyone get bored with her? And what the hell? He'd left her alone? He instinctively gathered her in closer.

"Is that why Kiki is so protective of you? She doesn't want another guy to treat you like that?"

"No and yes. She's that way more because of women than guys. Girls can be really mean, and even though I can't see their sneers, I sense them. If you close your eyes in a crowded room, you can sense all sorts of things. You learn to tune in to the way people breathe, the words they choose, the nervous tapping of a foot or hand."

"But why would women ever want to be mean to you? I was kidding at the café about the women sneering at you. Although, the guys *were* checking you out."

"From what Kiki tells me, it's not just me. She says women size each other up just like men do." She rested her head on his chest and said, "But when they do it to me, it's probably because I require extra attention from the person I'm with if I don't have my cane. I have to hold on to their arm or their hand. I don't know if women are jealous of the attention I get, or if it looks like I'm super possessive, when it's really a guidance thing. I mean, I love holding hands—don't get me wrong—but I can't find my way through a crowded party without something—my cane, or a friend who can see—or I'd be bumping into people right and left."

He knew it was more than that. Janie was a gorgeous woman, and she was sweet as summer rain, smart, and funny. She was the total package—and he knew enough women to know she'd be the target of jealousy.

"I promise you, honey, no matter where we go, I'll always stay with you."

Janie lifted her face from his chest, and he rolled them onto their sides and tugged her in closer.

Their mouths came together slowly, sensually. Her supple body melted into his, and her wet, willing mouth opened for him. Their tongues teased and took as the kiss intensified. She tasted of desire, stirring memories of when his mouth had been buried between her legs. Lust spiked down his spine, and he knew—*God, he fucking knew*—if he didn't stop kissing her, devouring her, enjoying every single sound she made, he wasn't going to be able to pry himself away. She was a spark to his inferno, and if she rocked her hips against him too many more times, he'd combust.

He traced her teeth with his tongue, willing himself to back away, to make his way out the door so as not to smother her with the very emotions swamping him. But she was too succulent, too enticing. She bit down on his lower lip, and he groaned with the erotic pleasure.

"Janie…" He wasn't sure if it was a warning or a plea.

"Testing the waters," she said through heavy breaths. "Research."

"Baby, if I don't leave, we're going to end up in bed, doing way more than *research.*"

He gazed lovingly into her eyes, knowing she could sense him doing so. She touched his cheeks, reading his emotions and, surely, his dirty desires.

"What if I want to do more than research with you?" she asked tentatively.

He didn't want *tentative.* He wanted surety. "When you do, there won't be a 'what if.'"

Chapter Ten

AFTER A RESTLESS night, Boyd got up early and went for a run. He'd helped Janie get ready for bed last night and taken her in another soul-searing kiss. The sounds of their kisses, their jagged breaths, and the feel of her willing, sexy body against him had nearly shattered his control. But he'd been honest about not sleeping around, and even though he knew with every fiber of his being that what he felt for Janie was bigger, and more real, than anything he'd ever felt before, he didn't want to assume she felt the same way. And more importantly, he couldn't chance that she might have been speaking out of a moment of passion and not from her heart.

He showered and dressed, arriving at Janie's by eight for their morning walk—or *wheel*—to the florist. He knew Kiki would help her shower and dress, but that didn't soothe the ache of missing her that he'd wrestled with all night, or the worry that she'd fall or forget about her ankle when she was half asleep and step off the bed. Images of her bruised shoulder and hip haunted him, and he couldn't shake the feeling that he should have stayed with her.

He texted Janie as he climbed into a cab. *How's my girl? Ready to go to the florist?*

She answered quickly. *They're not open this early on Sunday, but I miss you. Come over?*

He texted back, hoping she'd smile at his response. *Already on my way.*

A few minutes later Kiki let him into Janie's apartment. "Good morning, Romeo." Her dark hair was pinned up in a high ponytail that bounced with each step.

"Hey, Kiki," he said as he went to Janie. She was sitting on the couch, and then she was in his arms. He gazed into her eyes and kissed her sweet mouth. The unsettled feeling that had been his companion for the night drifted away. Her hair cascaded over her shoulders, and the bruise on her cheek had softened a tinge. The light blue top she wore set off her eyes, but it was the smile curving her lips that made his heart beat faster.

"You got more beautiful overnight," he said, before pressing his lips to hers again.

"And you got full of cheesy lines." She pushed her fingers through his hair and smiled up at him.

Kiki flopped into the recliner. "You haven't seen beautiful yet. Janie wouldn't let me put any makeup on her because of her bruise, but when she's all made-up, she'll knock your socks off."

"She already does," he said honestly. "Thanks for helping Janie this morning."

"Hey," Kiki said. "That's my line."

"Oh, the glory of being waited on hand and foot," Janie teased.

"How's your ankle?" He helped her settle back on the couch while Kiki breezed by on her way to the kitchen. He was glad to see the swelling had gone down.

"It's not as bad as it was," Janie said. "I tried using the

crutch when I got up, and with the brace it wasn't too bad."

"I told her not to, but there's no arguing with Janie," Kiki said from the kitchen.

"I was fine. Besides, I can't rely on you guys forever."

Wanna bet? The thought came so quickly it caught him by surprise. He blinked several times, as if he could clear his mind. No such luck. "It didn't hurt too badly to put weight on it?"

"Not too badly. Besides, I have to work tomorrow, so I need to get used to it." She squeezed his hand and said, "I can do this, Boyd. I know you're worried, but I'm stronger than you think."

"I know how strong—and how stubborn—you are, and I'd never try to change either. But I'd like to take a ride on the subway with you, just to be sure that you're okay on the platform. Unless I can convince you to take a cab to work?"

"There's no way I am taking a cab. I should be fine on the subway." She said it like it wasn't a big deal, but he saw unspoken worry in her expression.

He knew she might experience posttraumatic stress from her fall, and he wasn't about to let her go alone on her first subway ride after the accident. Especially since she'd need to navigate using her crutch and her cane at the same time. But he also knew her well enough not to *tell* her that.

"Would you like to try it together?" he offered. "We can take a short trip down to the flower shop, maybe grab breakfast, and if you're still not in pain afterward, we can try the subway."

"Okay, but I'm sure I'll be fine." She lifted her chin in that defiant way she had, and he couldn't resist kissing her right in the center of that adorably confident chin.

Boyd cleared the living room for Janie to practice with the crutch. With his arm around her waist, and using the crutch for support, she was able to say goodbye to the wheelchair.

Kiki joined them for their walk, and since the flower shop wasn't open yet, they stopped at a café for tea and muffins. It was good to see Janie laughing and moving her right arm more freely, although Boyd worried that the crutch might exacerbate the pain. She didn't need to use her cane when she had Boyd to guide her, but he worried about how she'd manage when he wasn't with her.

They were eating their muffins at a table by the front of the café when a plump woman with salt-and-pepper hair came out of the kitchen.

"Hey," Kiki said, waving to her. "It's Bonnie."

The woman frowned when she noticed Janie's ankle brace and the crutch beside the table.

"What on earth happened, Janie?" the older woman asked.

Janie told her about her fall, and Bonnie *tsk*ed and shook her head. "I'm so sorry. Is there anything I can do to help?"

"No, thank you. I'm in good hands. Kiki and Boyd have been helping me." Janie touched Boyd's arm. "Boyd, this is Bonnie Fletcher. She owns the café. Bonnie, this is Boyd. He's the one who found me after the accident, and he's a paramedic, so he knew just what to do."

"Nice to meet you, Boyd. A paramedic?" Bonnie said with a nod. "I guess you really are in good hands. If you need anything at all, Janie, groceries, someone to walk with you, whatever you need, I'm here. All you have to do is ask."

A short while later they left the café.

"Bonnie seems nice," Boyd said as they walked up the street toward the flower shop.

"We met her when we first moved in," Kiki explained.

"I think we went there nearly every morning the first month

we lived here," Janie added.

"Janie?" A dark-haired man stepped out from behind a newsstand.

"Mr. Gregory?" In Boyd's ear Janie said, "He's so nice."

"Looks like you took a spill." Wrinkles mapped his forehead as he looked Boyd over.

"I'm fine, Mr. Gregory," Janie said. "Just a little sprain."

Just a little sprain. As Boyd heard the words, he realized that Janie's insistence on her independence was more than just her being stubborn, or wanting to reclaim something she'd lost. This was truly just a minor setback in her eyes, and it probably should have been in his, too. Would he have worried so much if she weren't blind? Probably, because the thought of Janie tripping or further injuring her ankle killed him, but it bothered him that he even had to question himself. He made a mental note to be more aware of not being too overprotective.

Yeah, right.

What he felt for Janie was so strong, he wasn't sure he could tame those urges, but he'd try to keep them in check.

"Well, I won't hold you up." Mr. Gregory handed Kiki a newspaper. "On the house. Take care of Janie."

"You promised me a piggyback ride," Janie reminded Boyd.

"Hey, if my girl wants a piggyback, she'll have one." Boyd handed Janie's crutch to Kiki.

"Janie! He's already put his whole life on hold for you." Kiki took the crutch as Boyd lifted Janie onto his back.

"I'd never need to take the subway again if you'd just carry me everywhere." Janie kissed his cheek, and Kiki shook her head.

"For an independent pain in the ass, you sure are spoiled," Kiki teased.

Janie's hands slid farther around Boyd's neck, and she touched her cheek to his. "Oh, please. I had to go all night without him. That's hardly spoiled."

"Sounds like you missed me as much as I missed you." Boyd turned and kissed her.

"Here we go." Kiki rolled her eyes, then held the door to the flower shop open for Boyd to carry Janie inside. "If you two are going to be making out all the time, I need to find a hobby."

"Janie, sweetheart, what happened?" A tall, handsome man with sharp features and broad shoulders set his hand on his hip as his eyes rolled over Boyd. His brows lifted. "And who is this gorgeous creature carrying you around?"

Boyd held out a hand. "Boyd Hudson. *Chauffeur.*"

"Trick Myer, nice to meet you." He shook Boyd's hand, then turned his attention to Kiki. "My, my. Kiki, baby, what have I missed?" He leaned down and hugged her.

"I tripped," Janie said, lifting her hurt ankle.

"Off the subway platform," Kiki added as she set a bouquet of pretty, colorful flowers on the counter.

Trick gasped as Boyd lowered Janie carefully to the ground, holding her up around the waist.

"Careful, honey."

"Honey?" Trick kissed Janie's cheek. "You *have* been busy, haven't you, sweetie? Tell me everything."

Janie told Trick about her fall and about Boyd finding her. Trick held her hand and asked a dozen questions, all of which were clearly meant to assess Boyd as much as to find out about Janie's injury. Boyd was glad that Janie had another person looking out for her. A whole *village* of people, it seemed, which was quite unique for the city. A worry whispered through his mind. He was falling for a wonderful woman whose entire life was in New York, and if he got into medical school, his time there would soon be over.

BY THE TIME they returned to her apartment, Janie felt invigorated. She'd made it without too much pain on her first outing with her crutch, and they'd gotten new tulips for her bedroom. Kiki offered to return the wheelchair to the hospital on her way out for the afternoon, claiming that she was going to spend the day shopping, but Janie knew she was giving them privacy. She felt a little guilty, but she was dying to have some time alone with Boyd.

Boyd insisted on icing her ankle, just to be sure it didn't swell up again, and she got so involved in writing *Sinful Fantasies*, she didn't want to stop. She lay on the couch with her feet in Boyd's lap. He massaged her left foot while he read, distracting her from the scene she was writing. It was the first-kiss scene between the hero and heroine, and she wanted to get it just right. She remembered her first kiss with Boyd and how her insides had flamed and her stomach had gone a little crazy and tried to put that into words. It was harder than she'd imagined it would be. *Maybe a little refresher would help.*

"Can you help me with this scene?" she asked.

"Sure, but I'm not sure I'll be much help."

Oh, you have no idea. "It's the first-kiss scene, and they're stuck in a confined space." She went up on her knees and straddled his lap. "I'm thinking this position might be good."

His hands slid around her waist and cupped her ass. "This is an excellent position." His hair tickled her skin as he kissed her neck. "Perfect for making out."

He slicked his tongue up her neck, sending a bolt of heat right between her legs.

"And do you prefer my hands here"—she held his shoulders—"or here?" She wound them around his neck, bringing their chests together. Her nipples tightened. She never knew they could ache to be touched, but sure as heck, they were throbbing.

"Definitely there," he said huskily. His hands slid beneath her shirt and up her back. He gripped her shoulders and lifted his hips, bringing his thick arousal against her center.

"Oh, I like this position," she said breathlessly. "And…"

He sealed his mouth over her neck again, sucking and stroking his tongue over her flesh and driving her out of her mind.

"We're supposed…." She couldn't think, could barely breathe.

"First kiss," he reminded her as his hands moved sensually over her back, then up her rib cage, brushing the sides of her breasts.

"Yes—"

He lifted his hips again, and the friction was so enticing, so exciting, that she couldn't wait another second. She grabbed his face, and their mouths crashed together in a fury of want and need. Every stroke of his tongue made her want more of him. His hands pushed on her hips, driving his arousal hard against her core. She was wet, and so eager to have his strong hands on her, his naked body against her, that she felt out of control. But his mouth, his glorious mouth, was too good to leave even for a second. His kisses consumed her, and when he tangled his hands in her hair and tore his lips away—*No! Come back!*—he was breathing hard, and she was barely breathing at all.

His cheek touched hers, and she loved the closeness, could

feel his restraint in the tightness of his muscles.

"Janie," he said between heavy pants. "*God, Janie.*"

She rocked her hips against his arousal, and in one swift move she was beneath him, her hurt ankle hanging off the edge of the couch. Boyd perched above her, taking her in another greedy kiss. Her heart pounded as she tugged at his shirt.

"Off," she commanded.

He lifted up for half a second, and then he was bare chested—and lifting her shirt and bra up.

"You're so beautiful," he said before kissing her again. "God, I love your body."

His mouth came down over her breast, taunting and teasing, while his hips moved in perfect sync with his tongue, turning her nerves into live wires. He grazed his teeth over her nipple, then lavished the other breast with the same scintillating attention. Spreading her legs wider, she arched to meet every thrust of his hardness. The friction sent spears of heat between her legs, making her wet and wild. His mouth came down over hers, and he slid his hands beneath her ass, holding her against his cock and masterfully rubbing against her time and time again. Heat pulsed low in her belly, spreading outward, between her legs, into her chest, all the way to her fingertips. Her breathing became jagged, and she couldn't hear past the sounds of their kisses, their moans of pleasure. Her thighs tensed around his hips as he continued the exquisite rhythm, taking her higher and higher.

"Let go, baby," he said in a voice full of need and sex and—

Ohgodohgodohgod. He claimed her in another rough kiss as his shaft rubbed over the perfect spot one more time, and her world exploded. Lights and sounds and feelings that were too intense to name lifted her, engulfed her, made her senses spin and whirl in the space of a few seconds. She bucked and thrashed, abandoning herself to the volcano burning inside her. He kept up the torturously incredible pace—kissing, sucking, rocking her right through the last of her orgasm. Then his hands—soft, hot, tender—were on her cheeks, kisses trailed across her lips, her face, beside her ear.

It was all she could do to lie there and breathe, every muscle spent, as he carefully righted her top and held her, whispering naughtily in her ear.

"You're so beautiful when you come."

His words were edgy, dirty, and she *loved* hearing them.

"Was that okay for a first-kiss scene?" he asked teasingly.

Holy cow. She'd forgotten about the scene.

The sound of keys in the door sounded seconds before Kiki stormed into the apartment. "Forgot my purse—"

Janie felt her cheeks flame, but she wouldn't have given up those last few minutes with Boyd for anything. He scrambled off of her and shifted, facing Kiki. Suddenly Janie had tunnel vision. No longer was she thinking of their glorious make-out session but of Boyd not wanting Kiki to see his scars. Her hand moved to his back, and his muscles corded tight as he tugged his shirt over his head. Her heart ached at his need to cover up.

"Jesus, you two." Kiki's voice wasn't as light, and Janie knew she'd seen his scars. She heard Kiki walking into the kitchen, then returning to the living room.

"We need a signal," Kiki said, her tone lighter again.

Thank you for pulling it together.

"A sock on the door or something to warn me, because the last thing I want is to find you two buck-ass naked on the couch."

"Maybe it's time for us to start knocking on each other's

doors," Janie suggested.

"This is such a great problem to have. Sorry. I should have knocked."

Janie covered her face.

"Okay, I'm outta here again," Kiki said. "Next time I'll knock, but maybe you should go to the bedroom. I have to sit on that couch."

Janie threw a pillow in her direction.

After she left, Janie let out a breath. "Sorry. You didn't want her to see your scars, did you?" She kept a hand on his back, reading the tension as it seated itself deeper and wishing she could take it away.

He shrugged. "I just wasn't expecting..." He breathed deeply and turned toward her again. "How about we take that sexy crutch of yours down to the subway and try a ride?"

Subject changed but not forgotten.

Chapter Eleven

A SHORT WHILE later they were standing on a crowded subway platform. Boyd wondered again where all those people had been the night of Janie's accident. Janie gripped her crutch so hard her knuckles were white. The color drained from her face, just like it had drained from Kiki's when she'd seen his back. He should probably deal with that, bring it out in the open with Kiki, but right now he needed to focus on Janie.

"Honey, talk to me." He held her cane in one hand and kept ahold of Janie with the other. He was glad he hadn't given in and let her come by herself.

"I…I didn't realize how scared I was until this second."

"Maybe it's too soon. We can come back another day."

"No," she huffed. "God, I hate this. I need to do this. This is how I get around."

"What you went through was traumatic, and now you're trying to navigate with a crutch, which makes it even harder."

She shook her head adamantly. "I'm not afraid of the subway. I just need to get past the fear of tripping again."

"Okay. Do you want me to hold on to you? I can get people to move out of your way and give you space," he suggested.

"No. Please don't do that. That would be the worst. I need

to do this alone. I have to be able to get around. And it's not the crutch. It's like there's a knot of fear in my chest making it hard for me to breathe."

"That's totally normal. You can expect some free-floating anxiety after what you went through." He'd give anything to ease her panic, but he knew this was all part of the process of getting over the trauma of her fall. He'd gone through so many levels of adjusting after he lost his parents—panic every time the heat clicked on, when he smelled smoke from a grill or bonfire, and about a hundred other things that brought the fear of that night rushing back. He tightened his grip on Janie, wanting to comfort her.

"Okay. I'm okay." She breathed deeply a few times.

He heard the train coming into the station. The crowd began moving toward the edge of the platform, and fear fisted in his stomach. People were packed together like sardines, perched to lunge toward the doors. How the hell did she do this alone before the accident? How would she safely use both the cane and crutch without being trampled?

"We'll practice until you're an expert, but for this week, I'm going to rearrange my schedule so I can be here with you on your way to and from work."

She gripped the crutch tighter. "You don't have to do that. I can manage."

"I'm sure you can, but I'll be worthless to my team if I'm worried about you. I'm not trying to smother you. I'd just feel better knowing I was here with you, just until you can walk without the crutch."

JANIE'S HEART SLAMMED against her ribs as the train screeched to a stop. The familiar roll of the heavy doors sounded, followed by the rush of noise that reminded her of a fast-flowing river as people left the train. Voices and footsteps blended into a familiar tempo. She felt the change in direction as passengers began moving forward, and she froze.

Boyd's hand tightened around her. "Whenever you're ready."

Memories of her fall came rushing back: the silence beating around her, the sharp jolt of pain as her toe caught on the ground and her ankle twisted. The sinking feeling in the pit of her stomach the moment she realized she'd lost her balance, followed by the sheer, insurmountable panic that engulfed her seconds before she slammed into the rocky ground.

She clutched Boyd's wrist and shook her head. "Can't."

"It's okay, Janie." He wrapped her in his arms, and she knew he felt her trembling, and that made her angry at herself for being weak. A visceral reaction sprang from her lungs. "I hate this. I hate this so much."

"I know." He stroked her back.

He was so understanding, so comforting. She should be grateful, but it only made her more upset that she *needed* him to be that way. She pushed out of his arms as the mechanical voice came over the loudspeaker, telling passengers to stand clear of the closing doors.

"I'm sorry, Boyd. I'm not this pathetic." A sarcastic laugh slipped from her lungs. "Apparently I am. I just didn't know it."

"Christ, Janie. Give yourself a break. If I fell off this platform, I wouldn't be running right back on the train. You're not weak. You're human. Your accident is fresh on your mind, and your body is still fraught with aches and pains and bruises. It would be weird if you could just saunter onto the train without hesitation."

"Maybe so, but I can't afford not to be able to do this. We're not leaving until I can."

"And you call yourself pathetic?" He laughed, and she was glad for his levity, because it made it easier to battle her inner turmoil.

"Let's walk to the edge of the platform. I think I need to see that I can manage by myself over the bumps, where I tripped."

They spent the next few minutes walking up to the bumpy area, then back, and repeating it until the panic in her chest eased a little. By the time the next train pulled into the station, more people were waiting. Boyd was careful to let her lead, and she appreciated that, knowing he probably would have preferred to stand with his hands out to his sides, clearing a path for her to safely board the train.

This time as the passengers got onto the train, she made it to the bumps on the platform and then stopped.

"We'll get the next one," she said, feeling a little more confident.

She couldn't get on the next train, but she wasn't as panicked by the time the doors closed, and two trains later she and Boyd followed the crowd onto the train. The crutch made it awkward, and she was glad for Boyd's support. When they were on the train, he held her close.

"You're the bravest person I know."

"I am proud of myself for finally doing it, but it took me an hour to get on the train."

"You're talking to a guy who's still having trouble dealing with trauma from *years* ago. I think an hour is pretty damn impressive."

She took advantage of the opening. "Maybe it's time for you to face those demons. You told me that my blindness didn't define me, and you're right, but I feel like in some ways you let your past define you. Maybe you should talk to someone about your nightmares."

"Can we not talk about this, please? Not here."

The plea in his voice reminded her that he'd shared his loss in confidence with her, and she tucked away the conversation for another, more private time.

"Sure. I'm sorry," she said quietly.

He kissed her tenderly, without a hint of tension. "It's okay. I know you care, and I appreciate it."

They rode in silence to the next subway stop and crossed to the opposite platform to wait for a return train back toward her apartment. She had no trouble disembarking the train, other than the awkwardness of using the crutch, and it took her only two tries to get on the train home. The first train brought panic, but when the second arrived, she was able to push past the panic and board. That wasn't ideal, but it was progress.

On their way back to her apartment, Boyd called the fire-house and talked to Cash. Then he swapped shifts with someone so he could ride with Janie on the train all week. As much as she hated the idea of not being completely independent, she was relieved to know she'd have more time to get used to it before she was on her own.

"Cash invited us out for drinks tonight to celebrate Siena's brother Dex's newest video game release. He's one of the top video game developers in the country. It's probably going to be a wild night, so maybe we should skip it."

"Are you crazy?" she asked. "That sounds like a huge ac-complishment for him, and you're close to their family. We should definitely go."

"What about your ankle?"

"It's a sprain. I don't want you missing anything because of me. I'll be fine."

After a few minutes of debate, Boyd gave in.

It was a nice afternoon, and Janie wasn't ready to go back home yet. "You know, I just realized that I don't even know where you live."

"Just a few blocks away."

"Can we go to your place instead of mine? I'd love to spend time in your world for a while."

"You sure you're okay using the crutch? How's your ankle holding up?"

"Stop worrying. I'll complain if it gets too bad."

"You make a terrible liar."

A few minutes later they walked into Boyd's apartment building. From the moment Janie stepped inside his apartment it felt like home. It smelled like him, manly and confident. She tried to imagine him coming into the apartment last night, and wondered if he'd missed her as desperately as she'd missed him while she lay alone in her bed.

He showed her around the galley kitchen, which was small, like hers. The bathroom smelled even more like him. She ran her fingers over the furniture in the bedroom as Boyd described it to her.

"I'm afraid none of it's very unique. Dark wood, heavy furniture. Probably what most guys have, I guess."

She touched his comforter, which was thick and soft. She tried to imagine him living here, in this quiet apartment, without her. But every time she pictured him walking into the bedroom, or standing at the stove, she pictured herself nearby.

In the living room, she sank into the deep couch cushions. "Oh my God, this couch swallows me up. I love it."

"I love how you look on it." He propped her ankle up with a pillow on the coffee table and sat beside her.

"Tell me about your stuff. I want to get a mental picture of your world."

"There's not much to it. The couch is brown, and the coffee table doesn't match the bookcases, because I don't have very good taste." He leaned in and kissed her neck. "Except when it comes to my most recent girlfriend."

"Flirt," she said, loving his attention. "What about pictures? Do you have family photos?"

He reached across her and then set a frame in her hands and another on her lap. "This is a picture of my parents. It was taken on their anniversary the year of the fire. Their heads are touching, and they're smiling. My mom was really pretty. She was petite, like my sister, Haylie, who's barely five two. My dad was big, as I told you. Every time I see this picture, they look so alive and happy, it's hard to believe they're gone. Even after all this time."

"I'm sorry you lost them."

"Me too," he said softly. He handed her the other picture. "This is a picture of me, Chet, Haylie, and her little boy, Scotty."

"Do you guys look alike?"

"Chet and I are built the same, both over six feet tall, broad shouldered, like our dad. Chet played football in high school. I never did."

"Why not?"

"It wasn't my thing."

"Were you bothered by your scars?" He'd already told her

he'd avoided dating when he was in high school, and she assumed his insecurities had carried over to the locker room.

"Somewhat." He tapped the frame and changed the subject. "Haylie and Scotty both have big blue eyes, like you. Haylie's fairer than me and Chet, like our mom. This picture was taken at Scotty's third birthday party. He's sitting at the head of the table blowing out the candles. Haylie's got this look in her eyes, like Scotty's her whole world, which he kind of is. My parents would have gotten such a kick out of him."

"You must miss your parents."

"Every moment of every day." The longing in his voice was palpable. "That's the main reason I was hoping to get into a Virginia med school. To be closer to my family."

Her heart sank with the mention of him going away, but he'd said *was*, not *is*, and that surprised her. "Was?"

He lifted her chin and kissed her. "The idea of leaving you has got me rethinking my goals."

She didn't know how to respond. He'd lived his whole life with the intent of going to medical school. She couldn't stand in his way, even though she ached at the idea of him leaving. They may have known each other through work for a few months, but they'd only been seeing each other for a few days. It felt like they'd been dating so much longer.

"Did you apply to schools here?"

"I did, but I haven't heard from them yet. I don't want to talk about that right now. I've got my girl alone in my apartment for the first time." He gathered her in his arms and rubbed his cheek against hers, nipping at her earlobe. "How should we pass the time?"

"Well, I've had a pretty stressful day, having a full-on panic attack and all. I think a few kisses might ease the pain."

They were both smiling as their mouths came together. He traced her lower lip with his tongue and rained kisses along her jaw. "Does that help?"

"Mm, I'm not sure. Better keep trying."

She pulled his mouth to hers. She loved doing that, taking control when he wasn't expecting it. His kisses were hot and wet when he was caught off guard, and a few seconds later he took control, making them even hotter. He eased her legs to the couch and lay beside her. When he kissed her again, it felt like their entire bodies were kissing. Their chests crushed together, his arms engulfed her, and his eager arousal nestled firmly against her thigh. She slid her hands beneath his shirt, feeling the roughness of his scars. She'd wanted to ask him more about his family, how his brother and sister dealt with the loss of their parents, but all of that could wait. What she wanted more than anything was to disappear into the man who made her heart sing and her body hum.

Chapter Twelve

THE AFTERNOON PASSED in a flurry of kissing and talking, groping, and driving each other wild. By the time Boyd and Janie realized the sun had gone down, they were both flushed with desire. Boyd fought the urge to carry her into the bedroom and make love to her. He still wanted to wait until she was one hundred percent sure and not speaking from the heat of the moment. He wondered if they'd ever not be speaking from the heat of the moment. He couldn't keep his hands off of her. The thing that kept him in check was that he'd told Cash they'd meet him at Dex's celebration. If they went into the bedroom, there was no way they'd make it out before morning.

When they left to meet Cash and the others, his body was still thrumming. But all that lust settled when they took the train back to Janie's so she could change. She managed to get on the second train that came around, and this time she wasn't white-knuckling the crutch. Pride shone in her eyes, and seeing her so elated made his heart feel full.

While they were at Janie's apartment, Boyd took another look at her appliances. Kiki had told him where to find the stick-on buttons they'd used, and he wanted to make sure Janie felt as comfortable as possible at his place.

An hour later they walked into the packed bar. Boyd tugged Janie in tight against him, unable to avoid people bumping into them as they wound through the crowd looking for Cash. Janie seemed fine maneuvering her crutch, but Boyd was second-guessing their decision.

"You're so tense," she said in his ear.

"I wasn't thinking. This place is too crowded."

Janie placed her hand on his chest and looked at him like he'd said something wrong. He had no idea how she managed to put on makeup, but she wore just enough to give her cheeks a rosy blush, and a little coal-colored shadow above her eyes gave her a seductive look. The bruise on her cheek was less purple and more yellow, but it was no match for the glint of emotions in her eyes.

"If you're saying that because of me, I'm fine."

"Doesn't it bother you?" he asked. "All these people crowding you?"

She pressed her lips to his chest. "I'm here with you. That's all that matters."

"You're incredible." He kissed her, reminding himself not to smother her. If she said she was fine, then he had to accept that. It wasn't easy, dating someone so independent. Usually girls wanted more attention, but as she smiled up at him, he realized, she did want his attention. She just didn't want him to treat her like she needed special treatment. He shoved his protective urges as deep as they'd go. Then shoved them a little deeper. One more shove, and he figured he was below smothering level.

He could do this.

"Dude!" Cash pushed through the crowd, blazing a path for Boyd and Janie to walk through.

"Man, this is crazy." Boyd high-fived his buddy Tommy

Burke, another firefighter, and hugged Siena. "Tommy, this is my girlfriend, Janie."

He watched Tommy take in her bruised cheek, her crutch, and knew the second he realized her eyes weren't meeting his. He blinked a few times, as if he was processing the information, and then, true to Tommy's awesome nature, he embraced her warmly.

"Sorry to hear about your fall, but I've got to ask. What's a hot babe like you doing with a guy like Boyd?"

Boyd punched him in the arm.

"He's really good in bed," Janie answered easily.

Holy hell. Boyd tried to hide his shock.

Tommy and Cash burst out laughing.

"I knew I liked you," Siena said. "You look amazing. I love that outfit."

Janie looked hotter than any woman in there, in a pair of distressed jeans that hugged her sweet curves and a pink tank-style blouse. A chunky silver necklace spruced up the casual outfit, and she even managed to match her sparkly flat sandals to the necklace. Boyd would have to remember to ask her how she did that. He'd never given much thought to things like matching clothes or shoes, but Janie had opened his eyes to how much he'd taken for granted. He wanted to know how she did everything.

Dex Remington, Siena's twin, rose from a seat at the bar, bringing his fiancée, Ellie, with him. He shook his dark hair out of his eyes and pulled Boyd into a manly embrace. "Glad you could make it, bro." He turned to Janie and touched her arm. "Hi, Janie. I'm Dex, and this is my fiancée, Ellie."

"Hi, Janie. I'm so glad you made it out tonight." Ellie was a petite brunette. She and Dex had known each other as kids and had then lost touch for several years before reuniting right there in NightCaps. They'd been together ever since.

"Nice to meet you both," Janie said. "Congratulations on your game release. You must be so excited."

"Yeah, the fans' reception has been the best yet," Dex said.

"Boys and their games. Who knew they could play for a living?" Ellie sidled up to Janie, sandwiching Janie between her and Siena. Even though he was only a few feet from her, Boyd felt too far away.

He tried to move closer, but a tall blonde wearing too much perfume and too-tight clothing stepped in between them.

Siena said something to Janie, and Janie scowled. Boyd wished he could reach her, but short of pushing the woman out of the way, there wasn't enough room to maneuver around her.

"Hey there," the blonde said as she eye-fucked him. "Can I buy you a drink?"

Janie leaned forward and said, "You're wasting your time. He's deaf as a doorknob. I've been striking out for the past ten minutes."

Boyd bit the insides of his cheeks to keep from laughing.

"Seriously?" the blonde asked. "Shame. He's hot." She looked at Boyd again, then flashed a bold, lecherous smile at Dex and Cash.

Dex reached for Ellie.

"If she can't get his attention with a body like this," Siena said, nodding at Janie, "you haven't got a chance."

The blonde sneered at Siena before stalking away.

"Deaf? I can't believe you said that," Ellie said with a laugh.

"Totally cool, Janie," Dex said. "Way to claim your man. And, sis, nice barb."

"I've got my girl's back," Siena said as Cash put a possessive arm around her.

"Man, Boyd." Tommy elbowed him. "She's awesome."

"Tell me something I don't know." Boyd stepped forward and wrapped his arms around Janie. "Baby, you know I would have shot her down, right?"

"Yeah, but that was so much more fun." She held on to his shoulder as he leaned in for another kiss. "And I bet if I could see, she'd be giving me the stink-eye right about now."

"I can't believe she gave up because you said he was deaf," Siena said. "I mean, a man who's deaf and hot? How great would that be? He wouldn't complain about how much we talk, right?"

Janie laughed, and Boyd saw the blonde sneering at them. He pulled Janie closer, proud to be her man.

"I guess I shouldn't have worried about the crowded bar," Boyd admitted. "You really can take care of yourself."

"Someone has to look out for poor, handsome Boyd," she said in a mocking tone. "How did you ever fend off women before me?"

"The better question is, how can I keep you around so I don't have to?"

JANIE HAD SUCH a good time with Boyd and his friends, she forgot all about her ankle, until she asked Boyd to dance and tried to stand from the booth they'd taken over about an hour ago. She cringed and lifted her foot. Boyd's arm was around her waist, taking her weight off her foot in seconds.

"Careful, baby."

"I forgot about my ankle." She hooked her hands behind his

neck and leaned against him.

"We'll dance just like this. Keep your knee bent so your foot doesn't touch the floor."

"I've never seen Boyd dance," Cash said. "Have you guys ever seen him dance?"

The other guys hooted and hollered, and Boyd said, "Ignore them."

"Come on, big mouth," Siena said.

"Siena's dragging Cash up to dance," Boyd explained. She loved that he remembered she sometimes needed a few hints to know what was going on. "*Aaand*…here come Dex and Ellie."

"Aw, what about Tommy?" she asked.

"He's going up to the bar."

Janie leaned her head against Boyd's chest, reveling in the feel of his arms around her. She was so glad they hadn't skipped being there for Dex. Dex and Ellie were planning their wedding, and incredibly, they told Boyd they'd plan it around his schedule once he got into medical school. They really did treat him like family.

They danced to a few songs, and eventually they said good-bye to everyone and made their way back to Janie's apartment. The subway was less of an issue this time. She was comfortable using her crutch and stepping on and off the train, knowing that Boyd was with her.

Boyd set her crutch by the front door.

"I'll be here tomorrow morning to walk to work with you so we can practice using your cane and crutch on the subway, and then I'll disappear and come back to walk home with you after work."

She loved that he said *we*. "I don't want you to disappear."

He closed the sliver of space between them, pressing his

body to hers. "I can't imagine leaving you overnight, much less disappearing."

"Then don't." She fisted her hand in his shirt, not wanting to spend another night apart. One was already too many.

"Don't…?"

She could feel him searching her face. "Don't leave me. Stay with me tonight."

"There's nothing I'd rather do, but are you sure?"

"Yes. More than sure, Boyd. I want you in my bed, and not for any kind of research beyond my own selfish desires."

He cradled her face in his hands and kissed her deeply. He was so tempting, so deliciously warm and provocative. Her body melted against him as the kiss intensified. Anticipation coiled inside her, tight and hot.

"Janie…"

She didn't want him to put on the brakes. Need pounded inside her, begging for release. It took all of her concentration to force one word from her lungs.

"Stay."

Chapter Thirteen

JANIE DIDN'T WANT to overthink this. She wanted Boyd with a deep, aching need that burned between her legs and stormed in her belly. She'd thought all-consuming lust was something made of dreams and fantasies, but Boyd was *real*. More than six feet of firm muscle and loving words, with hands made for touching, a talented mouth that stole her brain cells with every kiss, and a steel rod behind his zipper that she wanted to feel inside her. But it was more than sex she craved from him. She wanted to experience the emotions he'd hidden so well from the rest of the world—hidden from her with his flirty facade and cool attitude—but now wore so boldly around her.

He lowered her onto the bed and carefully followed her down.

"Janie," he said against her cheek.

His voice—*God, his seductive, loving voice*—did her in every time he said her name. He sucked her earlobe into his mouth and grazed it with his teeth, triggering a torrent of pleasure through her.

"I don't want to hurt you. Your hip, your ankle, your side...I'm too heavy," he warned, but all she could think about was how much she'd been holding back since their first kiss.

He tasted her neck, slowly sucking her sensitive skin into his mouth, causing her to writhe and pant, to pull at his arms, his head, never wanting him to stop. And then he was gone—the mattress shifted, and she felt his movements as he pulled off his shirt and she reached for him. Her fingers met his warm flesh, the muscles flexing and taut beneath her touch. *God* she loved the feel of him.

"I don't want to hurt you," he repeated, his voice full of restraint and hope and something else, bigger, deeper. *Alive.* "We can wait until you're healed up. Even if I stay over, we don't have to…"

It wasn't just her body craving him now. With his caring words and careful touches, her heart was opening up to him, embracing him, wanting to sweep his goodness into a bundle and nestle inside it. But her body was on fire, and there was no way she would be able to sleep next to him without attacking him, despite her injuries. And she didn't *want* to resist him. She wanted Boyd—all of him.

"You'd deprive an injured woman?"

"Janie." He kissed her, still not putting any weight on her.

Oh, how she wanted to be crushed beneath him! To feel his powerful emotions as he took her, filled her, claimed her.

"I told you how many women I've slept with. How the hell have you gotten to me so quickly?"

"Destiny. You said it yourself. Now kiss me, Boyd."

His mouth swooped down and captured hers in a hungry kiss that shattered her restraint. She clung to his biceps, taking intense pleasure in the shudder that rolled through him. He stripped away her clothing, kissing every inch of her skin as it was revealed. Heady sensations whirled inside her as his mouth came down over her sensitive breast. She writhed for more, arching against his tongue as he teased her nipple, rocking her hips as he gripped her ass.

"Too many clothes," he said urgently, and sprang to his feet. She heard him stripping off his clothes.

Knowing he was naked brought her to the edge of the bed, wanting, needing, to feel more of him. She reached for him, and he guided her hands to his thighs. The pit of her stomach warmed, tightening like a fist. She ran her hands over his firm ass, fighting to control the smile tugging at her lips. She'd never been aggressive with her other boyfriends, had never wanted to touch them this badly, to bring them intense pleasure the way she did with Boyd. But with him, she couldn't have fought her desires if her life depended on it.

Heat rolled off his body as she pulled him closer. His hands framed her face and the muscles in his thighs flexed.

"Closer," she whispered.

"Janie, you don't have to—"

She closed her hand around the base of his arousal, inhaling his musky scent as she licked the swollen head. He hissed a word she couldn't make out, his hips bucking forward.

Loving his reaction, she licked him from base to tip, stroking him with her hand as she lowered her mouth over the head. She stroked and sucked, circling the head of his cock with her tongue. His body tensed, but his hands remained gently on her cheeks, tracing the edge of her lips, where they met his skin.

"I love to feel your mouth on me," he panted out.

Spurred on by his words, she took him deeper and quickened her pace. When he tangled his hands in her hair, he didn't rush or guide her. He held on tight as she teased and tasted, hearing restraint in his wanton groan.

"Janie. Stop."

She drew back and slicked her tongue over his swollen glans. "I want to taste you." She lowered her mouth over his arousal again and he groaned, making her sex twitch with need. She loved the feel of his smooth skin, the press of the large vein running up his shaft against her tongue. Cupping his balls, she coaxed him toward release.

"Janie," he ground out as he thrust harder.

Every thrust made her wetter between her legs. She sucked and licked, her cheeks hollowing out with each stroke.

"Janie...*God, Janie.*" He groaned as jets of salty-sweet come filled her mouth, and desperate words streamed from his lungs. "So good. *Janie. Janie. Fuck. Janie.*"

A hiss left his lungs as he withdrew from her mouth, sank down to his knees, and kissed her like he'd been waiting years to do it. She couldn't get enough of his taste, his tongue, as it plundered and pushed against hers.

"I need more of you, honey." He buried his tongue in her mouth again, their teeth clanking together as his hands found her breasts and squeezed her nipples, sending shocks of heat to her core.

"Are you on birth control, baby?"

"Yes." She'd been on birth control since college, something Kiki had drilled into her head for *those times when waiting isn't an option.* This was her very first time feeling that way. She'd have to remember to thank Kiki.

Kissing his way down her belly, he spread her legs wide and claimed her wet center as if he were claiming her mouth. He licked and sucked and kissed and stroked. Her legs tingled, her core tightened, and then suddenly she was in his arms, and he was guiding her legs around his waist.

"I'm too heavy to lie on top of you." His voice was gruff, restrained. "Is this okay?"

She felt the head of his rigid cock against her wetness and gripped his shoulders, surprised—and thrilled—he'd recovered so quickly.

"*Yes—*"

As he lowered her onto his shaft, they both moaned. She felt her body stretching to accommodate him, and it was the most exquisite feeling. So full, so tight, so complete. Her whole body awakened with his invasion.

"Jesus," he said against her neck. "So tight. So good."

Their mouths crashed together, and he filled her lungs with his hot, loving breath. With one hand under her ass, the other around her back, he raised and lowered her in time to each thrust of his hips. His tongue searched the far reaches of her mouth. She wanted to stay right there in his arms forever, to feel his emotions coursing through the muscles in his shoulders, the tension in his jaw. The raw and visceral grunts and groans he made blended with her moans of pleasure, all of which pulled her further into his fire. She felt an orgasm building, mounting, pleading for release. When he sank his teeth into her neck, lights exploded in her mind.

"Janie—"

His grip tightened, and the first pulse of his release stole her last thread of control. Her head spun, her insides clenched, and her heart teetered on a dangerous ledge.

He held her as aftershocks shuddered through them. His legs were shaking, matching the frenetic pace of her own trembling limbs. The scents of their lovemaking hung in the air.

"Honey." He slipped from her body and sat on the edge of the mattress, cradling her on his lap.

"Baby."

She loved that he was just as lost for words as she was. He kissed her cheeks, her neck, her lips, her forehead. His arms circled her. His emotions wound around him like a magnetic cable, binding with hers. She'd never felt more cherished, more desired, and as he breathed out her name, she nuzzled into his warmth.

"Are you okay, honey? Did I hurt your ankle?"

There he went again, watching out for her even though she'd promised to tell him if she hurt. He was so different from who she'd thought he was. Over the course of a few short days she'd felt his heart opening up to her in ways she could tell were difficult and meaningful. She wanted to be the person he trusted most, the person he wanted to share everything with— his dreams, his fears, and his tender heart.

"Hurt is nowhere near my radar."

He kissed her chin, her cheek, and finally—*finally*—her mouth. She wanted to disappear into his kisses again, and as he settled them onto the bed and curled his body around hers, she wondered if anyone would notice if they stayed in the bedroom forever.

Chapter Fourteen

"WATCHING YOU GET ready in the morning is like poetry in motion," Boyd said as Janie dressed.

She had a routine for getting ready for work and breezed through it effortlessly. Her clothes were color coordinated in the closet, separated by dividers in braille, which she read with a brush of her fingertips. Her jewelry was laid out in pretty wooden jewelry boxes, one for each type—silver, gold, sparkly—a system she and Kiki had devised in middle school.

They walked down to the subway, stopping to say hello to Mr. Gregory along the way. Boyd gave Janie a wide berth, letting her get comfortable using her cane and her crutch as she made her way along the subway platform. She sensed his presence like fall rolling in, steady and uplifting. She managed better than she thought she would as she followed the crowd onto the first train that arrived, holding her breath for only a few seconds as she crossed the bumpy area at the edge of the platform. Boyd moved in beside her, his strong arms quickly circling her waist.

"That was impressive," he said in her ear. "Your confidence is sexy as hell."

She tipped her face up, feeling his warmth on her forehead

as he lowered his lips and pressed a kiss there. "I told you I could do it."

"I never doubted you for a minute." The train came to a stop and the doors slid open. "But seeing it with my own eyes made me feel better."

They made their way up to the street and to her office.

"I'll put your bag on your desk," Boyd said. Then his arms were around her waist again and his body was against hers, bringing with it sexy memories of their lovemaking.

"It seems like a lifetime ago that we walked out of this office together," he said before pressing his lips to hers. "I hope things go well in the peer review meeting."

She'd forgotten completely about the meeting. "Thank you. Me too."

"I guess it's time for me to disappear, but I'll be back when you get off work. What time should I come by?"

"Five thirty?" They'd spent so much time together that the thought of not seeing him for hours made her long for him.

"Perfect." His hands cupped her cheeks the way he'd done so many times over the weekend, like he wanted her full attention so she didn't miss a word of what he had to say. "I better get out of here before someone sees us and you ruin my reputation for being a playboy."

"I hadn't thought about that. Do you think Clay will mind that we're dating?"

"If he does, I'll quit."

"Boyd, you can't do that." But she had no doubt he would if it came down to it.

"For you? Anything. But Clay won't mind. I'm a consultant, not a full-time employee." He kissed her again, and she listened to his footsteps disappear down the hall.

An hour later she was busy editing when her parents' ringtone sounded from her cell. She couldn't put their calls off forever, but she could keep it short.

"Hi." She cringed at her clipped tone.

"Hi, sweetheart. I've been trying to reach you." Her mother's voice was filled with the usual concerns: *Why didn't you call me back? How are you? I was worried about you. You should return our calls or we worry.*

Janie didn't have the time to go down that path because when she did, her mother took it as an opening to climb back into the oppressive spot she'd once occupied. She did what she had to do to keep enough space between them to retain her independence and apologized without leaving it open-ended. "Sorry, Mom. I've been busy at work. Everything okay at home?"

Her mother told her about her garden club, which she'd been a member of forever, and filled Janie in on her father's latest weekend of golf. Same story, different day.

"I don't understand why you don't return our calls, Janie. You know we worry. Anything can happen to you out th—"

As her mother proceeded to drill her, Janie tuned her out and finally cut her off. "Sorry, Mom. I'll try to return your calls from now on. I've got to run to a meeting." She hated lying, but she had no choice.

After ending the call, she was in a sour mood. She set aside her editing and hoped focusing on writing an article for the next newsletter might lift her spirits. But after writing about flirting and sensual innuendos all weekend, the very thought of writing an article about editing bored her.

She sat back, listening to the sounds of her coworkers talking as they walked by her office and thinking about the first-kiss scene in *Sinful Fantasies,* which made her think of Boyd and their toe-curling kisses.

Janie turned her braille device off of terminal mode, so no one could see what she was typing, and typed *How to write a kissing scene* into Google. After reading the first few articles, it became apparent that the people writing the articles were not blind, because the articles talked about seductive glances, lifting of lips, and other sights of two people coming together. She would have to imagine those things, having never really paid attention to them or experienced them when she was younger and had been able to see such detail. But she wouldn't have to imagine everything. With Boyd, she'd experienced the chemistry that elicited those responses and was thrilled when the articled described taking all senses into consideration when writing about a kiss. Sense of smell, sight, sound, touch…Maybe this would be easier than she'd imagined. She used those senses every day. She thought about setting the scene for the first kiss in her book and drew upon her first kiss with Boyd.

She pulled up her editing assignment on the computer, so anyone who might happen into her office would think she was working, and turned her attention to writing romance. Remembering the moments before their first kiss in the bathroom, she chose not to include descriptions of the cold sink beneath her or the way the walls had felt like they breathed and pulsed, because those weren't what she'd been focused on in those exciting seconds before their lips met. Her fingers flew across the keyboard as she wrote about her fictional heroine and hero, Candee and Kent. The synthesized voice program told her story through her earbuds.

Candee's heartbeat sped up as Kent stepped in closer. Anticipa-

tion prickled her limbs, and his masculine scent consumed her as his hips brushed against her inner thighs, nudging them apart and making her acutely aware of his thick, hard body.

Janie got lost in the fictional world she was creating. The desire that stormed through her characters made her just as hot and bothered as they were. She hadn't expected writing to be such a turn-on, but she was seven pages in, hours of work lost to the development of her characters' love story, and she didn't want to stop—or lose the heated, lustful sensation coiling low in her belly.

Kiki's ringtone pulled her from the moment.

"Hey," she answered.

"Janie? Why do you sound like you're having sex?"

Janie spoke quietly in case anyone was near her office. "Because I've been writing romance all morning instead of working, and oh my God, Kiki...I'm so flippin' turned-on I can barely see straight."

"Seriously? From writing?"

"Uh-huh. Thank God no one has come into my office. I'm sure they'd be able to tell." She fanned her face with her hand.

"Maybe you can call Boyd for a quickie at lunch," Kiki teased.

That sounded good to her.

"Speaking of which, he spent the night? I heard you leaving this morning. You guys are getting serious pretty fast."

"It was spur-of-the-moment. Do you think I'm making a mistake?"

"No! You go, girlfriend. It's about time you found a hot guy who treats you like gold."

"So you don't think it's a bad thing?" The last thing Janie wanted to do was slow their relationship down. She hadn't ever been this happy, or felt this alive, but Kiki was more experienced with men, and she valued her advice.

"Heck no. He's obviously crazy about you, and you're totally lost in him, which is a good thing. I've never seen you like you are around him. I know you can't see him, but you look at him like he's your everything."

"I do? I just…The things he says and does." Janie sighed dreamily. "Kiki, it feels so right, and it's all happening so fast." She was glad Kiki was happy for her, but she felt guilty for not spending much time with her this weekend. "I'm sorry you came home to help me and I spent all weekend with Boyd."

"No you're not." Kiki laughed. "And you shouldn't be. *I'm* used to being the one who monopolizes *your* time. It's kind of weird being on the other side of things, and I might be a little jealous, but I am happy for you."

"Jealous? You have dozens of guys after you all the time."

"Dozens of guys is a world away from one special guy. You're lucky, Janie. I'm truly happy for you."

A knock sounded on Janie's door, which she'd left open.

"Janie, the newsletter deadline was moved up." Tara Onyx, the office administrator, came into her office. "Oh, sorry. I didn't realize you were on the phone."

"It's okay," she said to Tara, then to Kiki, "I've got to run. We'll catch up soon." She ended the call and set her phone aside. "When do you need the article?"

"Four today instead of tomorrow morning. I've got to leave early today to pick up my brother from the airport. Does that give you enough time?"

She'd spent hours writing instead of working and hadn't even thought about the article since early that morning. She'd have to be more careful. "Sure. I'll send it over shortly."

After Tara left, Janie emailed her latest kissing scene to herself. Still revved up from writing the sexy scene, she opened a new Word document and let her friskiness come through the newsletter article.

Don't Get Caught with Dangling Participles...

BOYD WANTED TO make sure he was doing all he could for Janie to be comfortable in his apartment. He had no trouble finding the stick-on buttons he'd seen in Janie's apartment, but he called his buddy Heath, whose mother was also blind, for even more advice. Heath's mother had lost her vision after being beaten during a home invasion that left his father dead and their family in turmoil. Thankfully, Heath and his family were doing much better now, and Heath was more than happy to share the wealth of information he'd learned over the past few years. He'd turned Boyd on to a store in the city that specialized in devices for independent living for the blind. Boyd headed over to the store immediately after ending the call, and three hours later he was armed with products, games, and more.

The minute he got home he set to work. He began in the kitchen, carefully applying braille buttons over the front of the microwave controls, the stove, and labeling the cabinets so Janie could easily find the plates, cups, and glasses. In the bathroom he went a little mad with the braille label maker, labeling each item in the vanity. *Toothpaste, floss, Q-Tips.* He knew he was already in too deep to ever walk away from Janie when he got to the bedroom and emptied two drawers, labeling them *Janie's*. He'd bought special dividers for the closet like he'd seen in Janie's apartment, and he hung those up, too.

After labeling far too many items and controls, he moved extraneous items from his floor, as Heath had advised. Finally, with the apartment organized, he sent Janie a quick text.

How's my girl? How did the peer review meeting go? Did they like your writing sample?

Boyd checked his email while he waited for Janie's reply and found a letter from the University of Colorado School of Medicine. Praying they were inviting him for an interview, he clicked on the email and quickly read it. *Dear Mr. Hudson, We're pleased to invite...*

"Yes!" He pumped his fist.

His phone vibrated with a reply from Janie, and as he read it—*They loved my writing sample! They're discussing my promotion in the next management meeting. A good sign!*—his initial excitement over the interview waned.

He sank down to the couch, leaned his elbows on his knees, and rested his forehead in his hands. *What am I doing?*

He'd spent his life working toward medical school. He had to go on this interview. He couldn't push the opportunity aside for a woman he'd just met. But even as he typed his response and accepted the interview for the following week, he had a sick feeling in the pit of his stomach. His mind ran in circles. He'd known Janie for months on a casual basis, but he'd only *just* gotten to really know her, and already he was rearranging his apartment? His life? His future?

He sat back and closed his eyes, trying to imagine his life without Janie in it. He couldn't. The mere thought of it was too painful. He couldn't deny that he was falling hard and fast for her, but what would that do to his future? Her life was here, and his life here was temporary.

He returned Janie's text. *That's great news. Celebrate tonight?*

Dinner out?

His phone vibrated seconds later. *Tons of work to do tonight. Can we have dinner in and celebrate?*

Smiling, he sent off his reply. She was so driven. He loved that about her.

Anything you want. How about I cook?

Her response was immediate. *Perfect. Bring clothes to stay over?*

After showering and packing a bag, he headed down to the firehouse to clear his schedule, and hopefully, his mind.

THE FIREHOUSE SMELLED like spaghetti sauce, which meant Joe Arlen was cooking. Joe was a brash, thick-waisted, and heavily muscled Italian. He had a mop of dark brown hair, always sported at least three days' worth of beard, and what he lacked in manners, he more than made up for with his expertise as a firefighter and his mother's talents in the kitchen—*God rest her soul.*

Boyd popped into the recreation room, where he found Tommy and Cash watching an old Western. Their hair was wet, and they had that still-hopped-up-on-adrenaline look that came after fighting a particularly difficult fire.

"Tough one?" Boyd asked as he sat on the couch beside Tommy. His foot tapped out a nervous beat. Being in the firehouse brought up other stresses about leaving New York. These guys were his family, his brothers, and as much as he wanted to end up back in Virginia near his grandparents, siblings, and nephew, leaving these guys would be tough as hell.

"Four-alarm," Tommy said without taking his eyes off of

the television. "Went on forever. Just got back an hour ago."

Guilt settled heavily on his shoulders. "Sorry I wasn't there to help you out."

"No sweat. No fatalities. It's all good." Cash sucked back a Coke. "What're you doing here? I thought you needed time off."

"I need more time off, actually. I came to see who could swap shifts for the next week or so."

Tommy looked up. "What's up?"

"Med school interview in Colorado."

"How long you need?" Tommy kicked his feet up on the coffee table.

"Couple days, I guess." He didn't want to be away from Janie any longer than he had to.

"That's great news." Cash turned down the volume on the television. "Why do you look like you've got a stick up your ass?"

"Because, man. I've worked my tail off to get to med school, and now I've met Janie." He got up and tried to pace off his nervous energy. "Remember when you met Siena? How quickly did you know you loved her?"

"The first week, when he took our magazines away from us," Tommy said with a snicker.

Cash shut him up with a serious stare. "Right. I thought she was a big, snotty, gorgeous pain the first time we met, and within two days I wanted her to be mine and only mine."

"The man speaks the truth." Tommy picked up a magazine and opened it to a jagged-edged strip where a page had been torn out. "There used to be an ad right here, with a picture of Siena wearing nothing but a fur coat and heels. Jackass over here ripped it out."

"I don't blame him. You magazine masturbators would have made her sticky in no time." Boyd high-fived Cash. "I've got your back, man, but I'm a mess."

"You can't give up medical school," Cash said with a serious tone. "You'd resent her in no time."

"I know that. I'm not an idiot." He was so tightly wound he worried he might explode. "Or maybe I am an idiot, because going away to med school seems unimportant compared to spending time with Janie."

"After a weekend?" Tommy cocked a brow. "Go on the interview. You won't even hear back for a few weeks, and by then you'll have it all figured out. But don't throw your life away for a weekend. Janie's great, but..."

"Says the guy who spent three *years* pining for a woman who shall go unnamed," Cash said. Tommy had been stuck in the *friend zone* with a woman named Kelly, who'd strung him along like a puppy on a leash until a few weeks ago, when he'd finally worked up the guts to cut ties with her.

"Do *not* bring her up," Tommy warned.

"Who? Kelly?" Joe said as he sauntered into the room. "Hey, Boyd, I heard you were banging a blind chick. Scraping the bottom of the barrel?"

Rage flashed through Boyd. He grabbed Joe by the shirt and slammed him against the wall. "Take it back, asshole."

"Whoa, dude." Joe's smirk pissed off Boyd even more. He pushed him harder against the wall and Joe held up his hands in surrender. "What the fuck, man?"

"You think that shit's funny?" Boyd spat. "She's a person, Joe. A whole fucking person who happens to not be able to see."

"Boyd." Cash's hand landed on his shoulder, pulling him back as Boyd fought to keep hold of Joe. "Joe's just being a dick. He's not worth it."

Boyd tightened his fists in Joe's shirt and said through gritted teeth, "If you ever talk about Janie like that again, I *will* kill you." He threw Joe backward and paced the small room, feeling the walls pressing in on him. "Goddamn it, Joe."

"Dude, I was kidding." Joe rubbed his chest where Boyd's knuckles had dug into him. "I didn't mean anything bad about her. I was trying to say that no girl who could see would want you."

"Today's not the day to joke around," Cash said sternly. "Besides, that's not what you said, so think before you speak. Next time I'll let him have at you."

"Fuck." Boyd clenched his jaw, trying to regain control. He lifted angry eyes to Joe, who was looking at him like he'd lost his mind, and maybe he had. All he knew was that he didn't want anyone demeaning Janie in any way. Not even as a joke. She was too special, too good of a person, and she'd already fought that battle, hadn't she? He thought about how hard of a time she'd had finding a job, and that pissed him off again. Were people really that unknowingly cruel and shortsighted?

One glance at Joe and he knew Janie's assessment was right: People could rationalize anything in their own deluded minds.

"Sorry, Boyd," Joe said. "Stick around for dinner?"

That's how it was around the firehouse. They could fight, bitch a blue streak, and call one another out on shit they didn't want to face, but at the end of the day they'd always have each other's backs. Firehouse brotherhood was as thick as blood.

"Nah, thanks. Gotta go meet Janie."

Joe nodded. "Fair enough. And just for the record, from what these assholes said about her, you're lucky as shit. So try not to fuck it up."

As Boyd headed for the subway he wondered which he'd screw up—his future or his relationship—because he had no idea how to manage both.

Chapter Fifteen

JANIE HEARD BOYD walk quietly into her office, bringing with him his potent, masculine scent. Her stomach fluttered with anticipation, though she acted as if she didn't know he'd walked in. When his hands landed on her shoulders and his lips touched her cheek, she said, "Clay, stop. Boyd might catch you."

"Sleeping your way to the top, are you?" Boyd slid his hands to the nape of her neck, bringing their foreheads together. "I'd fight Clay for you."

"What if I had said Sin?" she teased, knowing he was at least a little jealous of Kiki's brother.

"I'd fight harder, because he's known you longer. I don't know how any man can know you and not fall head over heels—" He paused, and Janie's heart leapt. "In *like* with you."

She stood, using his chest for leverage. "Head over heels in like with me? I like the sound of that." Her fingers moved over his chest. "Hey. Your shirt? Where'd you get a shirt with braille on it?" A smiled crept up as she read it aloud. "'Would you like to proofread my briefs?' That might be the greatest shirt ever, and yeah, I'd totally like to *proofread* your briefs."

"Thought you might like that, almost as much as you might

like this." He placed a book in her hand, and her fingers played over the cover.

"A handbook on romance writing? In braille?" She went up on her toes and kissed him. "Thank you! I can't believe you got this for me. Where did you find it?"

"My friend Heath hooked me up with a great store today."

"Heath? He's the one who lent you the crutch and walker?"

Boyd handed Janie her crutch. "Yes, his mother is blind. And I think his fiancée's cat is, too. He's kind of an expert now."

"Well, you'll have to thank him for me. And thank you, Boyd. I can't believe you did all this."

"I Janie-ized my entire apartment. You'd be surprised how many things you can label with a nifty braille label maker."

"You did that all for me?" She ran her fingers over his shirt again and lowered her voice. "Do you have braille underwear on, too?"

"If you're a good girl, maybe you can find out." He kissed her again. "How was your day? Did you finish your newsletter article?"

"Yes, but I think Tara was a little surprised by the title." On the way out of the office she told him about how she'd spent her morning writing romance when she should have been working.

"You're really getting into this romance writing, aren't you?"

"More than I ever imagined I would. Of course, now I'll have to work extra hard not to miss my deadline for the manual I'm editing."

"Are you sure you don't want me to stay at my place tonight so you can get some work done?"

"Definitely not," she answered as they walked toward the subway. "It was hard enough being away from you all day."

Boyd guided her to the edge of the sidewalk and folded his arms around her. "Good, because I missed you like crazy today, and the last thing I want is time apart."

Right there on the busy sidewalk, with people hurrying past, he kissed her deeply. The sounds of the city faded away as she gave herself over to the kiss, and the next one, and the one after that.

After a while they ended their sensual assault and headed home, stopping at the market near Janie's apartment. Janie filled in Lisa, one of the employees she often chatted with, about her accident while Boyd picked up ingredients for dinner.

"You know everyone." Boyd effortlessly carried the groceries and held her around her waist as they made their way up to her apartment.

"Don't you know the people in the stores around your place?" she asked as she unlocked the door.

"I know them in passing. You know, a wave or a hello, but you seem to be friends with everyone."

"I guess. You must have escaped that small-town mentality of everyone being a friend. I know that's not true in a big city like this, but I was used to getting to know the people I see often, so I did." She closed the door behind them. "Do you mind if I change real quick?"

His arms circled her waist and his hot lips kissed her neck. "It was more fun when you couldn't manage that crutch so easily."

"Mm. Wait until you see what I can do with two good ankles."

He held her face between his hands, and she felt him gazing at her. She loved that he didn't shy away from really looking at her. It was all these little things he did that added up to the magnificently caring person he was.

"Honey, there are so many things I can't wait to do, like make love to you properly, the way you deserve to be loved."

The way he said *loved*, full of emotion, made her heart skip a beat.

"I thought last night was pretty incredible." She touched his shirt again, reading the message there. She wanted to get her hands on his briefs, all right, but reading was the last thing on her mind.

"Beyond incredible, but I want to lay you down beneath me. I want to love every inch of you without worrying about being too heavy, or moving too hard or too fast. When you're healed up, I'm going to spend an entire evening lavishing your gorgeous body with attention."

"You're full of promises, aren't you?"

"Only promises I intend to keep." He gave her ass a little pat. "Go get comfy."

Using her crutch, she headed for the bedroom. "Dirty talk. Put that on our list for tonight."

He laughed. "What list?"

From behind the bedroom door she said, "I'm starting a list of things I need to research for my story. It's lacking dirty talk, plot, and kinky sex. Oh, and I'm still a little stuck on the sci-fi aspect. Maybe you can help me out with a few of those."

DIRTY TALK? HELL yeah, he'd like to fill her sexy, smart brain with dirty talk. *Kinky sex and sci-fi?* What was he thinking when he said those things to her? *That she'd never want to write a romance with all that in it, much less hang out with a guy who*

said those things. It had been a knee-jerk reaction to protect himself from getting too involved with her.

Epic fail, Hudson.

Boyd drizzled oil in a large pot of boiling salted water and added linguine. In another pan he melted butter, olive oil, and garlic, while Janie sat at the small wooden table looking enticing as hell in a white cotton skirt and purple tank top, typing on her braille device.

She inhaled deeply and said, "That smells incredible."

"My grandmother taught us all to cook. Shrimp scampi is one of my favorite quick meals."

"I cook Pop-Tarts really well."

"You heat me up really well, too." He leaned in for a kiss, and she pressed her hands to the sides of his head, holding him as she lifted up on one foot, deepening the kiss.

The garlic and butter sizzled, and Boyd reluctantly broke their connection to tend to dinner. "You should patent your lips."

She began typing again. "I'm stealing that for my book."

"Of course you are." He loved watching her write. Her face went from serious to playful and back again as her fingers flew over the keyboard. "Are you working on your book now?" He sautéed and seasoned the shrimp, filled two plates, added a touch of lemon juice and a sprig of parsley, and joined Janie at the table.

"Linguine and scampi, madam." He handed her a fork and a napkin. "It's hot, honey, so be careful."

"You spoil me. Thank you. I'm catching up on the editing I put off to write this morning."

"Don't blow your promotion over our bet."

"I won't. I want the promotion, but the more I write romance, the more I love it. I am having a little trouble, though. I wasn't kidding about needing help. The articles I read said to write what you know, but that's not going to work. So let's get started with dirty talk." She looked at him expectantly.

"Um…"

"*Dirty talk.* You know, sexy things you say to a woman to turn her on." She speared a shrimp and took a bite.

Boyd's fork stopped midair. "You want me to sit across from you while we eat dinner and talk dirty?"

"Sure. That'll work." She moved her braille device closer. "I can take notes while you talk."

Christ. "Baby, that's not going to happen."

"What? Why?" Her shoulders slumped, and she looked so damn cute he knew he didn't stand a chance of resisting her.

He reached across the table and squeezed her hand. "Because, first of all, I don't have standard lines, or whatever it is that you're looking for. I say what comes to me at the moment."

"Okay, so repeat what you said about making love to me." Her fingers hovered over the keyboard.

"Janie…"

"Please? How can I write a hot romance that you'll love if I don't know what you like?"

"*You're* what I like," he said more gruffly than he'd intended. How the hell was he supposed to talk dirty over dinner, like they were talking about the weather?

She brought his hand to her lips, sliding her tongue over his rough palm.

"Please?"

He set his fork down as she sucked his fingers into her mouth.

"Baby, we're going to do a lot more than talking dirty if you do that."

She shook her head. "No, we're not. Tonight's research is just dirty talk."

He came around the table and shifted her chair so she was facing him. She brought her braille device with her. A smile tugged at her lips. She looked so damn beautiful, with a rosy blush on her cheeks and a seductive look in her eyes, perched to take notes like a sexy librarian. He gently parted her legs and knelt between them, sliding his hands up her calves, beneath her skirt, and along her outer thighs.

"You look incredibly sexy right now, with your thighs spread wide for me and your lips waiting for my mouth to claim them."

Her trembling fingers hovered over the keyboard. Aroused by her reaction, he brushed his lips over hers, a whisper of a kiss, and her fingers stilled.

"How dirty do you want to hear?"

She seemed to think about that for a second, her fingers perched over the tiny pins. "Filthy," she whispered, making him instantly hard.

He pushed his hands farther up her hips, careful of her bruises, and lifted her forward, until her panties met his erection.

"Feel that, baby? Feel how hard you make me?"

With one hand on her hip, he slid the other beneath her hair and cupped the back of her head, angling her just so as he took her in a slow, intoxicating kiss. He kissed her until her breathing shallowed and her hands moved from the device to his arms.

"That's it, baby. Be with me."

Tangling his hand in her hair, he had to remind himself to

push away the loving words on the tip of his tongue and fulfill her dirty talk fantasy slash research mission.

"I love when you kiss me like you want me to strip you bare and take you right here on the table." He slid his hand between her legs, stroking her through her damp panties. "When your body quivers with need. Hot." He kissed her again. "Wet." He sucked her tongue into his mouth. "Ready."

"Don't touch, only talk. *Research.*" She moved trembling hands back to the keyboard and typed, much slower this time.

"Torture, baby," he whispered against her neck, and moved his hands to her thighs, his thumbs resting lightly against the damp material.

"I can't wait to feel all your slick heat swallowing me deep."

"Dirtier," she said breathlessly.

He'd held back using raunchy words. They didn't feel right, but he hated to let her down. "I want to taste your sweet pussy, baby, to feel your naked, hot flesh against mine as I bury my cock deep inside you."

She stopped typing and spread her legs wider, an invitation Boyd wasn't about to ignore. He brushed his thumbs over her panties.

"I want to sink my fingers, my tongue, into you."

"Ohmygod," she said in one long breath. She gripped his biceps, desire written in the flush of her skin. "Touch me."

He pushed his fingers beneath the thin material and sank two fingers into her.

"Fuck," he whispered against her lips, then claimed her mouth in a sensual kiss as he crooked his fingers deeper into her succulent heat, furtively seeking the spot that would send her over the edge.

"You're so tight, baby." He couldn't continue using that

language—not with Janie. Not when he wanted to love every inch of her. "I want to bury myself deep inside you and make love to you slowly, until you feel like you're going to explode, holding you on the edge of ecstasy, begging for more. I want to feel your nails digging into me as you cry out my name and make you come so many times you can't think."

"Boyd..." She rocked her hips against his hand, her legs wound around his thighs.

He sucked her lower lip into his mouth and bit down just hard enough for her to make it sting. She whimpered.

"Sorry, baby. Got carried away." Her head fell back with a pleasure-filled moan, and he continued his relentless pursuit of fulfilling her naughty request. "I can't wait to see your face when you come on my mouth again." He kissed the pulse at the base of her neck, feeling the erratic beat against his tongue.

"More," she begged.

Boyd hesitated for a second, trying to gauge how far she wanted him to take the dirty talk, and in that flash of hesitation she gripped his biceps tighter, pushed harder against his fingers, and said, "Talk dirtier."

"I loved seeing your lips wrapped around my cock as I fu—"

"Ohmygod, this is so hot." She grabbed his head and kissed him hard as a climax gripped her. Her body pulsed around his fingers. He swallowed her cries of passion, holding her hip so she couldn't escape the intensity as he took her up, up, up, over the edge again.

"I'm so hard, baby." He needed more, but he wanted her to have control. This was her dirty-talk game.

She pushed his shoulders, guiding him lower, and he was more than happy to comply, devouring her essence as she pulled at his hair, arched against his mouth, and trembled and shook when she finally gave in to another intense release.

"Take me, Boyd. Take me now," she pleaded.

He tugged open his jeans and pushed them down his thighs.

"That doesn't sound very dirty, baby." He squeezed the base of his cock to keep from losing it. She wanted dirty talk, and he wanted her to feel safe enough to give it right back if she wanted to.

She was quiet for a moment, her body writhing against him, her fingers digging into his skin. "I want to feel you deep inside me."

Boyd loved that she didn't get too down and dirty. She was sexy as hell without being raunchy—although he'd have loved it either way. One hard thrust buried him to the root. She wrapped her arms around his neck, pulling herself off the edge of the chair, taking him even deeper. Caught up in their emotions—their dinner and her notes forgotten—dirty talk went out the window, replaced with the sounds of their lovemaking.

Chapter Sixteen

WHEN THEIR BREATHING calmed and their limbs finally worked again, Boyd carried Janie into the bathroom and ran a bath.

"You've carried me a lot lately," she said as she settled between his legs, leaning her back against his chest, feeling safe and loved.

"If we keep missing meals, you'll be able to carry me," he teased. "I'm starting to think your hurt ankle was all part of your evil plan to win the bet."

He poured body wash into his palm and began washing her shoulders. His hands felt so good caressing her skin.

"*I'm* doing all the work. I have to write the story." His hands slid deliciously over her breasts, making her hot and bothered all over again.

"Somehow it seems like you're doing more taunting than writing, under the thinly veiled guise of *research*." He gathered her hair over one shoulder and kissed her neck.

"You love every minute of it. I feel like the luckiest girl in the world lately, and not just because we're having mind-blowing sex." She held up her hand and he poured soap into it. She lifted his legs beneath the knees, washing them, and loving the feel of his body embracing her from all sides. She relaxed back against his chest again.

"You don't even have to touch me and you blow my mind. Why do you feel so lucky?"

"Everything at work is going well, and it looks like I have a real shot at getting the promotion I've been working toward. That's a biggie, because I'd finally be a writer instead of just an editor."

"*Just* an editor? Baby, editing is every bit as important as writing. You make sure the text flows and is perfect before the public sees it. Don't knock my girl like that."

She loved hearing him claim her. "You're right, and I love editing. But since I started playing around with writing romance, everything's changed. I feel energized when I'm creating instead of polishing. I wanted to write so badly when I got out of college, and a few weeks later I was forced to bury those dreams. I haven't let myself go there—mentally, I mean—for a very long time. I know it was just a silly bet, but you inspired me to try something I probably never would have done otherwise."

"We've stirred up your creative juices."

She pulled her knees up to her chest and turned in his arms. Her ankle felt much better, but she still had to be careful not to twist it too far to either side.

"It's more than that, Boyd. You didn't just challenge and inspire me in that way. You make me feel safe enough to explore lots of things."

"Ah, we've released your inner vixen." He wrapped his arm around her waist and nuzzled against her neck.

"It's bigger than that, too. Being with you makes me feel happy and *whole*."

He touched her cheek, and she covered his hand with hers. She found herself doing that a lot, wanting more of him. More of a lasting connection.

"Honey, you make me feel happy and whole, too. I tried to imagine my future without you in it, and there was nothing to imagine. It's like there was life before Janie, and then there was life with Janie. There was nothing else."

She felt his muscles tense. "But?"

"No but." He lifted his face to hers and brushed his thumb over her cheek. "I was invited to interview with a med school in Colorado next week."

"Wow, that's..." *So far away.*

"Far." He sighed. "Let's get dried off and we can talk about it."

He helped her from the tub, and as they dressed, she wrestled with her thoughts.

"You're going on the interview, aren't you?" She'd never hold him back, not from something this important. But that didn't stop the devil on her shoulder from begging her to tell him not to go.

They sat on the couch, and Boyd held her as they talked, which only made it harder for her to separate how she felt about him from what was best for his future.

"Yes. I'm going for the interview, but it doesn't mean I'll go to school there. I just—"

"Don't explain. You have to go. I'm glad you're going." He deserved to live out his dream, but that didn't stop the new, and apparently clingy, girlfriend in her from nearly choking with the realization that the man she was falling for might actually move away. He'd been up front with her the whole time, hadn't he? He hadn't tried to hide it, and yet it still felt like a surprise.

This was ridiculous. It was an interview, and she couldn't hope it didn't go well. She wasn't that selfish.

Was she?

After a second of reflection, she decided she definitely was *not* that selfish. She wanted Boyd to achieve everything he'd ever wanted. She forced down the clingy woman clawing to get out and managed, "Would you like to practice interviewing? It's only fair, after you helped me practice talking dirty."

He drew her in closer and kissed her, a sweet, languid kiss that made her feel like she was his whole world—and made the idea of him leaving hurt even more.

Chapter Seventeen

BY WEDNESDAY EVENING Janie had come to grips with Boyd's interview. She'd even managed to squash that clingy woman inside her. Boyd's perspective of letting their relationship take its natural course and figuring it out later seemed okay. *For now.* He'd said it would be weeks before he knew anything one way or the other, and a lot could happen in a few weeks. Look how much had happened in a few days.

Janie and Boyd had spent the last few nights together, and although Janie was used to being independent, she reveled in their being a couple. Just this morning they'd walked down to the florist before work and bought fresh flowers. When they'd returned home, they'd run into Kiki as she was leaving for work. She'd teased Janie about being spoiled and Boyd about being whipped. Boyd had teased her right back, and Janie was just glad they got along so well. She couldn't imagine life without either of them.

They'd taken a detour on the way home from work. Boyd said he wanted to show Janie a waterfall. True to his promise, Boyd continued to accompany Janie to the subway before and after work. She'd become an expert, cruising along with the crutch in her right hand and her cane in her left, although once she'd proven that to herself and Boyd, she tucked away her cane and held on to him instead.

"A waterfall?" Janie asked as they left the subway station. "I've lived here for years and I've never heard of a waterfall in the city."

"I told you you've been hanging out with the wrong people. Stick with me and I'll show you a few things around here you might have missed."

"Like dirty talk?" Janie teased. "I definitely missed out on that."

She heard his smile, which was something new. She could usually sense his smile based on his voice, but during their intimate moments, she'd become familiar with the sounds of his moods separate from his words. When he smiled, he exhaled a tiny happy breath, and when he was turned on, that breath turned guttural, and she imagined the look on his face was sinful.

"That was all you, honey." He pressed his lips to the tender spot beside her ear. "Not that I minded skipping dinner to fulfill your dirty-talk fantasy."

His sexy, deep voice stroked over her cheek, making her whole body shudder. She heard the unmistakable sound of rushing water, bringing her back to their adventure.

"I hear it!" She was mystified by the idea of a waterfall in the city. "Where exactly are we?"

"Greenacre Park. Cash and Siena turned me on to this little slice of paradise when I first moved here."

"I like them even more now."

"They're great friends, and they are crazy in love with each other, which I used to tease Cash about, but now…"

"Now?"

"Now I understand how he fell for Siena so quickly. You know I'm crazy for you, baby." He tightened his hold around her waist. "We're walking into the park now."

Crazy for me! Crazy didn't begin to explain her feelings for him. He made her want in ways she hadn't ever wanted before, feel things she had only read about. But it was the way he looked after her, without doing so because of her blindness but because he truly cared about *her*, that made her heart turn over every time she thought about him.

She tucked those intimate feelings away and focused on their unexpected date.

"It feels cooler. And it's so loud. The waterfall completely drowns out the road noise. That's amazing." She felt like she'd been plucked from the city and dropped miles away from the concrete jungle.

"The waterfall's only twenty-five feet high. Can you imagine how loud Niagara Falls would be? Maybe one day we'll venture there, too."

Janie lingered on that thought and the future it implied. "I'd love that."

"Me too." He guided her toward the sound of the waterfall. "We're buffered from the road by walls and locust trees on either side, and they've created beautiful sitting areas with plants and trees. There's a wooden trellis over the entrance and another over one of the sitting areas. It's gorgeous."

"It sounds incredible."

"Water trickles down a wall to the left of the falls and flows into a narrow stream along the right side of the park, with rocks covering the bottom, so you feel like you're really in a park."

"I can't believe people don't talk about this place all the time."

"It's really pretty. Feel this." He placed her hand on something cool and smooth. "It's a granite bench, and behind it there are plants. Here, feel." He placed her hand on thin, rough leaves. "And this." He knelt, bringing her down with him, and placed her hand on delicate flower petals, then lower, on a wide planter, that felt cold and rough, like stone.

"The flowers are yellow and red, and there are peace lilies, which I only know because my sister loves them. They have big leaves and tall-stemmed white lilies that grow much higher than the leaves."

She loved that he described things that other people might take for granted. "The mixture of granite and flowers is such a contrast," she noted. "I love that. Can we go near the waterfall?"

"Baby, you're going to *feel* the water. That's why I wanted to bring you here. When I'm away on the interview, maybe you'll think of us here, where we both can *feel* the water and smell the earthy plants instead of the city streets. I wanted to go someplace where I could experience what you experience."

"Usually people want to know what I see, not what I experience otherwise. You have no idea how much what you just said means to me." She reached for his cheek and drew him into a kiss that she hoped said it all.

"I have one favor to ask," Boyd said as they continued walking. Droplets of water landed on her arms and face.

"Oh! Do you feel that?" She touched the wetness on her arm.

"We're at the base of the falls. You can't walk any closer or you'll fall in."

"Will it embarrass you if I get on my hands and knees to feel the water where it pools?" She knew the answer before she even finished asking the question, because Boyd didn't want her to miss out on a thing.

He kissed her palm, then pressed it to his cheek, and she knew he wanted her to feel his smile. She loved that smile.

"Nothing you do will ever embarrass me. Will it embarrass you if I do it, too, and have someone take a picture of us so we can always remember it?"

Boyd and his pictures, another thing she loved about him. He wanted to remember everything they did. And that he wanted to get down on the ground with her made her feel even more in sync with him. "No, but I'll always have a picture of it in my mind."

"I know you can't see the picture, but I can describe it to you in the future."

He asked a man to take their picture. "I gave him my phone. Let's touch the water." He helped her down to her knees, careful of her ankle.

Her hands and knees were instantly soaked, and she laughed, because the whole thing—a waterfall in the middle of the city, sharing this moment with Boyd, and knowing some stranger was making Boyd's desire to memorialize the moment come true—felt magical.

"I should have warned you."

"No, it's better this way."

He held her hand and lowered it to the water, which was colder than she'd anticipated.

"Don't move your knees any farther forward or you'll fall in. Can we take the picture so this poor guy can get on his way?"

"Oh gosh, yes. Sorry." She turned and felt Boyd's arm circle her shoulder, and then his lips were on her cheek. Surprised, she turned in to the kiss. Boyd's warm hand slid to the nape of her neck, drawing her deeper in to him.

"These are great pictures," the guy said.

She'd gotten carried away and forgotten about the guy taking their picture.

"Ohmygosh," she whispered.

Boyd chuckled and gave her another chaste kiss.

"Thank you," he said to the guy. He reached for the phone, keeping one arm protectively around her.

"You scramble my brain," she said a minute later as their fingers skimmed the water.

"Honey, you scramble my life, and I wouldn't have it any other way."

Chapter Eighteen

FIVE O'CLOCK SATURDAY morning Janie was sitting in bed reviewing notes on her braille device while Boyd slept beside her. They'd stayed up late last night watching *Star Wars*. Boyd described the scenes as Janie took notes, but she'd been more enthralled with the effect the movie had on Boyd and the way he described the scenes to her than the story itself. He really got into the action, the way she got into romance, and it helped her to understand his fascination with the genre.

Yesterday she'd finally been able to walk without the crutch, which made her commute that much easier. She almost hated to forgo the crutch, because it meant that she wouldn't need Boyd with her when she took the subway. He'd modified his schedule so much for her, taking day shifts at the hospital while she was at work and having the guys at the firehouse cover his schedule there. She didn't need to inconvenience him anymore, no matter how much she enjoyed sharing their morning commutes. Boyd didn't let her pine over their lost time together. Without missing a beat, he'd gone right back to telling her how much her cane turned him on. He'd filled that hole with his cheesy lines, leaving her no room to pine for anything.

Boyd mumbled something in his sleep that she couldn't

make out. She stopped reading and listened more carefully. He continually offered to stay at his place, but she loved sleeping cocooned by his body too much to want to sleep without him. They'd be forced to do so when he went to Colorado for his interview, and until then she wanted as much time with him as she could get.

His breathing quickened and his legs suddenly jerked. She placed her hand on his arm and was surprised to find his skin damp with perspiration. He mumbled again, and she realized he was having another nightmare. He'd had one Wednesday night, and though it had lasted only seconds, it had shaken him up pretty badly.

Janie set her braille device aside and whispered, "Boyd?"

His breathing quickened.

She touched his chest, feeling his frantic heartbeat. "Boyd, wake up."

He bolted upright, gasping. She startled and drew back, unsure if he was awake or not.

"Sorry, baby." His voice was husky, strained. He cleared his throat and squeezed her hand. "Did I wake you?"

"No. I was reading my notes from last night, but you were saying something that I couldn't understand. Are you sure you're okay?"

"I'm fine. I didn't mean to startle you."

"Do you want to talk about it?"

"Not really." He sat up beside her and took a few deep breaths.

She'd shared so much of herself with him; she wanted him to trust her enough to share this part of himself with her, too. But she could hear in his voice that he wasn't ready to talk about it. At least not yet.

"Did watching the movie help last night?" He sat up beside her. "Did you come away with any helpful notes?"

He was a master at subject changes. He'd done the same thing after his nightmare Wednesday night, but Janie didn't want to give up as easily this time. She decided to try a different tactic.

"Yes. Tons. You claim not to be good at creative writing, but your descriptions were so vivid, I felt like I was *in* the movie."

"That's because I wasn't creating the scenes, just telling you what I was seeing."

Janie was glad he was breathing a little easier now. "I think I can learn from you. I'm not great at describing settings. I think my writing reflects too much from my perspective—textures, scents—and needs more fleshing out of visuals. Can you help me?"

"Help you win the bet, you mean?"

She heard the smile in his voice. "I want to modify the bet. Take the romance festival off the table altogether."

"I'm listening." He pulled her in closer.

"I'm really loving this whole process. The writing makes me see things differently and brings us closer together."

"Sounds like a sales pitch. What's the hook?"

She playfully smacked his arm. "I'm serious. I need help with descriptions, and I need some ideas for romantic places my characters can go. If you help me, and I finish the story, I'll still go to Comic-Con with you. Even if you hate my story."

"I'm liking this so far." He tucked her hair behind her ear and kissed her cheek.

She swallowed hard, readying herself for what she was sure would be a negative reaction. "But in return you have to share your nightmares with me."

Boyd was quiet for so long she feared he might storm out. She remained still, waiting for him to respond. He shifted beside her, and then his fingers laced with hers and he kissed the back of her hand.

"Honey."

She heard so many things in that one word. *Please don't make me do this. Why? This is too hard. Even the thought of it hurts.* What she didn't hear was a definitive *no*, and that was enough to give her hope.

"I think it might help," she explained. "I know it won't be easy, but life isn't easy, Boyd. What you went through was a million times more traumatic than my fall, and you helped me face that right away. I don't know how long it would have taken if I'd tried to do it on my own, but I know going through it with you helped tremendously."

He went quiet again, and when he said, "I'll think about it," she clung to the hope that he'd eventually come around.

"WHERE ARE WE going?" Janie asked as they stepped off the subway later that morning.

"You said you needed help with romantic places for your characters to visit. We're doing a little romantic research." Boyd had been even more shaken up by his most recent nightmare than he wanted to admit. This morning the nightmare had roped Janie into the burning house, and that had scared the shit out of him. So much of what Janie had said made sense. He should talk about his nightmares, but the very thought of it brought renewed panic. He needed to get out of his own head for a while.

"Some things in life are better as surprises." He was glad she could walk without her crutch now. It allowed him to hold her closer, and he wouldn't worry as much when she took the subway without him next week.

"You were my best surprise yet."

He took both her hands in his. The sun's rays reflected in her eyes and took his breath away. Cluing Janie into what was going on around them came naturally now. At the hospital it had been instinct to calm her fears, but ever since, he'd simply wanted her to be a part of everything he experienced.

"The sun is shining down on you, and, Janie, you're so beautiful. I wish I could show you how sweet and pretty you look right now."

She pressed her hands to his chest and said, "You just did."

It was easy to forget how transparent he'd become to her. She rose onto her left toes, favoring her right ankle, and he met her halfway for a kiss.

They made their way inside the museum, and Boyd guided her toward the exhibit. He pushed open the exhibit doors, and as they walked inside, he tried to experience those first few moments through Janie's eyes, inhaling the pungent earthy scent and listening to the sounds of people talking.

"Boyd? Where are we? It smells like we're in a greenhouse."

"The butterfly conservatory at the American Museum of Natural History. Have you been here before?"

Her eyes widened. "No, but now I'm excited."

"There are gardens on either side of us, with flowers and leafy green plants. Butterflies are everywhere, on the plants, flying up by the lights."

"One just flew by me," she said with a laugh. "I felt it by my cheek, right?"

Seeing the excitement in her eyes filled him with joy. "Yes. It was brown with yellow stripes. So pretty."

"I love this. Tell me more. What colors are they?"

"There are so many. There's one with amber on the bottom of the wings and black on the tips, and oh, there's one that's bigger than the others, with mostly black wings, but there are spots of white on them."

"The flowers, tell me about them."

Boyd told her about the pink and white flowers beside them, and as they made their way through the exhibit, he tried his hardest to explain everything without leaving out a single detail.

A butterfly landed on Janie's arm, and she held her breath.

"Don't move. It's a beauty, with dark brown at the tips of its wings. The color gradually gets lighter as it gets closer to its body. If you move slowly, you might be able to lift your arm without it flying away and feel the wings on your cheeks."

As she lifted her arm, Boyd cupped his hands around the butterfly to keep it from flying off. She held it beside her cheek, and when he moved his hands the butterfly remained, as if it wanted Janie to share in the magical moment, too.

Seconds later the butterfly flitted away.

"Did you see that?" She reached for Boyd. "Thank you for this. I might never have come here."

"This might sound hokey, but butterflies are kind of symbolic for both of us. We're both in a place of change in our lives. You're evolving with your writing, getting to the heart of who you are, revisiting your dreams, and I'm"—thinking about dealing with my past—"thinking about med school."

"That's not hokey at all. It's incredibly romantic." She

wound her arms around his neck. "Looks like I chose the best research partner around."

As they walked through the exhibit, Boyd continued describing the plants and flowers and Janie touched each one. But his mind kept drifting to his interview. He had to fly out tomorrow, and every hour that passed felt like a ticking time bomb. It was hard to believe that two weeks ago he'd been able to keep his distance from Janie, and now the thought of going away for two days made him ache inside.

"Stand here." Janie stopped beside a garden overflowing with lush greenery and dozens of butterflies flitting about. "Close your eyes for a second."

"Okay, baby. My eyes are closed."

"If you listen carefully, you can hear them flapping their wings. When I was little my father and I watched a show on butterflies, and I learned that some species chirped in defense, which I didn't know. The more interesting thing was that when they flapped their wings, their bodies made a noise, or maybe it was the actual movement that made the noise. I'm not sure what it was, but tell me what you hear."

Boyd tried to tune out the voices of the other people in the room. He wondered if having seen the butterflies and knowing there was a family a few feet away and an older couple standing by the entrance talking affected his ability to separate the sounds. He was surprised at how much effort it took for him to really tune those noises out and focus on only the butterflies.

He thought he'd be able to name the sounds quickly, but as he listened, he found himself searching for words and coming up empty for what seemed like several minutes. Finally, he said, "It almost sounds like rain, or shifting papers."

"Rain," she repeated. "I wasn't thinking that, but I can

totally hear that now. But *shifting papers?*" She laughed, and Boyd brought her into his arms.

"Okay, butterfly expert, what does it sound like to you?"

He fought the urge to open his eyes, even though he wanted to see her face as she concentrated on what she heard. Experiencing the world from Janie's point of view was becoming even more important to him. He wanted to hear what she heard, feel what she felt, sense what she sensed, so he could figure out how to make every experience even better.

"It sounds enchanting, like a breeze rustling through autumn leaves after they've fallen to the ground."

"That's so much more romantic than shifting papers. No wonder you're the romance writer and I'm the dirty talker."

After they left the museum they went for a walk through Central Park. Boyd had been trying to figure out how to talk to Janie about his nightmares, but every time he thought he could do it, the words wouldn't come. He held Janie's hand as they crossed Bow Bridge, feeling so lucky to be with her. The last thing he wanted to do was lose her—over school, over his past, over *anything.*

"I've been thinking about what you said this morning. I know it can't be easy being with me when I have nightmares and then being shut out of that part of my life, and I'm sorry, Janie."

"It's okay. I understand."

He wrapped his arms around her and kissed her. "It's not okay, although I appreciate your patience. You deserve someone who will share everything with you, and I'm trying. What happened to my family, and the nightmares I have, aren't easy for me to talk about, but I *want* to be able to talk about them with you. I just don't know how yet."

"I know, and I don't want to push you into something you don't want to do."

"I appreciate that, too, but what you need to know is that I've never even *considered* sharing these parts of myself before. Until you."

Chapter Nineteen

"HOW MANY TIMES are you going to push that button?" Kiki asked as she applied dye to Janie's dark roots.

Without answering, Janie pushed the button on the talking digital frame Boyd had given her earlier Sunday afternoon before leaving for the airport. His voice came to life, describing the pictures, telling her he was crazy about her and that she was beautiful, among other sweet things that made her dizzy with delight.

"That was sweet of him, and those pictures are cute. Even the one with you sticking out your tongue."

"That's only because he's in the picture. With those dark roots you keep telling me about, I must look awful."

Kiki yanked her hair. "It's because you're cute no matter what, goof. You know, when I left town last Friday morning, you were happily working toward your promotion, writing newsletters that were drier than dirt, and spending evenings either out with me or curled up on the couch reading smut. And now you're writing smut and working toward what exactly?"

Janie sipped her margarita. "At the moment I'm working on finishing this deliciousness." She'd spent all afternoon writing, and even though she knew she'd probably want to rewrite the story a bunch of times to get it just right, it was finally coming together.

"Right, and…"

"I'm still waiting to hear about the promotion, spicing up the newsletter a little, and—"

"A little?" Kiki laughed and painted more dye on Janie's roots. "I don't think 'Manual Manipulation' is spicing it up *a little*. The guys in the office will be walking around with hard-ons from the title alone."

In the most professional voice Janie could manage, she said, "I believe there's a place in everyone's life for double entendres."

"I guess so, but what does Tara have to say about it?"

Janie shrugged. "I haven't turned it in to her yet. I'm sure it's fine. Besides, I can't help it. All this sexy writing I'm doing has made me think differently. When I'm on the subway I sit there hoping to hear something that inspires a scene."

"And when you're with Boyd you're memorizing every touch."

"Not really," she admitted. "I start that way, thinking I'll use it somehow, but then my brain just turns off and fails to think past how much I want him, how much I love the things he says, or how good it feels to be in his arms."

Kiki turned on the timer and sat across from Janie. "And now he's interviewing in Colorado and you're here pretending like you're not waiting for him to call or text."

"Pretty much." She held up the margarita. "This helps."

"Janie, have you guys talked about what's going to happen when he gets accepted to med school? Will you go with him?"

"We talked a little, but it's too early to think about that. We haven't been dating that long." The statement was true, but her heart didn't seem to care how long they were dating. It already belonged to him.

"Anyone can see how serious you two are. Boyd changed his work schedule for you. He's here every night, and when you said goodbye earlier, you had tears in your eyes, and don't try to tell me you didn't."

"Okay, so I miss him. Is that a crime?" She set her drink on the table and sighed. "I don't know how to feel, Kiki. I've never liked anyone this much before. I wish I could *see* him, and not because he's hot. I dream about seeing his eyes, seeing the emotions I feel from him when we're together. You *know* I've never dreamed about that before."

Kiki sighed. "Wow."

"Knocked me for a loop."

"Do you love him?"

Janie had been wondering that herself lately, because the feelings she had were so strong. "I don't know. *Maybe?* It's too soon for that, isn't it?"

"Does he know that?" Kiki asked. "Because the way he looks at you…Janie, if a guy looked at me like that…"

Why do you think I want to see his eyes? "Let's talk about something else, because you're making me miss him more."

Like a true friend, Kiki circled back to Janie's writing, and after they'd finished with Janie's hair, they decided to spice up her story. Janie had been reading the handbook Boyd had given her, and one of the key elements she'd learned was the need for diversity in her sex scenes. They sat on the couch with their drinks and Janie's laptop and braille device and typed *interesting sexual positions* into the Google search bar.

Kiki read the headlines. "'Ten WTF Positions You've Never Heard Of.' Like there are any *I* haven't heard of?" She scoffed as

Janie navigated to the next article. "'Top Forty Sexual Positions.' Perfect."

Janie's hands flew over the pins, reading the copy beneath the pictures.

"Speed bump?" Janie laughed. "That sounds funky, but it's just missionary with a pillow under your butt."

"You'd be surprised what that pillow can do."

"Really?" Janie made a mental note to try it with Boyd. "What's this? 'The Waterfall'? Straddle the guy and lean back so your head hangs toward the floor? Who would do that? I'd get dizzy."

Kiki laughed. "I'd probably throw up. How about this one? 'Lust and Thrust.' Do it on the stairs!"

"The neighbors would love that."

They surfed the site, laughing about the names and the awkwardness of the positions—*Sultry Straddle*, *Edge of Heaven*, *Corridor Canoodling*, and *the Good Spread*. Janie took copious notes to share with her hunky research partner.

Chapter Twenty

COLORADO WAS GORGEOUS. The air was crisp and fresh, and the campus had an incredible view of the mountains in the distance. As Boyd toured the campus, pride settled around him. This was what he'd worked so hard for, to one day be exactly where he was: interviewing for medical school. In his mind's eye he had only childhood visions of his parents, and many of his memories were too fuzzy to form detailed pictures of them. But photographs kept visions of his parents' forever-thirtysomething smiling faces alive. It saddened him that his parents had already missed so much of his and his siblings' lives: high school and college graduations, the birth of their grandson, all of their children's accomplishments, big and small. He imagined his father's rugged face, his dark, serious eyes, and his mother's bright blue eyes, which he saw every time he looked at Haylie, filled with the same pride he felt, commending him for his hard work and dedication.

Hard work and dedication.

He'd definitely worked his ass off to get there, and yes, he was damned proud. But he couldn't deny the difference in the way he felt today as he toured the facilities compared to when he'd interviewed and toured the campus in Washington State before getting together with Janie. Then he had prayed to get accepted to any school. He didn't care if he had to go halfway around the world to attend medical school. He'd have done whatever it took to make it happen. But today his excitement was tempered by the woman he'd left back in New York. Being here brought new awareness and, with it, mixed feelings about going away to school at all, much less this far from Janie.

He tried to picture Janie there with him. Surely she'd enjoy the clean, less stressful area compared to the hustle and bustle of New York City. They could experience a completely different type of lifestyle than in the city, hiking, taking walks in the woods, maybe even fishing. He'd have to remember to ask Janie if she'd ever gone fishing.

They could get a place with a view of the mountains and a nice patio where she could write instead of within the four walls of her tiny apartment.

"We're only eight miles from downtown Denver, and there's public transportation available," his tour guide, Anthony, a third-year medical student, explained.

Janie could work in Denver. It was a big city, with plenty of booming businesses. How hard could it be to find a job there?

"Is paratransit available in town and on campus?" As he asked the question, he remembered how difficult it had been for Janie to find a job. She'd given up her dream of being a journalist because people were too shortsighted to see how talented she was. *The sighted were too shortsighted.* His gut clenched and fisted tighter with the thought of her going through another painful job search.

"Yes, there are options for various paratransit companies. The admissions office can provide you with that information."

Boyd was getting way ahead of himself. Even if there were transportation options, would Janie want to move away from her job? From Kiki? From the life she'd created there, in the community where shop owners looked out for her? Was it fair to ask her to consider it after dating for such a short time? Would it be fair after a month? Six months? A year? Would it ever be fair to ask her to move away from the life she'd built?

Moving presented all sorts of logistical complications for sighted people, including figuring out which areas were safe and which weren't. As Anthony talked about the campus, professors, and community outreach, Boyd realized that he assessed safety in the first ten seconds of arriving in a new location. Hell, he'd done it when he'd taken a ride through town last night, visually inspecting the cleanliness of the sidewalks and roads, taking in the businesses, looking for vagrants and trying to discern sketchy parts of town. He'd assessed Anthony in three seconds flat when they'd met. How would Janie do that? She obviously knew how to assess her surroundings, but had she been able to mentally map the city only because Kiki had helped her to learn what areas were safe and which ones weren't? He'd be happy to help her, but how long had it taken her to find her comfort zone? To figure out which people she met in her daily travels—at the café, the flower shop, even the newspaper stand—were safe to be around? Boyd had lived in the city for years and he still didn't have those close-knit community-based relationships.

By the time Boyd sat down for his interview, he realized that not only was he getting ahead of himself, but he didn't have enough knowledge to assess the viability of *any* location for Janie—and it wasn't his place to even consider doing so.

The dean of admissions shook his hand and introduced himself. "Tell me, Boyd, why do you want to be part of our program?"

Boyd recited the answers he'd been memorizing for weeks, each the perfect blend of his desire to be a doctor, the school's reputation, and his personal strengths and goals. A few weeks ago he'd given a slightly modified answer to the dean of admissions in Washington. He'd been outwardly confident and determined to make his mark and establish himself worthy of a coveted spot within the prestigious institution.

Today, while he felt the same confidence in his skill set and worthiness, his motivation wasn't as pressing as it had been. The only thing he was certain of was that even though he and Janie had talked on the phone last night for more than an hour and she'd be in his arms tomorrow, being this far apart sucked. He missed her. *Desperately.*

As Boyd drove back toward the hotel, his motivation became crystal clear.

He never wanted to be separated from Janie again.

JANIE WAS FINISHING up the last of the edits on the ARKENS handbook when Clay called and asked her to join him in the conference room.

"Good luck in there," Tara said as she passed Janie in the hallway.

Janie had turned in her latest newsletter article that morning, and Tara hadn't said anything about the title. Surely Clay wouldn't call her into a closed-door meeting for something like that, would he? The management team wasn't scheduled to meet this week, either, and she couldn't imagine what else he might want. With butterflies swarming in her stomach, she knocked on the door and stepped into the conference room.

"You wanted to see me, Clay?"

"Janie, come in, please."

She listened carefully for sounds of others who might be in the room, but they appeared to be alone.

"How's the ARKENS handbook coming along?" he asked.

"Fine. I should be done by the end of the day. I just want to go over a few things again to make sure I didn't miss anything."

"You're always very meticulous. We appreciate that." Clay sighed, in that unemotional way that made him difficult to read.

"Thank you." *Very meticulous* had to be a good sign. She breathed a little easier.

"As you know, we'll be discussing your promotion in the next management meeting. I expect that will go very well, as you're a dedicated, hard-working employee. Your skill set speaks for itself."

"Thank you," she said again, feeling a little more confident.

"You're welcome. You probably haven't heard about this yet, and I ask that what I say will be kept confidential."

"Of course."

"We're working on expanding TEC over the next few months, and what I wanted to talk to you about was what that could mean for you. I know you're interested in writing, but if the expansion comes through, as we expect it will, then we'll need to hire more senior editors as well. Those editors will need to be brought up to date on our practices and procedures, and I was thinking of pitching the idea to our team of you heading up a once-a-month training seminar for new editors. If, of course, you'd be interested in doing so."

"A training seminar? Clay, thank you for your vote of confidence, but that's not a role in which I've ever imagined myself." Training? What would that be like? What if she agreed and hated it? What if she agreed and wasn't able to pull it off?

"Janie, when I hired you, you made it very clear that your

blindness would never hold you back, and you asked me to let you prove yourself." For the first time since she'd worked there, she heard emotion—*excitement*—in Clay's voice. "You've proven yourself, and I think you have tremendous potential. You're one of our star editors, you get along with everyone, and your writing is not only clear and concise, but you have a way of connecting with your readers no matter what the topic, which is critical to what we do."

"Thank you. Your praise means a lot to me." She was practically bubbling over with excitement, knowing he thought so highly of her.

"You missed a lively discussion about the Oxford comma in the lunchroom the other day, which stemmed from your article. Who knew people had such strong opinions on the topic. Even if your latest newsletters have been a little more risqué than we're used to, they have been discussion starters."

She hoped her cheeks weren't turning pink as a wave of embarrassment washed over her. "I'm sorry about that. I've been doing a bit of creative writing lately, and I guess it carried over."

"Don't be. I assume you're just trying to spread your wings, show that you have abilities beyond the norm. The article was stellar, and I think the title actually got people reading, which was brilliant."

Brilliant? That was much better than *inappropriate.* "Thank you."

"If you're not opposed to the idea of training, I'd like to go over a general outline of what I had in mind."

Janie listened as Clay explained his ideas. She was so thrilled with his praise, and his faith in her that she silently thanked the heavens above for the day they'd met. She couldn't wait to tell Boyd about her new opportunity.

Chapter Twenty-One

BOYD STOOD OUTSIDE Janie's apartment door Tuesday evening with a backpack over his shoulder, a bouquet of white tulips in his arms, and a swarm of bees wreaking havoc in his stomach. He shouldn't be nervous to see Janie after they'd spent almost every night for nearly two weeks together, but he felt like a kid picking up his prom date. She'd told him all about her new opportunity at work, and it made what he had to discuss with her even more important. When she opened the door, wearing the smile he'd envisioned every minute they were apart, his heart nearly leapt from his chest.

"Hi." He wrapped his arms around her, breathing her in and exhaling the invisible bees. She was finally in his arms again. "Two days seemed like a lifetime. I never want to miss you that much again."

"Then stop talking and kiss me already."

Their mouths came together like dance partners, slowly, sensually, in perfect sync. He drank in her sweetness, the feel of her hands sliding around his waist, bringing their bodies even closer.

He drew back, his gaze rolling over her beautiful face. "I missed you so much, honey." His lips came coaxingly down on hers again, and he felt her smile as they kissed.

"I feel that." She pushed her hips against his arousal.

He laughed softly. "I can't get anything past you, can I?"

"Why would you ever want to?"

"Hey, lovers!" Kiki called from the living room. "Get in here before you catch the hallway on fire." She rose from the couch as they came inside. "Aw, you brought me tulips? You're such a sweetie pie."

"You brought tulips?" Janie felt for his hands and he handed her the bouquet.

"Hey, Kiki," Boyd said. "How's it going?"

"Great, except I've got every word that you recorded in the digital frame memorized." Kiki winked.

"My girl liked her gift?" he asked as he nuzzled against Janie's neck.

"I loved it, and I love the flowers. Thank you." She inhaled deeply and then held them for him to do the same. "What do you smell?"

"Flowers," he said.

"Fail." Kiki carried a vase of water from the kitchen.

"Smell them again." Janie held the flowers beneath his nose. "Do you smell anything specific?"

He inhaled again. "They smell like fresh flowers."

"I think they smell like honey and light. It's one of my favorite scents." Janie let Kiki take the flowers. "Thanks, Kiki. Will you please put them on my desk?"

"Yup, and I'll get the blindfold."

"Blindfold?" He held Janie again. "Are we doing more research for your book? If so, please tell me Kiki isn't joining us, because I'm not good at sharing."

"Thank goodness for small favors." She went up on her toes

and kissed him.

"No research. You've done all this stuff wanting to experience life the way I do, and I thought I'd show you my world in a different way."

"Honey, I want to experience all of your world." He ran his fingers through her hair, the dark roots now as blond as the rest. "Your hair looks really pretty. I guess Kiki got her hands on it."

"She did. Someday I'll show you pictures of me with my natural color hair."

"You could be bald and you'd still be the sexiest woman around."

She kissed him again. "I've missed your cheesy lines."

"But they never sound cheesy coming from Boyd, which is weird. Do you have a brother, by chance?" Kiki handed Janie a blindfold. "Don't get it sticky." She laughed and grabbed her book from the couch.

"I do have a brother, but he's in Virginia." Boyd shrugged his backpack from his shoulder, thinking about Chet, his slightly surly brother.

"Bummer," Kiki complained. "Well, I'm taking off now that the photo narrator is here."

"See you, Kiki," Janie said as Kiki headed out the door.

"Honey, when you asked me to stay over, I forgot to tell you that I have to be at the firehouse tomorrow at seven for my shift. Would you rather I stayed at my place so I don't wake you too early?"

"Not a chance." She tugged him by his collar toward the balcony. "I want my big, strong fireman with me. I've already gone too long sleeping without you."

She pulled open the balcony door. Headlights split the darkness below as she led him outside. Sounds of cars and people tangled together, livening the warm evening air.

"Sit next to me." Janie pulled him down beside her on the cold concrete balcony.

"Do you want me to grab chairs or a blanket for you to sit on?"

"Nope. I just want you with me. Blindfolded."

"You sure you don't want to move this to the bedroom?" He slid the blindfold over his eyes.

"Maybe later."

Her words sent lightning to his core.

"But for now..." Her fingers grazed the blindfold. "Is it weird that I get a little rush of control, or power, knowing you're now shrouded in darkness?"

"Is it weird that hearing that turns me on?"

"NO, BECAUSE IT turns me on to say it." Janie had missed him terribly. When they'd talked last night, she'd told him about where she'd grown up, and she'd tried to describe what it was like to grow up by the water and how her view of her hometown had changed as her vision worsened. She wanted to help him understand what it had been like for her to lose sight of everything she knew and loved piece by piece.

"Baby, what is this dangerous game you're playing?" He slid his hand up her thigh, burning a handprint through her jeans.

"It's called experiencing the evening Janie style. Kiki and I do this sometimes. I thought it might be fun."

"Everything with you is fun, but I have to admit, it's a little unsettling not being able to see where the noises are coming from."

"Right? That takes some getting used to. My vision didn't change all at once, as I've mentioned. It was gradual. I used to panic when I'd suddenly realize that I was straining to see things I used to see clearly, or that I could no longer see a streetlight when it was right in front of me."

"That would be scary for anyone."

"I know. There was this moment in seventh-grade choir practice when I realized I could no longer see my teacher silhouetted at the front of the class. I only told Kiki. No one else. But I was petrified. I remember another time when I woke up from a nap and my world was darker. I call those moments 'hiccups,' because they jolt me into awareness. It's kind of the same thing with the blindfold."

Boyd put his arm around Janie and kissed her. "I wish I could have been there with you. Not that I could have done much, but I wish I could have been there so you wouldn't have been so scared."

She knew if he had been, he would have reassured her. Just like he had so many times since she'd fallen.

"I didn't mean to go over my visual history, but when we're together, I want to share all of myself with you. And, well, this is all part of me."

"Janie, I want that, too."

"I know you do. I just wanted you to understand that even though I had years to get used to losing my vision, I experienced that same sensation sometimes of feeling ungrounded because I suddenly couldn't see the source of a noise."

She felt him searching for her hand.

"You'll get used to finding my hand, too." She held his hand, enjoying the strength and comfort and how perfectly they fit together. "And figuring out where body parts should be."

"I don't think I'll have trouble with your body parts, honey."

"Yeah, probably not," she said with a smile. "I think when I lose my vision completely, it might be a relief. Because now I keep wondering when it's going to happen."

"So eventually you won't be able to see shapes if lighting and contrast are just right?"

"*And* if I look out of my peripheral vision and get up real close like a freak," she reminded him.

"Baby, you're not a freak. Please don't ever say that again. It really bothers me when you say things like that."

"I'm sorry. I was kidding. *Sort of.* It is kind of freaky to do what I have to do to make out even the slightest shadow."

"When you said you could see me at the park, it was like I'd died and gone to heaven. Not that I needed you to see me, or was hoping for it, or anything like that. It was a total surprise. Like a gift I never expected. And you were so excited, it made the moment even more special."

"I'm not wishing that away, but I accept that one day that'll be gone, too."

"Then we'll take advantage of it now, while you're able."

He not only understood her on too many levels to count, but he wanted to experience everything *with* her. Not just deal with her loss of sight as it happened, but make every moment count, and that made her heart so full she felt speechless. It was an easy silence between them, one that spoke of their deep connection.

Janie rested her head on Boyd's shoulder, and once she'd soaked in the things he'd said, she found her voice again. "How do you like the darkness?"

"It forces me to use my other senses. Without seeing the

source of the sounds, I'm separating them, cataloging them in my mind without realizing it. Car horns, a guy yelling, the sounds of your breathing."

She loved the way he weaved her into his thoughts.

"I have a confession to make," he said.

"A naughty confession? Should I take notes?"

"You really do have romance on the brain."

"I blame you. Okay, you may confess your sins."

"Only if it's a sin to have been attracted to you since the first time I saw you."

She lifted her head from his shoulder, surprised by what he'd said. "That's not true."

"Fireman's honor."

"There is no fireman's honor."

"I wasn't a Boy Scout, so...Honest to God. It's the truth. The first time I saw you at TEC, you were in the reception area talking to Clay, and something about you—*everything* about you—caught my attention. You were smiling. God, Janie, I adore your smile." He brushed his thumb over her lips. "And you exuded confidence that took my breath away. I remember sitting there, unable to look away."

"Did you know I was blind right away?" The question slipped out before she could stop it, and she found it strange that while she didn't think her blindness defined her, it was the one thing she wanted to know. Was she fooling herself? Or would that always be a lingering insecurity?

"No, honey. You were looking right at him, and when you turned away, that's when I noticed your cane. You had it in your right hand, but I hadn't seen it because it was blocked by your body. It took a second to register, like noting you had blond hair, and that was it. After that morning, I thought about you nonstop."

He pulled her in closer. "That's why I acted like I always had someplace to be, or flirted, so you'd think I was the kind of guy you'd never want to be involved with. That's why I couldn't ever stick around and talk to you for too long. Every time I saw you, my stomach got funky. But with medical school looming, I didn't want to take the chance of getting close to you."

Her heart swelled with love for him, for his honesty, and for all these things she never knew about him but now were making her want to crawl into his lap and tell him how much she cared.

"But...?"

"But now I have, and I'm in too deep to walk away. Can I take the blindfold off? I want to see your face."

"Yes." She wished she had a blindfold she could take off.

He tucked her hair behind her ear. "Janie, this is so hard. I can't turn my back on medical school, and I can't turn my back on you. I don't have the answers we need right now, or the answers you deserve, but I know I want to be with you."

"I want to be with you, too, and I'd never ask you to walk away from med school." Her mind raced. Would they have a long-distance relationship? Would he eventually want her to move with him? Would she want to? Or, something she didn't think she had in her—but who knew what anyone was capable of when dealing with emotions of the heart—would she ever ask him to stay in New York?

"I know you wouldn't, but I also know you're wondering where we go from here, just as I am."

She touched his face, feeling the tension there and wishing she could admit how much she wanted those answers.

Unable to find the right words, she went for levity, hoping to quell the ache inside her. "So, you stalked me, then you fell for me…"

"Fell hard for you," he said with a serious tone.

"And now?"

"Now you deserve concrete answers about medical school and my plans, but I don't have them."

She dropped her gaze, not wanting to think about losing him. He curled his finger beneath her chin and lifted her face. He never let her get away from facing the hard things.

"Janie, I'm trying to be up front with you, so neither of us gets hurt."

"Maybe you could not be so up front, and we could just live in our little circle of happiness until you know for sure." *Put off the inevitable. Give me another few weeks of bliss with you.*

"Honey, I'll never be dishonest with you. Knowing that I don't have an answer about us and that it will take time to figure out how to deal with my past, do you still want to be with me?"

Janie didn't hesitate. "Yes. Without a shadow of a doubt, I want to be with you. If we get a day, a week, a year, or only this moment right now, I want to be with you."

He touched his forehead to hers. With a voice full of emotion, he said, "Thank you, baby. Because I can't imagine another day without you."

Chapter Twenty-Two

LATE WEDNESDAY NIGHT Boyd and the guys were back at the firehouse after a busy day. Luckily there wasn't much to the calls they'd received—a quickly contained gas leak, a smoking dryer, vehicle accidents, a medical emergency, and a few others. Boyd called Janie while he had a moment alone, which was rare at the firehouse.

"Hey, baby. How's my girl?"

"Missing you. I can't believe I have to sleep alone tonight."

He hated taking a night shift, but he'd had no choice. "Just for one night. I'll be back tomorrow. What's your plan this evening? Are you and Kiki going out carousing?"

"Kiki's working late again tonight, so I'm diving into my romance writing."

"Maybe we can play with your blindfold and think up a few more sexy scenes when we see each other."

"I thought you'd never ask," she teased.

"You don't have to wait for me to ask. I'm always hungry for you, baby."

"Speaking of hungry, I'd really like to take you out to dinner tomorrow night."

"Take *me* out to dinner? How about I take you out to dinner?"

"This is my treat. A nonprofit group is hosting a Dining in the Dark event tomorrow. A portion of the proceeds go toward charities and causes concerned with visual impairment, and if you want to experience what it's like to be visually impaired, this is a great way. You eat in complete darkness, and trust me, you'll be surprised at how different it is."

Cash came into the room and flipped on the television. Boyd looked up as Tommy flopped onto the couch.

"Sounds good, honey. I've got to run. The guys just came in, but I'll see you tomorrow." He didn't care what they did as long as they were together, but he loved that she wanted him to experience more of life from her view as much as he wanted to do it.

After he ended the call he opened his laptop, trying not to think about how much he already missed her.

"What's up, dude?" Tommy stretched his legs out across the couch, flashing a crooked grin at Cash.

"Move it, Burke." Cash crossed his arms and looked down his nose at Tommy.

"What crawled up your ass and died?" Boyd asked.

"Nothing," Cash snapped.

"Bullshit." Tommy sat up, giving Cash room to sit down. "Siena's got a modeling gig with Gunner Gibson."

"The football guy? So what?" Boyd pulled up his email and began weeding through spam.

"So, he's the guy—"

"Tom," Cash growled. He turned to Boyd with a serious look in his eyes. "It's not Gunner. Tom's just fucking with me. I don't give a shit about the gig."

"Then what is it?"

"Haven't slept much lately." Cash leaned back and closed his eyes. "We're trying to get pregnant."

Boyd snickered. "Damn, that's a good thing, Cash."

"Yeah, except it hasn't happened yet, and Siena's bummed. Hell, I'm bummed. But I can't let her know that." He leaned forward and rested his elbows on his knees. "We spend our youths trying not to get chicks pregnant, and the one time I want to..."

"It'll happen," Boyd assured him, although what did he know about these things? All he knew was that his buddy was having a hard time and he wanted to make him feel better. "Remember when you were a rookie and all the experienced guys would sit around telling stories about the fires they fought? Remember sitting around wishing for a fire?"

"Yeah." Cash cracked a smile. "We couldn't wait to get into the belly of the beast. To become one of them."

"We were so foolish," Tommy said.

"Yeah, because who the fuck wishes for a fire?" Boyd had never wished for a fire, though he played along with the others because that's what rookies did. He'd already experienced his first fire, and he'd lost far too much. His prayers revolved around saving the people in the fires.

"It eventually happened for us all," Tommy said.

"And hopefully this will, too." Boyd turned back to the computer, silently praying that Cash and Siena would make their dream for a family come true. He knew firsthand how important family was to them. He'd never thought much about having children. Until Janie, he'd never thought past making it to medical school. Now, as he skimmed his emails, he pictured a little baby girl, with Janie's lips and beautiful eyes, nestled in Janie's arms.

Smiling to himself, his eyes caught on an email from the admissions office of the University of Virginia School of Medicine. The image of Janie and a baby wrestled for his attention. His finger hovered over the mouse, no longer certain what he hoped for. A future with Janie was what he wanted, but he knew the dedication and long hours of studying for medical school would require, and his past relationships had shown him exactly how far good intentions got people. The time he'd put into his studies had cost him every relationship he'd ever had, and Janie hadn't even had a taste of his dedication to anything but her. How could he expect her to understand when that changed?

And it would definitely change.

Might as well get this over with. He clicked on the message and scanned the invitation for an interview.

"Hot damn," he said under his breath.

"Good news?" Cash asked.

He wasn't sure if it was good news or not, but it was *news*. "I got an interview at UVA." This was what he'd hoped for, what he'd worked toward. He should be elated, but as he thought of leaving Janie again, his muscles corded tight.

What the hell am I doing? If he felt this way about leaving her for the interview, how would he feel if he got accepted?

JANIE WROTE LIKE a fiend Wednesday night, staying up well into the wee hours of Thursday morning. It was either that or sit around thinking about how much she missed Boyd. Pouring her emotions into her characters, she'd plotted, schemed, and given them more angst than they probably deserved. But how could she not, when she and Boyd had no idea where they were going to end up?

Luckily, Thursday flew by. Clay arranged for Janie to consult with the human resources department on proper training techniques and to select materials that would make the training easier for her. She hadn't had much time to think about the program, but the one thing she wanted to make sure of was that she used effective teaching techniques so there was no miscommunication. She and the human resources team came up with a system that seemed foolproof, using PowerPoint presentations, which could be read via her braille device, and clearly outlined instructions for employees in a handbook.

There would be weeks of work ahead of her to devise a complete plan, but the more she fleshed out her ideas, the more excited she became about the prospect of both opportunities that were hanging in the wings. She spent hours putting together an outline for the orientation packet for the program and turned in a rough draft of what she was thinking to Clay at the end of the day.

"You've really put some thought into this," Clay said.

"I figured I'd jump on it so you would have it for the meeting with the managers."

"Great initiative, Jansen. Sit down, please."

When Janie's world had gone from definable shapes and images to shadowy contrasts, making everything she did that much harder, she used to wonder what people thought about every move she made. She rarely worried about those things anymore. As she sat in a chair across from Clay, bigger worries hovered over her. Like where she and Boyd were headed.

"You realize that if I go to bat for this position, I'll need a commitment from you to stay here at TEC."

"Yes, sir. I realize that." The truth was, she hadn't thought about it, but it made sense. She was happy there. Or at least, *relatively* happy. She liked the people and the work, even if it wasn't as much fun as the writing she was doing on her own. Although, now that she was thinking about it, she realized that she'd been secretly hoping this romance story might lead to something more. She'd even been thinking about giving her story to Kiki and Sin to get their opinions. And if they liked it, then maybe she'd give it to a few more people.

But she was jumping the gun and apparently missing out on what Clay was saying, because as he said, "Does that sound acceptable to you?" she had no idea what he was referring to.

"I'm sorry. I—"

"Don't be sorry. It was a lot to ask. I knew that a two-year commitment might be pushing our luck, but it was worth a shot."

Two-year commitment?

"I'll convey that to the management team. I think we can work with a standard one-year commitment."

"One year." She was on the verge of not one but two promotions and Boyd was possibly going away to medical school. Could she commit to a year?

"Yes, that's reasonable, don't you think?"

Of course it was a reasonable request, but...

"I think TEC got really lucky when we hired you, Janie."

How could she not commit to the man who had given her a shot when no one else would?

Chapter Twenty-Three

BOYD LEANED AGAINST Janie's dresser, watching as she put on a pair of dangling silver earrings for their date to Dining in the Dark. She wore a simple navy blue dress that hugged her hips and accentuated her waist, looking anything but *simple*.

He pushed away from the dresser and wrapped his arms around her from behind. "You look so pretty. It's a shame we'll be in the dark, because I'd like to stare at you all night."

She turned, pressing her hands to his dress shirt. "There are benefits to it being pitch-black. You can't see anything, but that means no one else can see us, either. And I do need some inspiration for my next chapter."

"Oh, baby. I love dating a romance writer." He pressed his lips to hers and she wound her arms around his neck, eagerly returning the kiss. Boyd had been waiting for the perfect time to tell her about the interview in Virginia, but the longer he waited, the more anxious he became.

She drew back from the kiss and flattened her palm over his heart. He knew she felt his mounting tension and lifted her hand, kissing it tenderly.

"You okay?" she asked sweetly.

"How can I not be? I've got my girl all to myself and two

days off work."

"You have the weirdest schedule."

"If I worked regular hours I never would have walked out of the office with you the night of your accident, and that makes everything worthwhile."

"Yeah, lucky for me I forgot my phone."

"One day I'm going to bronze that phone." He couldn't resist stealing another quick kiss. "I do want to talk to you about something, though. I was invited for an interview at the Virginia med school I applied to. The one near my family."

Her whole face brightened. "That's fantastic! When?"

He knew she had mixed feelings about his going away and was overwhelmed by the unselfishness of her response. "That's what I wanted to talk to you about. I'd really like you to come with me."

"To Virginia?"

"Yes. I'd love for you to meet my family. We can stay with Haylie. She's only thirty minutes away from the school. It would mean a lot to me if you'd come with me, and if you want, we can stop by your parents', too. Make a four-day weekend out of it."

She nervously nibbled on her lower lip. "When is your interview?"

"I haven't scheduled it yet, but I was thinking that if the interview was next Friday, we could drive down Thursday, or take a train, or fly. Whatever you want. And come back on Sunday so you don't miss too many days of work."

"Next week? Wow, I'd really like to, but I'll have to talk to Clay."

"I know the timing's not great, since he just brought up the training position."

Her brows knitted and her expression turned serious. "I really want to go, but we don't need to stop by my parents. This is *your* trip; let's keep it that way. And I don't want to inconvenience your family. Maybe we should think about staying at a hotel."

"Baby, don't be silly. My family won't think we're an inconvenience. They'll adore you, just like I do. And Haylie will be thrilled to have another woman around, though Scotty might drive you batty, because he's three."

"I love kids. He won't bother me."

"You love kids?" A smile tugged at his lips. "Funny you say that, because Cash and Siena are trying to get pregnant, and it made me think about us, and kids, and a future together."

"Boyd…" Her gaze softened.

"I know it's too soon to think about those things, but I couldn't help it. What do you say? Will you try to come with me to Virginia?"

"Yes. Yes!" She went up on her toes and kissed him. "There's nothing I'd rather do." Her stomach growled and she said, "Except maybe eat."

"Then let's get that sexy little butt of yours in gear. Stop lollygagging, talking about futures, and trips, and other nonsense. We have some dirty dining to do."

JANIE HAD BEEN to Dining in the Dark events with Kiki and Sin once when he visited, and she'd gone with a few other friends, but being there with Boyd felt completely different. Just like when she'd blindfolded him the other night on her balcony and felt a rush of excitement at being the one familiar with the sensations Boyd was experiencing for the first time, tonight she felt an adrenaline rush as they were led into the restaurant with a line of other diners. Each person walked with their hand on the shoulder of the person in front of them as the host told them what to expect and led them through what he described as a *pitch-black room* to their table.

"I can't see anything," Boyd said, with one hand on her arm, the other fishing around, she assumed for a chair. "Here you go, honey."

After she heard him find his seat, she reached across the table. "Can I hold your hand? It might make you feel more secure."

He reached across the table, knocking the silverware into the plate. "Sorry."

"That's okay. That's what this experience is about, getting a feel for living without sight. It's even different for me, because I have some light perception, but suddenly I'm thrust into total darkness, too."

She slipped her foot out of her sandal and ran it up Boyd's calf. "Maybe giving us something else to focus on will help."

He leaned forward and knocked over an empty glass. "Damn. Sorry, baby."

"That's okay," the waiter said as he arrived at the table. "Better now than when it's full. I'm Taylor and I'll be bringing your dinner shortly. What can I get you to drink?"

"I'll have tea, please," Janie said, still teasing Boyd's leg with her toes.

"Tea it is, and you, sir?" Taylor asked.

"I'm not sure I can be trusted with a full glass."

Janie slid her foot along his inner thigh, feeling the tension in his leg and loving it.

Boyd cleared his throat. "I'll have a glass of water, please. Thank you."

She waited for the waiter to leave before teasing him. "Flustered?"

"Baby, you'd have to do much more than that to fluster me." He shifted his chair closer and moved her foot between his legs.

"Oh my," she whispered, running the bottom of her foot along his erection.

Boyd slid his hands up her calf, then slowly back down. "Too bad they don't have bench seating."

When he ran his hands up either side of her leg again, his fingers grazed the skin just above her knee, sending a thrill through her. She pushed her chair as close as she could to the table, pressing her foot harder against him and allowing his fingers to climb farther up her thigh.

"Your tea, ma'am." Taylor set a cup of tea in front of Janie.

She hadn't even heard him approaching. "Thank you."

"And your water. Dinner will be out in just a moment. Can I get you anything else?"

"No, thank you."

Janie heard the restraint in Boyd's voice and wondered if Taylor did, too. She massaged his arousal harder with her foot.

"Janie," he warned.

She felt him moving around, then his stockinged foot slid beneath her dress and between her legs. *Oh my!* His leg was strong, and his foot was big and mind-blowingly talented.

"Two can play this game," he said seductively.

The ball of his foot moved in a slow circular motion, applying the perfect amount of pressure while his hot hands stroked up and down her calf, stealing her brain cells a handful at a time. When he rocked his hips, pressing his hard length against her foot, she realized she'd been so lost in his touch that her foot had gone still. One hand continued rubbing her leg and his other hand covered her foot, holding her tight against his erection. All the while Boyd's foot nudged her legs farther apart and continued his teasing assault through her panties. Shuddering with the precision of his efforts, she held on to the edge of her chair to keep from climbing across the table and straddling her man right there in the restaurant. She tried to focus enough to speak, because she wondered what other diners were thinking about their silent seduction. But her mouth was too dry to get out a single word, and what they were doing felt so taboo, so naughty and exciting, that her whole body was vibrating.

When the waiter brought their food, Boyd barely eked out a *thank you* and Janie couldn't have said a word to save her life. Heat flooded her veins as he pressed and stroked and drove her out of her mind. When he lifted her foot from between his legs and set it on the floor, it jarred her from her lusty haze.

"Sure, I'll walk you to the bathroom," Boyd said out of the blue. His foot slid away, and Janie clamped her mouth closed to keep the needy whimper from escaping.

In the next breath he was standing beside her, helping her to her feet. "I've never put a shoe on so fast in my life." His strong arm curved around her waist as he spoke into her ear, walking so fast she could barely keep up. "I'm holding on to the ropes, following them because I can't see a damn thing. I think we're rounding a corner. Jesus, where are the—"

She heard doors swing open and Boyd swooped her through them. "Locking the door," he said huskily as he held her against the door and engaged the lock.

"Are we alone?" She sounded so desperate. Her body burned

and shivered at the prospect of Boyd's hands on her.

He answered her with a hard kiss and a guttural moan that made her insides sizzle. Need seared through her veins as his hands gripped her thighs and he lifted her leg to his hip.

"Need you," he said coaxingly before his mouth claimed hers again.

He drew back urgently, sliding one hand beneath her ass and into her panties. "Need you so badly."

She felt his eyes like lasers on her face as his hand moved between her legs, stroking her erotically. As always with Boyd, it was the emotion in his voice, the love in his touch, the heat coursing through his body and into her own, that stoked her heart and spurred her on.

His fingers pushed into her, bringing all her nerve endings to life. She grabbed his head and kissed him with cruel ravishment, unwilling to stop from taking her fill. With his mouth latched on to hers, she dropped her hands to his pants and wrestled with the zipper.

He pulled away—*No! Come back!*—"You sure, hon—"

"Don't ask. *Take*, Boyd." He was so careful with her, and right now she didn't want careful. She wanted to be wild with him—only with him.

She'd never had bathroom sex. Kiki had, and Janie had wrongly judged her best friend. This was hotter than any fantasy she'd ever imagined. She couldn't stop this if she wanted to— and holy mother of sexiness, she did *not* want to.

Boyd tore her panties down, and she kicked them off as he pushed his slacks down and lifted her—so easily and urgently— and lowered her onto his thick shaft. She cried out in pleasure and he claimed her mouth again, drowning out her sounds with his plundering, hot tongue. She loved his mouth, the way it consumed hers, possessed every bit of her as he was buried deep, stroking her insides with exquisite mastery. Her back was against the door, and her thighs tightened around his waist. A firestorm of sensations whirred and spun on every inch of her skin. Lust burned and coiled in her core, tighter and hotter with every stroke. Her nails dug into his biceps as his mouth pushed her remaining sanity to the edge. She clawed and grasped, fending off her mounting orgasm, wanting this scorching heat to go on and on. He thrust and panted out her name— "Janie"—his thighs tightening like rocks below her.

"Love you so much," he said in a heated breath against her mouth.

His words tore through her, pulling her own confession to the tip of her tongue, where it hung, lost in sensation as he thrust harder, impossibly deeper, and sent her spiraling over the edge in a sea of red, blue, and yellow. Colors she hadn't seen in years spiraled before her, as sweet release finally—blissfully— pulled them both under.

Chapter Twenty-Four

BOYD HELPED JANIE clean up and fix her pretty dress, but all he could think about was what he'd said. He hadn't planned it, hadn't even registered how deeply he felt it. But his love for her was powerful and all consuming. They left the restaurant in a whirlwind of kisses and laughter, without ever eating dinner. The moon shone brightly against the evening sky, and the lights of the city looked as electric as he felt. But as they walked along the busy sidewalk, he realized Janie had fallen silent, and he hoped he hadn't freaked her out.

He wasn't experienced in matters of the heart, and he wasn't sure how or when it was appropriate to confess his feelings. But they were out there now, his heart laid bare between them, and he wasn't about to reel it all back in.

Once inside Janie's apartment, the silence—and his confession—seemed to intensify. Boyd's worries shifted and morphed into bigger, more problematic worries. Had he taken things too far in the restaurant? Had she given in because she'd felt trapped? Or because she was lost in the moment, as he was, but now she regretted it?

The idea that he might have unknowingly pushed her too far was too much to bear.

He took her hand and led her to the couch. "Sit with me?"

Her eyes drifted to her lap, where she fidgeted with the edge of her dress.

"Talk to me, baby. I can't take the silence." He drew her face toward his and tried to read her expression, but he had too many emotions rivaling inside him to see clearly.

"What are you thinking, honey? Did I take things too far when you'd planned such a romantic dinner? I'm so sorry. I—"

She pressed her finger over his lips. "Please don't do that. You're too careful with me, Boyd. You gave me the chance to stop us, and I appreciate that more than you know. Please don't worry about that. I'll tell you if I want to stop, or if I'm uncomfortable."

His heart soared knowing that he hadn't somehow disrespected her, or pushed too hard, and just as quickly he came back down to earth with the only other thing her silence could mean.

"Then it was what I said."

"It was what you said," she admitted. "And the way you said it. I felt your words as if they were moving through me."

"And it's too much too fast?"

Her sweet lips curved up at the edges and hope floated in again.

"No. It isn't too much too fast. It was feverish and unexpected, and it brought an explosion of emotions more powerful than anything I've ever experienced."

"That's good, right?" He felt like they'd become a handful of puzzle pieces tossed in the air and he was waiting for them to settle. To see if they still fit together. He knew they did, but did Janie?

"It's scary and sort of astounding." She paused, her face

serious. "Did you mean it? Do you love me?"

"More than I've ever loved anyone or anything." His confession was fast and truthful, but as soon as the words left him he felt completely, utterly exposed and vulnerable.

"I feel like I've been trying not to fall in love with you. Every second we're together builds on the last. I wake up and smile, because I'm in your arms. When I'm writing, it's my feelings for you that pour onto the page. You mentioned a future, children, and I fought hard not to see those things with you, because our lives are so up in the air right now."

Relief swept through him. She was falling for him, too. That was enough to soothe his worries. They had time. It would probably be weeks before he heard back from the schools, and even then, if they weren't ready to make a decision, maybe he'd table medical school. Wait another year and focus his applications in and around the city.

"I didn't say I loved you because I needed you to say it back." Even if he wanted to hear it, it wasn't the reason he'd said it. "I said it because I couldn't hold it back. I adore you, Janie. I don't want to scare you off or put pressure on you. I just...love you."

"I'm struggling to make sense of it all. You might be going to med school and I'm up for promotions, and at the heart of this crazy time of our lives, I feel these intense emotions for you—"

"I'm trying to make sense of it, too. But we don't have to figure it out now. We have plenty of time."

"But you're probably going away to med school, which you should. It's everything you've ever dreamed of."

"Only because I didn't know I should be dreaming of you." It had taken him years to find Janie, the only person to break through the barriers around his heart and evoke emotions in him he thought he'd lost in the fire.

Her sweet, soft laugh floated into his ears. "Why do I love your cheesy lines so much?"

"Because you know they're true. Yes, I've always dreamed of going to med school, but now I realize med school is missing one very important thing. An incredible woman who dove into a bet without a moment's hesitation, who pulled herself out of danger, and who somehow managed to wake up my sleeping heart."

Chapter Twenty-Five

JANIE HAD ALWAYS loved traveling. She loved experiencing new things—people, places, cultures. She hadn't traveled many places, so her cultural explorations were limited to a few childhood trips with her parents and, in college, weekend trips with Kiki. That was the extent of her *real* travels, but through the books she read, her adventures were far and wide.

She'd never been frightened by new experiences or too worried about finding her way around unfamiliar places. But even after a week of getting used to the idea of going to see Boyd's family, she was as nervous as she was excited. Clay hadn't hesitated to give her time off, and when she'd told Boyd she could go, he'd twirled her around with delight.

As they retrieved their luggage at the airport, Boyd held her hand. Sounds of the luggage carousel mixed with rushing footsteps and blips of conversation. He leaned in close, and the spike in adrenaline that she'd come to expect raced through her. Would she ever get used to the effect he had on her?

"I've got to let go for a sec to grab our bags, but I'm right here."

She listened as he situated their bags, and then his hand circled her waist.

"Let's blow this taco stand, gorgeous."

They picked up the rental car and drove toward Boyd's hometown. Every mile brought renewed nervousness. Boyd talked the whole way, describing the scenery as they left the city and entered rural Virginia. His voice was soothing and reminded her of the night of her fall.

"Doing okay?" he asked.

"A little nervous, but I'm okay."

"My family's going to love you. You'll see."

"I hope so. I was just thinking about the night of my fall. I don't think I've told you this before, but I love your voice."

He kissed the back of her hand. "You do, do you?"

She nodded. "It's soothing and emotional. Sometimes I know you're smiling because of how you say something, but I touch your face to be closer to those emotions. I'll have to watch that while we're here. I can't be pawing you around your family."

"Baby, don't ever stop touching me. I don't care who's around."

They drove in silence for a few minutes, the fresh air blowing across her cheeks through the open windows. Janie rested her head back, breathing in the floral, grassy scent that reminded her of home.

"We're entering Meadowside. You'd love the sign. It's been there forever and looks like it's never been repainted. There's a meadow of sunflowers and a big yellow sun cresting over the mountains. Across the top it says 'Welcome to Meadowside,' and across the bottom it reads, 'Where hills are high and hearts are full.'"

"I like that. Is it true? Are the hills high and hearts full?"

"The hills are pretty high, but not like out West. And

hearts? You tell me. A few more turns and we'll be at Haylie's."

When they arrived at Haylie's, Boyd turned off the car, leaned across the seat, and kissed her.

"Don't worry, okay? They'll love you, but if you feel overwhelmed or uncomfortable, we'll stay at a hotel, okay?"

She nodded, too nervous to speak. *What if your family doesn't like me? What if they think you should be with someone who can see?* Oh God! Was she really worried about that?

Boyd came around the car and helped her out. "Do you want your cane?"

"Yes, but just leave it folded. If you're with me, I'm fine, but if you want to go off with your family, I might need it. Oh, and there's a gift for Scotty in my bag."

"You bought Scotty a gift?"

She heard him fishing around in her bag. "Just a toy car Kiki and I picked up while you were at work."

"Uncle Boyd!" The high-pitched voice sounded bumpy, like Scotty was running toward them. A moment later she heard the little guy slam into Boyd's legs, and Boyd lifted him into his arms.

"How's my favorite little buddy?" He kissed him loudly.

"Good," Scotty said. His voice was so cute, Janie wished she could hug him, too. "Is dis Janie?"

"Yes, *this* is Janie, and she's very special to me, so be good to her." Boyd leaned closer to Janie and said, "He has a hard time with 'th.'"

"Hi, Scotty. I've heard a lot about you." She reached a hand out, which Scotty touched with his tiny fingertips, then launched himself toward her.

"Whoa, buddy. Slow down." Boyd held him until Janie got a grip on his wiggling body. "You okay with him?"

"Sure, just take my cane." She hefted Scotty onto her hip and held up the gift-wrapped toy. "Uncle Boyd and I brought you a little something."

Scotty snagged it from her hands and tore it open.

"Scotty!"

"Haylie," Boyd whispered to Janie. "Hey, sis."

She heard them embracing.

"You must be Janie," Haylie said. "Scotty's not very shy. Do you want me to take him?"

"No, I'm fine. I love kids, and it's so much better than him being uneasy around me." Her nervousness faded away with the distraction of Scotty tearing open his gift.

"You didn't have to bring him anything. That was so sweet of you," Haylie said. "Say thank you, Scotty."

"Fank you," he said in that sweet voice that made her heart squeeze.

"Come on," Haylie said. "Chet's out back with Gram and Grandpa."

Boyd guided her around to the backyard, where Scotty tried to wiggle out of Janie's arms.

"It's okay," Haylie said. "The yard is fenced, so he can't escape."

"There they are," an older woman, who Janie assumed was Boyd's grandmother, said. She heard Boyd embrace her.

"Hi, Gram. I missed you. Janie," Boyd said with pride in his voice, "this is my grandma Evelyn and my grandfather Lee."

"It's such a pleasure to meet you," Janie said as Evelyn embraced her. She was petite and smelled like homespun sunshine.

"Fair warning, little miss," Lee said. "I'm coming in for a hug."

Janie laughed as his arms circled her. She was surprised by

his size. He had to be at least six feet tall.

"Hey, big brother." Chet's voice was deep, though not as deep or soothing as Boyd's. "So this is the woman who made Boyd slow down and realize there's a whole world out here."

"It's a good thing you can't see the smart-ass smirk on his face," Boyd said as Chet hugged her. "Or his ugly mug, for that matter."

"Let's see." Janie reached up and touched Chet's stubbly cheeks. "Your jaw is wider than Boyd's, and, oh, look at that." She reached up to his ears. "Your ears are bigger, too."

"You know what they say about big ears," Chet teased.

"Actually, if you really knew"—she lowered her voice—"you wouldn't want to announce it."

Chet scoffed. Janie giggled.

"Oh, I do love her, Boyd," Haylie said.

"I'm kidding," Janie said. "But I wouldn't say he's ugly, Boyd."

Chet's arm came around Janie's shoulder, and she could feel Boyd's burning stare.

"But he's no Boyd, that's for sure," Janie added, reaching for her man.

"Christ," Chet mumbled.

"Jealousy will get you nowhere, Chet," Evelyn said sweetly. "Let's get to know our lovely guest."

While Boyd caught up on his family's lives, they peppered Janie with questions.

"Do you have any siblings?" Evelyn asked.

"No. It's just me."

"Boyd said you're from Peaceful Harbor," Lee said. "That's not far from here. How did you end up out in New York?"

"I must have known Boyd would be there," Janie teased.

"That's reason enough to go the opposite direction," Chet said.

"Leave him alone," Haylie chided him. "He's just jealous that Boyd has you, while he has, well…the guys at the firehouse."

"Right, and any woman I want," Chet retorted. "And you and Scotty to look after, but we're not talking about me."

Haylie touched Janie's shoulder and said, "You are so lucky not to have older brothers. I swear, while Chet smothers me here, Boyd smothers me from afar."

"It's called love," Boyd said.

Janie thought about Kiki and Sin and assumed all brothers were overprotective.

"If by love you mean controlling," Haylie said. "Then yeah, maybe. Anywho…Back to Janie. How'd you end up in the Big Apple?"

Janie explained that she'd gone away to college with Kiki, and they'd decided that the best place for a journalist was New York or DC, and DC was too close to her family. Although she didn't tell them that part.

Boyd was as attentive as always, without being overly so. He held Janie's hand, asked after her every so often, and she noticed he also asked after Evelyn and Haylie. She was relieved that he didn't smother her or make her feel like she was different from the others. She hadn't realized she'd been worried about that, but she must have been. Maybe she'd always worry about feeling like a burden to the people she cared for, or maybe one day that, like her ability to see people's faces, would simply fade away, too.

"I'm glad you and your friend moved to New York," Evelyn said when Boyd got up to push Scotty on the swing. "I haven't seen Boyd this happy in years."

"I'm glad, too," Janie answered.

Over the course of the afternoon, as Janie got to know Boyd's family, she learned a few new things about her smart, confident, loving boyfriend, too. He doled out lessons about sharing to Scotty and reminded him that he should always listen to his mommy. When he spoke with his grandmother about her apparently famous cinnamon apple pie and to-die-for ribs, he wasn't just making small talk. He was using the guise of cooking to find out other things about her, like if her arthritis had been acting up: *Are you still handling the mixer like a pro? Does Gramps have to carry the trays yet?* But it was when he was talking with his grandfather, reassuring him that he really was considering coming back to Virginia, that Janie got the biggest glimpse into Boyd's heart. She couldn't be sure if his family heard the hesitation in his voice, but she heard it loud and clear, and she wondered if it had been there the first time he'd told her that he hoped to return to the area. Or if that hesitation was born from the fact that they were a couple now.

She'd seen his wounded soul the day he'd shown her his scars and again each time he had nightmares. She'd sensed his need for closure, but what she'd somehow overlooked, and what became increasingly clear as the sun began to set and Haylie carried Scotty inside for a bath—but not before getting another hug and kiss from his treasured uncle—was that Boyd needed his family, too. If the hesitation she'd heard was because of their relationship, she couldn't come between him and his family. Not when he clearly needed them in his life. He might call the guys at the firehouse family, but there was no replacing the hearty laughter of shared childhoods or the ache of loneliness that embraced them and bound them together when their grandfather brought up how much Boyd looked like their father.

They'd moved into the living room, and the room grew silent. Sadness hovered like another person in the room. She felt their loss as if she'd experienced it, too. Boyd's hand rested on her thigh. She laced their fingers together, hoping to comfort him.

She hadn't known Boyd's parents, but she had the sheer pleasure of being loved by the man they'd raised in the few years they'd shared. The man she wanted to help overcome the ghosts that haunted him at night. He'd become her friend, her lover, and everything in between.

As the Hudsons brought her into their close-knit family, she felt guilty for blowing off her own family. How could she have taken their love for granted when Boyd's family had lost so much?

BEING HOME BROUGHT harsh reminders of why Boyd had run so far away after high school. Memories hovered around every corner—in the pictures that hung on the walls, in the eyes of his grandparents when they looked at him a certain way. Even the inflection of Haylie's voice sometimes brought flashes of memories. Most memories were good, but the overwhelming need to keep his siblings safe was still oppressive.

"Come on," Chet said as he tugged Boyd up to his feet. "Let's get the card table set up." Their family had always gathered around the card table. Even when their parents were alive it was a weekly thing. Family game night was a highlight of Boyd's youth. It was a part of their memories the fire couldn't steal.

"I brought braille playing cards if you want to play," he whispered to Janie, who was talking with his grandmother.

Janie's eyes widened with disbelief. "You did?"

His grandmother smiled up at him with an approving nod.

"The store Heath told me about. Same place I got the shirt with braille on it."

"And my book," she reminded him as she rose to her feet and hugged him. "You never overlook anything. Thank you."

"I'm just competitive. You keep saying you're going to win our bet, and I want to win something. I'm pretty good at gin rummy."

"You suck at rummy." Chet grabbed the back of his shirt and dragged him toward the stairs. "I'll bring him right back, Janie."

"She's pretty great," Chet said as they descended the stairs.

You have no idea. "Yeah, she is." Boyd grabbed the cards and a few folding chairs.

"I'm happy for you." Chet lifted the card table and ran his eyes over Boyd's face. "Gramps said you look at her like Dad used to look at Mom."

"Did he?" Every time someone said he resembled his father he was struck by a strange mix of emotions. Pride, love, and a little guilt for being alive. Chet's gaze was expectant, as if he were waiting for more of a response. But Boyd's mind slid back in time to the night of the fire. If only he'd gotten up. If only he'd done something.

"You okay?" Chet's brows knitted.

"Huh? Yeah. Sorry." Maybe he should finally ask Chet if he'd heard a noise, too. Shit, he couldn't do that. If he didn't hear it, then he'd know Boyd could have saved their parents, and how could Chet ever forgive him for something like that?

Chet's lips quirked up. "It's been years since you've been serious with a woman. It's fuckin' with your head, isn't it?"

The spark of amusement in Chet's eyes, the trust and friendship they shared, was right there before him, loud as a billboard. But he didn't deserve that trust. *Fuck.*

"Hurry up, you guys!" Haylie called down to them.

"We're coming!" Chet hollered. When he lowered his voice and said, "By the way, the last guy Haylie called you about was a douche. Thanks for cluing me in," Boyd was thankful for the change of subject.

"Christ, she can't catch a break. Sorry. When she told me about him, something felt off. I don't remember what it was, but that's why I told her I wanted you to check him out, but it was the night of Janie's accident, and I forgot to text you." Haylie had met Scotty's father when she was visiting a college friend. He'd promised her the world, but when she discovered she was pregnant, she'd found out he was engaged to another woman. Boyd and Chet had always looked after her, but after that they had stepped it up a notch—*or twelve.*

"No worries." Chet patted him on the back. "Maybe if you get into UVA and move back here, you'll take over eyeballing the men in her life so I can move on to eyeballing a few ladies of my own."

As they headed upstairs, Boyd wondered if he could ever really come back to the place where his nightmares' roots were too deep to avoid.

Chapter Twenty-Six

DRESSED IN HIS best dark suit, a crisp white shirt, and a blue tie Haylie said made his eyes *pop*, Boyd drew Janie in for *another* kiss.

"I'll miss you today." He'd had another nightmare last night, endlessly searching for the cause of the noise he'd heard before the fire erupted, and Janie had been right there for him when he woke up, soothing him out of the cold sweat that engulfed him. He'd feared that his nightmares would keep him from ever having a lasting relationship, but Janie was still there. Just as loving and caring as ever.

"I'll miss you, too," Janie said, "but I'm so proud of you."

Haylie came out of the kitchen carrying Scotty, whose fingers were covered with red jam. "You're still here?" She'd taken the day off work to show Janie around town. Their grandmother had offered to watch Scotty.

"Leaving soon," Boyd assured her. "Thanks for showing Janie around today."

"No prob. I plan on clueing her in to all of your most embarrassing stories." Haylie's blue eyes danced with the tease.

Boyd shot her a deadpan stare.

"Now get out of here before I let Sticky-Hands Scotty touch

that handsome suit of yours." She disappeared down the hall.

"I'm going." He stole one last kiss from Janie. "For good luck."

"You don't need luck. They'd be crazy not to offer you a spot." Janie took her hand in his and put something cold into his palm. "I have faith in you."

He looked down at the round silver charm hanging from the key ring and rubbed his thumb over the bumps.

"It says 'Born to be a doctor' in braille. That way just you and I know what it says."

He closed his hand around the charm, swamped with emotions, and embraced her. "I love this, and I love you." She still hadn't said she loved him, not in the three words he craved, but Janie showed her love for him in everything she did.

"You don't mind that it's in braille? I wasn't sure…"

He gazed into her eyes. "Honey, it makes it that much more special. Now you have to teach me to read braille."

"Do they sell braille shirts for women at that store?" she whispered seductively.

"I love the way your brain works."

Her smile reached her eyes. "Maybe we'll be able to fit in braille lessons between our romance research."

"Oh, baby." He pulled her against him and kissed her again.

"You need to leave, or you'll miss your interview. It's true, you know. You were born to be a doctor, so go make it happen."

After another chaste kiss, he was out the door. He took the long way out of town, avoiding the past that haunted his nights—and drove toward a future he might not be able to accept.

IT WAS A nice, sunny day. Haylie and Janie walked the few blocks into town and spent the afternoon meandering in and out of shops. The streets were quiet, and the people were friendly, stopping to chat with Haylie and introduce themselves to Janie. It was a far cry from New York City.

"I have to admit," Haylie said as they left a gift shop, "I was nervous about asking if you wanted to *see* the town. I know that's probably not the politically correct way to ask."

"Just the fact that you admitted that places you on my list of favorite people," Janie said with a smile. "Most people clam up instead of asking things like that. I love that you asked if I wanted to see the town. Seeing, for me, means so many things. Getting a feel for the town's vibes, the people. You've seen that I love exploring the shops. I couldn't keep my hands off of the ceramic animals in there."

"They are cool, aren't they? Careful of the curb." Haylie touched Janie's elbow as they stepped off the sidewalk.

She'd noticed that Boyd's whole family was courteous with her, but not overly protective, and it made her even more comfortable. Last night when they were saying good night to everyone, their grandparents had both told her how glad they were she'd come. And when Chet embraced her, he'd said, *Thanks for making my brother so happy.* She loved that they were affectionate and had welcomed her into their circle. And even happier that her initial worries of feeling like an imposition were unfounded. Scotty had jumped into her arms first thing this morning, and she'd eaten up every second of his chattering tales.

"Would you mind if we stopped into the bookstore? We're at the curb." Haylie took her arm as she stepped onto the sidewalk. "I want to pick up a new book for Scotty."

"Are you kidding? I love bookstores!"

"Really? But…" Haylie's silent question hung in the air.

"But I can't read the books. There is that little inconvenience." She laughed. "I love the smell of bookstores, and when they have coffee shops and comfy chairs. Some bookstores have audio clips I can listen to, but not many. And nothing is more fun for me than being read to."

"Really? Does Boyd read to you?"

"Yes, sometimes," she admitted. She felt like she was exposing something intimate, even though it was such a little thing. Thinking of Boyd the day they were at the park, and how he thought her privacy wasn't a little thing at all, made her smile.

"Can I ask you something?" Haylie asked. "If I'm crossing a line, then please tell me to shut up."

"Okay."

"Does Boyd talk to you about our parents?"

She'd been expecting a question about what it was like to be blind, which people asked her often. This took her by surprise. "A little."

"I'm only asking because he doesn't talk about them with us, and it worries me."

Janie thought of Boyd's nightmares and how reluctant he was to talk about them. She wanted to ask Haylie about them. Did she know he had them? Did he ever discuss them with her? Did she have nightmares?

But that also felt too intimate to share. If Boyd had kept them to himself, then it wasn't her place to speak of them. Instead, she told Haylie the same thing she told herself.

"One thing I learned as my vision worsened is that moving forward is all about adaptation. Look at all Boyd's accomplished and where he's headed. He's obviously found a way around whatever he is or isn't talking about."

Haylie looped her arm with Janie's, and Janie loved the connection. They'd spent so much time talking—about the town, Scotty, and Haylie's hopes to one day meet someone who would love Scotty as much as she did—Janie already felt close to her.

"I guess that's just another reason my brother is so gaga over you. You see more than we sighted people do."

Gaga. Boyd had made that abundantly clear, but Janie reveled in Haylie's assessment for a moment. "I'm gaga over him, too."

A few minutes later Janie inhaled the woodsy, inky scent of the bookstore. Haylie's arm was still linked with hers, but she didn't want to assume that Haylie would stick with her, so she continued using her cane.

"Hi there." A happy female voice carried through the store.

"Hi, Amber," Haylie said. The unique *tap, tap, tap* of a dog's nails approached alongside footsteps. "This is Janie, Boyd's girlfriend."

"Hi, Janie. I'm Amber Montgomery. I didn't know Boyd was back in town."

A fluffy dog brushed up against Janie's leg. "Oh. I guess your dog's friendly?"

"Yes. That's Reno. He's my seizure dog. He might lick you to death."

As Janie reached down to pet the dog, her hand accidentally stroked over Amber's. "Sorry."

"Don't be," Amber said easily, taking the discomfort out of the situation.

She wanted to say she was sorry Amber had seizures and to find out what type of seizures she suffered from, but Janie didn't want to make her uncomfortable. She realized she was suddenly on the other side of the fence and understood the hesitation people had toward asking her about her blindness.

"He seems like a sweetie." Janie crouched beside the friendly, fluffy pup. "I always wanted a guide dog, but I live in New York City and it's too hard. There are so many people and noises. I envision being dragged down the block as the dog runs after a scent or chases someone rushing for a cab."

"I can only imagine. My mom trains seizure dogs, and she's thinking about expanding her business to guide dogs, too. You should come by and talk to her."

"I'd love to, but I probably won't be getting a dog anytime soon."

"I didn't mean it like a sales pitch," Amber explained. "I just thought you might enjoy coming by to see them. I'm sure my mom would love to talk with you, pick your brain, and all that."

Most people were so careful about not mentioning her blindness. She much preferred the way Amber took it in stride.

"I'm not sure if we'll have time this trip, but I'd love to talk to her. Maybe I can call her?"

They talked for a few more minutes about the dogs, and Amber took Janie on a tour of the store while Haylie searched for a book for Scotty.

"I've got a small braille book section." Amber showed her a bookshelf that had about two dozen books. "I'm constantly trying to get more, and I hope to add an audio section, too."

"I was just telling Haylie how much I love listening to audiobooks. Gosh, you're so lucky to own a bookstore. You must love your job."

"I like the quiet, and disappearing into the worlds of incredible authors, but like with any business, there are downsides. So many people read on ereaders these days that I'm constantly looking for ways to bring more attention to the store."

"Have you thought about hosting a monthly book club, or starting a newsletter that goes out as a mailer with coupons for ten percent off a purchase, or doing a special poetry reading night?"

Reno rubbed up against Janie's leg again.

"Reno likes you as much as I do. You're full of great ideas. I'll have to jot some of those down. Maybe we should swap email addresses so we can talk about these types of things." Amber led her up to the checkout counter. "This is my card. What's your email?"

Janie gave Amber her email address.

Haylie joined them a few minutes later. "Janie's writing a romance novel. Maybe you can carry it when she's done."

"I'm just...I'm not...It's nothing." She'd forgotten she'd told Boyd's family about their bet.

"Books are never nothing," Amber said. "I'd love to be a beta reader for you. I'm a romance junkie."

"Really? It's probably not very good. It's the first time I've tried my hand at romance. Anyway, it's not done yet."

"You'll have to let me read it, too. I have zero romance in my life, besides the snuggles of my little man." Haylie's voice was full of love.

"That's more than I have," Amber said. "My love life exists between the covers of books."

"Mine used to be that way, too," Janie admitted. "It's true what they say about finding your soul mate when you're not even looking."

"Soul mate," Haylie said wistfully. "I thought Scotty's dad might be my soul mate, but he was just a liar."

"I'm sorry." Janie didn't know what happened with Scotty's

dad, but she realized she'd called Boyd her soul mate, which was something she hadn't even shared with Boyd yet. "I didn't mean soul mate. I meant…"

"Oh, please, you meant 'soul mate.' It's written all over your face," Haylie said with a laugh. "Scotty's dad *was* a liar, but Boyd's not. He's just a little too big brotherish sometimes. When we lost our parents he stepped in as Mom, Dad, and protector, making me change my clothes in middle school if I wore something he thought was too short or too tight. He pushed Chet to study more than my grandparents ever did. I remember them getting into wrestling matches over it. I'm sure it's an eldest thing magnified by the loss of our parents, but I'm glad he's not that way with you."

Boyd had been protective of Janie but not overly so.

"It's definitely an eldest thing. Grace, my oldest sister, practically tried to live our lives for us when we were younger." Amber tucked her business card into Janie's pocket. "Don't lose my card. We'll have a Skype party and celebrate your book when it's done. Maybe we've just discovered the next Nora Roberts."

Janie didn't know about all that, but she felt a kinship with Amber and Haylie, and it was wonderful to feel so at ease. They settled into a comfy couch, with Reno at their feet, and compared their favorite books, favorite romance tropes, and somehow Janie ended up telling them all about the night of her accident.

"It was the scariest, and the best, night of my life." They'd been talking for hours. Customers had come in and out of the store, greeted by Reno and Amber. A few of the women had sat with them and chatted for a few minutes before making their purchases and moving on. Janie was drawn to the easy pace and the people in Meadowside, where friendships seemed to matter more than the next text or email.

She'd fled a small town much like this because of overprotective parents. She imagined Boyd growing up here, embraced by the warmth of this community, and she wondered if moving away had less to do with the college he'd wanted to attend and more to do with escaping something, too.

Chapter Twenty-Seven

BOYD AND JANIE spent Saturday touring all of Boyd's old favorite haunts. He showed her the schools he'd attended, the fields where he'd played Little League—his father had coached the team—and the creeks where they used to have parties and get into trouble. After dinner with his family and a round of gin rummy, which Boyd won, his grandparents went home, and he and Janie went outside to catch the tail end of the sun dropping below the horizon.

"Don't you miss this?" Janie rested her head on his shoulder and sighed.

"Watching the sunset?"

"All of it. The serenity, the pastures. Air that doesn't smell like exhaust. Being with your family, who obviously adore you. Seeing the people you grew up with."

He shrugged. "You're a long way from your family, too."

"And you're avoiding the question." She lifted her head and kissed his cheek.

"Are you sure you don't want to stop by and see your folks tomorrow?"

"I'm sure. I'll call them at some point." She rested her head on his shoulder again. "Seeing how close your family is makes me miss mine. I'm going to try harder to be more understanding toward them."

He kissed her temple, and she wrapped her arm around his knee. "You have the most remarkable ability to face everything head-on."

"What's the alternative? I've drawn a line in the sand with my parents, and they've done their best to respect it. But I'm realizing that it shouldn't be my way or the highway. They're family. Their biggest crime is that they love me *too* much."

"So what's the answer?"

"I'm not sure," she said. "Maybe I'll start by not getting my back up every time they call. Give them the benefit of the doubt instead of expecting the worst."

They fell quiet, and Boyd's mind drifted to his nightmares. He loathed them, but did he expect them? Was he going to sleep every night expecting the worst?

"Are we going to talk about what we're not talking about?" Janie asked.

"Probably not." He was wondering when she'd get around to asking about the one place he *didn't* take her.

She turned to face him then with a serious gaze, which told him she wasn't going to let him off that easily.

"Okay, go ahead," he relented. "What do you want to know?"

"You took me everywhere today, except…"

"The site of the fire. Do you blame me? Why would I ruin a nice afternoon?"

"Maybe you can find some good memories there, too, mixed among the difficult ones." She said it so sweetly, as if he could see ice cream with marshmallows on top if he tried hard enough. It was that confidence, that strength, which he'd admired since he'd first met her, that had drawn him to her like bees to honey.

"It's not happening, Janie. The memories there are rough."

"But you said your mom's gardens were her favorite things. Why not take a quick ride over and see them?"

He lifted her under her arms and set her on his lap, tucked her hair behind her ear, and kissed her cheek.

"Why do you try so hard?"

"Why don't you?" she challenged.

"I do. It's just not that easy." He leaned in for a kiss, and she pulled away.

"Nothing in life is easy. We've already established that."

"Janie," he groaned.

"I'm not asking you to talk to me about anything. I just think seeing something happy, like the gardens your mom loved, might not be such a bad thing."

"I must love you to even be discussing this. What do you hope to accomplish with this garden visit?"

"Maybe taking the edge off of the memories for you."

"It's not going to happen." He lifted her off his lap and rose to his feet. "But I have a feeling you need to see where it all went down, so let's go."

They drove in silence, every mile making his skin feel tighter. When he turned off the main road toward the property, the country road was pitch-black, save for their headlights. He made the final turn into the long gravel driveway, remembering the last time he'd visited and feeling like his throat was closing up.

"You okay?" Janie ran her hand up his arm, and he knew she felt his tension.

"Sort of." He left the engine running and the lights on, aimed at the gardens. He wanted to describe the gardens, to let

Janie experience their beauty, but he couldn't, because what he felt wasn't beautiful. "Five minutes, okay, honey? I'm not into self-torture."

He stepped from the car and went around to help Janie out. Her arms circled his neck, and she went up on her toes, her hands pressed flat on his chest.

"We don't even need five minutes." She kissed him. *Deeply.*

Her hands slid around to his back as the kiss intensified. Myriad emotions gripped him. Fear and worry were shifted and pushed by love and lust. She made a sweet, sexy noise in the back of her throat, bringing a smile to his lips.

"Trying to drive me crazy?"

"Trying to replace difficult memories with happier ones." She grabbed his ass and squeezed.

"Careful," he warned her, before taking her in another mind-numbing kiss, which he realized had been her plan all along. He eased away from the kiss, went back for more, then drew away again.

"Thank you," he whispered.

"I think I should be thanking you for giving in. I know it's hard to be here." She took his hand and placed it over her heart. He felt the frantic beating against his palm. "That's partially because I was worried about you coming here and partially because of those kisses."

She moved his hand over his own rapidly beating heart. "What's yours from?"

"Being here. Being here with you." He embraced her and closed his eyes, feeling the beast at his back, flames licking at his neck, and willing away the silent screams that haunted him.

Chapter Twenty-Eight

BACK IN NEW York, everything felt too fast, too crowded, too loud. It took a full week for Janie to settle in to her comfortable stride, which she realized wasn't all that comfortable. It had been so nice walking through Boyd's hometown with his sister and exploring the area with him. When they were out at his childhood home, she felt tension building inside him, felt the way he seemed to cocoon her body from the property, as if his memories were living, breathing things inhabiting the land itself and they could hurt her, too. He hadn't said anything after they returned to Haylie's house, but that night he'd held her tighter than ever before. Although he didn't have a nightmare that night, they'd been back from Virginia for ten days, and he'd had a few since. She hoped he would continue to open up to her and that eventually they might get to the root of the nightmares so he could move past them.

Boyd was back to working at the firehouse, but today he was working an afternoon shift at the hospital. He was scheduled to consult at TEC again next week, and she wished he was there now so they could sneak in a few minutes together. She was nervous about her promotions, which she should hear about any day.

Needing something to focus on, Janie turned to her romance writing. She'd gotten in the habit of getting up early and writing, which had the lucky side effect of putting her in a sexy mood by the time Boyd woke up. Their mornings together were wonderful. They made love often, but other times they just talked. She could no longer imagine waking up without him.

Making sure her braille device was not in terminal mode, which meant her computer monitor remained on her latest newsletter article, Rock-Hard Editing, she furtively researched science fiction heroines. This morning she'd left her heroine, Candee, on her way to Kent's comic book store, wanting desperately to win his attention from his coworker, a spandex-wearing, purple-haired vixen named Kenisha. Janie had never been into costumes or role-playing, but she had a feeling that if Candee could pull it off, she'd finally land Kent for good. After a few minutes of research, she had her answer. According to the online comic forums, no comic book junkie worth his salt could resist a girl dressed in a skintight outfit like Black Widow, who was amazing with her hands and—according to 150 forum members—looked kick-ass wielding a gun.

Get ready, Kenisha, because my girl Candee is on the prowl.

Janie's lips quirked up as another idea came to mind. Googling costume stores, she found one nearby and headed out for an early lunch break. What was better than hands-on research?

"Janie," the receptionist said as she returned an hour later, armed with what she hoped would be a fantastic surprise for Boyd. "Clay's looking for you. He said to send you into the conference room as soon as you arrived."

Her stomach flipped. Was this it? Would she finally have her answer about the promotion?

"Okay. I'll just drop this stuff in my office first. Please let him know I'll be right in."

She paced her office, trying to calm her racing heart. What if she didn't get the promotion? What if she did? She'd let Kiki read the first three chapters of her romance story, and she'd loved it so much, Janie had sent the chapters to Amber and Haylie for a second and third opinion. Not only had they loved them as much as Kiki had, but they wanted to read the rest. As silly as it sounded, even in her own head, it gave her hope that maybe one day she really could write a romance worthy of publication.

That hope made her more confused about the promotion. She did want it, but maybe that was driven by the fact that if she was turned down, it said something about her abilities. *Well, wouldn't that suck?* To be told she wasn't good enough to be a technical writer?

Maybe she didn't *want* to be a technical writer.

But what if she wasn't good enough as a fiction writer *or* a technical writer?

Great. Now her stomach hurt.

With her stomach knotted and her mind spinning, she headed down the hall, focusing on the tapping of her cane instead of the hammering of her heart.

"HEY THERE, LOVER boy," Kelly said as she approached the desk where Boyd was taking emergency calls in the hospital. "How's our favorite patient?"

"Janie's great. All healed up and beautiful as ever."

Kelly leaned her hip against the desk and crossed her arms. "So you *are* dating her. I wondered."

"We weren't dating when she came in, but yeah, we're pretty serious, actually." *Pretty serious* sounded like the understatement of the year. They'd practically moved in together. Kiki had even started knocking before entering Janie's apartment, instead of using her key.

"Good for you. She seemed really nice, and she probably needs someone like you, a little overprotective, openly affectionate."

"She doesn't *need* anyone, but I'm glad she wants me."

"I didn't mean it because she's blind. I meant that you probably make a great boyfriend."

He matched her crossed arms and narrowed his eyes. "Thanks, but I'm not overprotective."

"Ha!" She shook her head. "How many times have I heard you reeling off a list of questions to Haylie about some guy who'd asked her out?"

"That's different. She's my sister, and she's a single mom."

"I guess." She slid an elastic band from her wrist and tied her hair back with a sigh. Boyd knew she was at the tail end of a long shift, but her blue eyes still danced with energy. "Janie's a lucky girl. I could tell the night you brought her in that you were taken with her. I think you called her 'honey' a dozen times."

"Did I?" He still wasn't sure where that endearment had come from, but it had come easily then and even easier now. His phone vibrated and he pulled it out. "Oh man."

"What?"

"An email from UVA med school." Adrenaline spiked through his veins.

"Well, open it already." Kelly's eyes widened with interest.

He hesitated, afraid of what the message would contain.

Rejection? Acceptance? He didn't even know which one he was hoping for anymore.

He opened the email and scanned it quickly. He read it a second time to make sure he'd read it right. *Holy shit. I got in.* They wanted a decision within two weeks. Two weeks? How could he decide his future in fourteen days?

"Well?" Kelly fanned her hand. "I'm excited. Did you get in?"

"It's not that kind of letter," he lied. "It's just a follow-up."

He thought he'd have more time to figure out what to do, what he wanted. What Janie wanted.

It had taken less than a week for Boyd to know he wanted Janie in his future.

How long would it take for him to decide if he was willing to give up his dreams to keep her there?

Chapter Twenty-Nine

JANIE WAS BOUNCING with excitement while Kiki tugged and twisted her hair into a side braid.

"Would you sit still?" Kiki chided. "I still can't believe you're dressing up like some giant slug's slave."

"I'm Princess Leia, *thank you very much*. And the giant worm is Jabba the Hutt. Boyd loves science fiction—you know that." It was Wednesday evening and she couldn't wait to surprise Boyd with her costume.

"You dated a guy who loved history and you didn't dress up like Betsy Ross." She laughed. "That would have been hilarious, though. She's so *not* sexy."

"If I'm making my heroine seduce her man looking like Black Widow, shouldn't I experience role-play seduction first? They say write what you know."

"I could write a wicked novel." Kiki snorted with laughter.

"No kidding. I'm getting there," she said proudly. "Besides, this is a celebratory night. I haven't told Boyd about my promotion yet. I'm trying to figure out what to do first—seduce or share my news."

"Have you thought about the fact that he might not be as pleased as you are over your promotion?" She tugged a little too hard on Janie's hair, and Janie knew she was doing it to kick her brain into gear.

"He hasn't heard from any med schools yet, so what would you have me do? Turn down my promotion?" She'd wrestled over that for a while on the subway ride home, but it wouldn't make sense to give up what she'd been working for *just in case* Boyd got into medical school.

"I just think you have to be careful about the messages you send him. You were so excited after me and those other girls read the chapters you shared. You were talking about finishing the book and trying to get it published. That's something you can do from anywhere. But taking a job with a one-year commitment? That's a whole different story."

"Clay was there for me when no one else would give me a job, and Boyd hasn't said anything about me moving anywhere with him." She didn't mean to sound upset, but she'd been trying to ignore the elephant in the room ever since they returned from Virginia.

"Do you want to go with him wherever he gets accepted to med school?" Kiki's hands stilled on Janie's hair.

Yes, but I don't want to leave you. "Can we talk about something else? I was excited to talk with him about it and to show him this outfit, and now I'm nervous."

"Well, that's no good, is it? We'll have no nervousness on the night of your very first sci-fi seduction. I'm sorry I brought it up, but I am your best friend, and tough love comes with the territory." Kiki finished braiding her hair and laid it over her right shoulder. "Only you could pull off a one-sided eighties braid. You look gorgeous."

"Do I?" She patted her hair, feeling the tight braid. "There's not much to the costume." She wore a robe over the bikini-style gold and maroon costume. "Do you think I look ridiculous?" She stood and opened the robe.

"Holy shit, Janie. You look like a million hot-ass sexy bucks! I can tell you right now that if you answer the door in that outfit, you are not going to get one word out of your mouth before he's all over you."

"We'll go with that, then, because that sounds perfect." She reached for Kiki, and Kiki moved into her embrace. "I know Boyd and I need to talk about things, but tonight I just want to be happy."

"And that's exactly what I want you to be. I just don't want you to get hurt."

"Neither do I." *Which is why I'm not letting my career go down the drain just because I'm falling in love.*

BOYD WORRIED THE whole way to Janie's apartment. Virginia was a world away from New York and from everything Janie had. Her job, Kiki, the comfort of the life she'd built there. But what if it was the only medical school to accept him? What if he didn't get an offer from a New York school? It didn't seem likely at this point, since he hadn't received an invitation to interview. He'd spent years working toward medical school. Years putting everything else in his life on hold.

Until Janie.

He rubbed his thumb over the key chain she'd given him. *Born to be a doctor.* It might be more accurate if it read, *Born to love Janie Jansen,* because nothing else seemed as important as being with her and making her happy. And making Janie happy meant making sure she was comfortable.

He shoved the key chain in his pocket as Janie's apartment door opened, but he didn't see her.

"Honey?" As he stepped inside, Janie pushed the door closed from behind it.

Boyd's thoughts shattered to oblivion. Janie stood before him nearly naked, wearing the Princess Leia slave costume that every man in his right mind had drooled over—and she looked a hundred times hotter than Carrie Fisher ever could.

"Hi," she said so seductively it sizzled.

His gaze dragged down over her beautiful face, lingering at those cupid lips that never failed to make his heart stutter. She raised her brows just a hair, as if to say, *Wanna play?* Oh, hell yes, he wanted to play. His eyes dropped further, taking in the golden collar circling her neck, connected to a plastic chain she held in her left hand. Her skin was oiled up, slick and alluring. His eyes traveled farther south, to the velvet bra laced with gold serpentine designs barely containing her breasts.

He stepped closer and stroked a finger over the golden arm cuffs circling her upper arms. He opened his mouth to tell her how sexy she looked, but all that came was a rush of hot air. He dropped his hands to the crisscrossed thin gold straps of her itsy-bitsy bikini bottom, from which a wine-red skirt hung between her legs. He couldn't wait to rip *that* off. His eyes traveled over her luscious curves again, to her sweet bowed lips, then higher still, to the smoldering flames in her eyes that had him closing the gap between them, bringing her body flush with his.

"I missed you," he finally managed.

"Welcome home, Han…Hans…" The slight tremble in her voice amped up his arousal. She'd stepped way outside her comfort zone—*for him.* For them. And she looked incredibly sexy. Little did she know that costumes weren't necessary, although appreciated at this very second. She was all he ever needed, all he ever wanted. Sweet, sexy, smart Janie Jansen. His strong, independent temptress.

"Han Solo? Baby, I'll be anyone you want me to be, just as long as I get to devour you."

Her eyes danced with wickedness. "I hope you brought your lightsaber."

Their gazes held, and it didn't matter that she couldn't see him. He was certain she was the only person on earth who saw all of him. His strengths, his weaknesses, his fears, and his dreams. He crushed their bodies together and brushed his lips over hers. His hands skimmed along her luscious thighs, to her sweet, nearly bare ass.

"Boyd," she whispered. Her hands pushed into his hair as she lifted up to meet his greedy mouth.

After one wild and messy kiss, he drew back, slowing them down and savoring the moment. He slicked his tongue over her lower lip, kissed the corners of her mouth, her cheeks, her chin. Every kiss, every touch, every inhalation of her seductive perfume, brought waves of desire. He wanted to let her play out her fantasy—whatever it might be in her beautiful mind. But he was no match for the emotions that swamped him. His body was an inferno, burning from the inside out. Her tremulous breaths, the tightening of her grip on his arms, told him she was wrestling the same primal urges.

When she whispered his name, full of lust and sex and greed, his restraint snapped. He captured her mouth in a desperate kiss. Her body sank into his, her softness yielding to his strength, as he took the kiss deeper. Heat pulsed through him, sending his thoughts spinning away. He swooped her into his arms, never breaking their connection, and carried her into the bedroom, where he laid her on the bed and followed her down.

She was everything he ever wanted. He felt drunk on her, lecherous with his inability to restrain himself around her. That worried him as they moaned and groaned, kissed and sucked. He forced himself to draw back, panting for air.

"I love you, Janie, so much I ache when we're apart."

Her swollen lips remained parted. Her skin was flushed with desire as she blinked up at him. "I know."

She tugged him in for another kiss, and he lost himself in her taste, her touch. Her sexy costume sailed down to the floor piece by tiny piece, followed by his shirt, jeans, and the golden collar with the chain that offered too many enticing options to cast away for good. Finally, nothing separated them besides a slick sheen of heat. She lifted her knees and wound her legs around his waist as she grabbed a pillow and shoved it under her hips.

"Research," she breathed against his neck as her wetness enveloped the head of his cock.

He entered her slowly as their mouths came together again, tongues stroking to the same rhythm as their lovemaking. She made the most delicious noises, sweet, sensual moans that disappeared down his throat. The pillow allowed him to drive deeper, to love her more completely, but it wasn't enough. He wanted her every way possible, wanted to see her face as she came again and again.

Lacing their fingers together, he pinned her hands beside her head, moving slowly inside her, seeking the spot that turned her moans into a gasping, pleading, orgasm. Her breathing shallowed.

"Boyd," she panted out seconds before her eyes slammed shut. She arched up as her hips bucked, quaking with each thrust, pulsing around his heat. Her climax went on forever, seriously testing his control. Just as it began to ease, he quickened his pace, growing desperate for release but wanting to take her higher. Letting go of her hands, he wrapped her in his arms and rolled them over so she was on top, giving her the advantage of control. She rode him hard, her breasts bouncing against her creamy skin. Her face was flushed, and her eyes beaded on him in a mask of pure erotic ecstasy.

He rolled her nipples between his fingers and thumbs, and her moans became heated pleas. He rose, pressing her breasts together and taking both nipples in his mouth, sucking, teasing, as she clawed at his head, holding him in place as another intense orgasm tore through her.

"Boyd—"

His desire mounted, aching, throbbing for release. Every sweet clench of her heat nearly made him blow, but he wasn't done. He rolled them onto their sides and drew her knee up his hip, holding their bodies together, grinding inside her. He gazed into her eyes, determined to love her completely, until she was fully sated.

Their bodies moved in perfect harmony. Her knee tightened against his side. Heat slid down his spine, pooling at the base.

"Let go, baby. One more time. With me."

She touched her forehead to his shoulder, clutching at his arms. He felt her strength dwindling, knew she was close to spent as she whispered against his heated flesh, "I'm with you. I'm always with you."

As if they'd both been waiting for those words, they surrendered to their passion. Waves of ecstasy washed through Boyd as

Janie's body melted against him, full of love and trust.

Over the course of a month she'd become his world. He'd spent the afternoon searching for answers, and he no longer sought anything. All his answers were right there in his arms.

Janie.

Janie. Janie. Janie.

Chapter Thirty

JANIE DIDN'T TELL Boyd about her promotion Wednesday night. She'd been too spent to do anything but sleep after they made love. The next morning they both awoke before dawn. As they lay nose to nose, Boyd's fingers traced the dips and curves of her hip and waist. Her hand rested lazily on his forearm, riding the tender movement as they talked about everything and nothing at once.

"Favorite color?" she asked.

"Blue, like your eyes." He kissed the tip of her nose. "Childhood fear?"

"Boogeyman. I thought he lived in my closet and watched me sleep at night."

"If I'd have known you then, I'd have checked your closet every night to show you he wasn't there, and I'd have held you so you felt safe."

"Your childhood fear?" she asked, then added, "Before the fire."

He was quiet for a beat, and when he answered, his hand stilled on her hip.

"Bees. They used to scare the bejesus out of me." His fingers began working their way along her waist again. "Biggest fear now?"

Janie had been sure of many things in her life. She'd known she needed to move away from her parents in order to find her independence. Embarrassingly, she'd known she needed Kiki by her side in those early years, to remind her that she was strong enough to act on that independence. And now she knew without a doubt that Boyd was her one true love. She'd known it for a while. Maybe even since shortly after they met. But she hadn't been ready to admit it aloud until now.

He was the one she wanted to share her news with, even if, as Kiki had mentioned, he might not be thrilled with it. He was the only other person besides Kiki whom she felt completely comfortable with, whom she could count on, and whom she wanted to always be there for. Boyd had his own demons, and she knew it would take time for him to deal with them, but she wanted to be there when he did.

"Losing you," she said honestly.

"Not happening." He kissed her tenderly.

She placed her hand on his cheek, and he covered it with his own.

"You want to read my reaction."

"Yes," she whispered, not at all surprised that he'd figured that out. "I got the promotion to technical writer." She felt his cheeks lift with his smile.

"Baby. I knew you would." He kissed her again, more deeply this time, and it warmed her from her head to her toes. "I'm so happy for you."

"They asked for a one-year commitment." She held her breath.

"Breathe, baby. Whatever you want, whatever you need, we'll make it happen."

"But...You're not upset?" Did that mean he wouldn't want her to go with him if he got into medical school?

"Upset? Of course not."

"But what if you get—I mean, what about *when* you get into medical school?"

"We'll figure it out. Aren't you happy about your promotion? Isn't this what you were working toward?"

"Yes." But she was no longer thrilled about it. Was she sending the wrong messages to him, by saying she wanted the promotion? Was Kiki right? She couldn't let this go any longer. They needed to talk about the possibility of him leaving and what it would mean to their relationship.

"Then this is a great thing," he assured her.

Janie drew in a steadying breath, determined to let the elephant in the room out of the cage.

"Boyd, can we talk about us? I feel like we're in limbo, and I know we're talking about big, life-changing decisions, but you know me by now. I need clarity."

He sat up, leaned against the headboard, and tucked her against his chest. Janie felt like her world was spinning, or maybe their worlds were colliding, and yet Boyd seemed calm as a summer's day. He was always calm and steady. When she had her accident, he'd been her rock, and ever since he'd remained just as steadfast in his confidence, his future, *their* future somehow working out. Why, then, did she feel like her world was careening while she waited for the conversation to move forward?

Boyd kissed her temple, and she tried to steal a little bit of his calmness to tether her worries. It didn't work.

"Okay, honey. Let's talk."

Now she was too nervous to lay it all on the line. What if

her line and his line somehow veered off, running parallel, or worse, in opposite directions? He wrapped his other arm around her waist and nuzzled against her neck.

"Want me to start?" he whispered against her cheek.

Could her heart pound any harder? "Maybe."

"I love you; you know that. I've made no secret of my feelings for you."

She turned in his arms, wanting to be closer to him as she bared her heart. The feel of his expressions, his face, his body, had become so familiar, she'd created a mental image that stayed with her through the day. She could picture every expression based on the sound of his voice.

"Boyd, I know how much you care for me. I feel it in everything you do and say. And I think I've been pretty honest about how hard I've worked to establish my independence. I never thought I'd ever want anything else. No matter how many times I dreamed of being the heroine in a romance novel, or finding a man who would love me like you do, I never really craved it like other girls did."

"I understand," he said sadly.

"I don't know how you can, because I haven't let myself understand it until recently. I never craved love because I never knew how wonderful it could be. I've been smothered by my parents, and I have Kiki and Sin, who love me, but it's different. I never knew how incredible it could be to share my life with someone like you. I never knew that anyone other than Kiki would not only understand my need for independence but also respect and encourage it. But what's really surprising is that I never knew how much I could love you, or that I would want to make room for you in this life I've built for myself." Her voice escalated with the excitement she felt inside her and the love she had for him.

"My independence has moved over, making room for my love for you. Does it sound silly to say I love you so much that I want to be independent *with* you?"

She heard the little puff of air that came with his smile, and she laughed softly. "I know. What kind of writer says something so contradictory? But it's how I feel. I want to be with you. I want to look into our future and see our lives as one."

YOU LOVE ME. Those three words wound around and around his heart, through his veins, to his very core. Boyd felt like he'd waited a lifetime to hear her say those words. If he'd had any doubts about how far he would go for Janie, she slayed them right there and then. Even in her confession of love for him she remained steadfast in her need for independence, and that solidified his resolve about the offer from UVA.

"Baby, you can't imagine how happy that makes me. I want nothing more than to be with you, and I'd never try to steal your independence."

"It feels so good to say it. I love you, Boyd." She pressed her lips to his again, her whole face smiling back at him. "I love everything about you. I love your strength and your vulnerability. I love that you've lived your whole life toward something you really want and that you made a silly bet with me that opened my mind to so many fun things. I love the way you and Kiki tease each other. The way you are with your family."

Boyd searched for words to express the way his heart felt full to near bursting, but everything paled in comparison to the intensity of what he felt.

Before he could find the right words, she said, "I feel like my love for you has been trapped inside me for too long. I feel so much better, like our love can breathe now, and feel, and *grow*." Her sweet lips curved up as she leaned closer. "So if you get into medical school, would you want me to go with you?"

Boyd's heart nearly stopped. What did UVA have to offer besides close proximity to his family? What did Virginia have to offer Janie? She was what really mattered. He'd waited this long to return home. He could wait another year.

"Go with me?" he said lamely, still pulling his thoughts together.

She nodded. "Isn't that what we're talking about? Where we go from here?"

"Yes, of course." But he was still soaking in the fact that she loved him.

"So...?" Her brows knitted together. "Should I tell Clay I can't make a full-year commitment? I don't want to accept the position and then break my promise."

Boyd felt like he was in the belly of the beast—but it wasn't the flames engulfing him; it was his love for Janie, his need to protect her, to keep her in the environment she'd become accustomed to. To keep her with Kiki. *Christ, your best friend since third grade.* Sure, she was excited, and she would move with him if he asked, but would she be happy someplace else? Would she grow to resent him for giving up the promotion she'd been working so hard toward, for moving her to a strange city?

Who was he to ask her to upend her life and start over without her best friend, without the mental mapping she'd become so accustomed to? That would be selfish, wouldn't it? *Damn right it would.* Boyd had lived selfishly for enough years.

It was time for him to put the woman he loved ahead of himself.

"This is what you've worked for all this time," he reminded her. "You can't turn it down. I'd never ask you to turn it down."

"But what about when you get accepted to medical school?"

It was no longer a matter of *when* he got accepted. Now it was all about when he got accepted to the *right* school. A school near Janie's world. His mind reeled back to all he'd done to get his apartment ready for her, and he had to wonder if even back then, for Janie, he'd been subconsciously heading toward this decision.

"Hopefully I'll get accepted to a school here. There's still time." They had nothing but time. She loved him, and that was all that mattered.

Chapter Thirty-One

JANIE FLOATED THROUGH the morning, finally feeling settled. She and Boyd picked up fresh flowers from Trick before work. When they came back to the apartment to fill the vases, they fell into each other's arms, getting lost in each other again. Before she knew it, they were twenty minutes late. Janie grabbed her purse and phone as Boyd headed for the door.

"I've got to flag a cab to get to the station on time." He kissed her quickly. "Meet me downstairs for another kiss?"

He stepped outside the apartment door as she zipped off a text to Clay letting him know she was running late and scheduling a meeting with him for later that morning to discuss her promotion. She hurried down after Boyd, hoping she hadn't missed him. As she pushed through the front doors to her building, car horns and people rushing by inundated her senses. But through it all, she heard Boyd's sure and steady voice and made her way through throngs of passersby to steal one last kiss before heading for the subway.

"Chet, I know what I'm doing." Boyd sounded harsh, almost angry. Janie slowed to listen, wondering if he'd seen her. "There's nothing to talk about. Turning down UVA is the right thing for both of us."

The world skidded to a halt. Everything around her faded away, leaving only Boyd's words playing in her head. *Turning down UVA is the right thing for both of us.* Someone bumped into her shoulder, shaking her from her trance and jostling her bag from her arm.

"Janie!" Boyd's voice sailed into her ears as her bag tumbled to her feet and she fought for balance.

He was by her side, murmuring something—in his phone? To her? She had no idea. His strong arm steadied her, and it was then that his voice broke through her confusion.

"Honey, are you okay?"

She heard him gathering her things, but it wasn't *her* Boyd. Her Boyd would never make a decision like she'd just heard.

He hooked her bag on her arm. "My cab's waiting."

He was breathing hard, and she was barely breathing at all.

"You're turning down UVA?" It was all she could do to get the vile words out.

"Janie, we're late. There's no time to talk about it right now."

She was shaking, angry and sad at once. "Are you turning them down?" She didn't mean to yell, but she couldn't stop. "We just said…We just talked about doing this together."

"Janie. I'll get into a school here next year. You can finish out your promotion. Moving to a new city, away from Kiki, away from everything you know, would be stressful. Overwhelming. You don't need that. Not after how hard you worked to move up."

The little air remaining in her lungs left her. Whatever he said next was a blur. She was too focused on four words—four words that, when strung together in this scenario, made her sick to her stomach with rage. *You don't need that.* "You promised never to treat me like I was different."

A horn sounded from beside them.

"One second, please!" Boyd hollered—to the cab, she assumed. "Can we talk about this later? I think it's best if we wait. You have everything here, support from the community, friends, a job you love. You know the transportation system. You need to be here, and I need to be with you."

The horn blasted again. Once, twice, three times.

"Goddamn it. I'm late, babe. I have to go," Boyd gave her arm a gentle squeeze, the way he had so many times since they'd been together. It was a loving, nurturing touch, but after everything he'd said, it felt wrong. It felt controlling.

She wrenched her arm free and stepped back on shaky legs. "You have no right to make those decisions for me. You obviously have no idea what's best for me. And you want to know what else? I think you're using me as an excuse. I think you're afraid to move back to your hometown."

She was spouting mean, hateful words, but they were truthful, too, and she was powerless to stop. "You risk your life every day for others, but you're so afraid to risk your heart—to face your past—you don't even see it. You should have let me in, Boyd. I was worth the risk."

She had to get out of there before more anger spilled out.

With her heart in her throat, she stalked into the crowd and headed for the subway—leaving Boyd to call after her, and eventually, she assumed, to climb into the cab and walk out of her life for good, taking her shattered heart with him.

Chapter Thirty-Two

BOYD FELT LIKE he'd been sliced open and left to bleed out. He'd thought he was doing the right thing. How could things have gone so wrong? As the cab drove toward the firehouse, he replayed the scene in his mind. Her words cut like a knife.

Was he using her as an excuse?

Was he afraid of going back home for good?

Boyd took out his phone and rubbed his thumb over Janie's image on the screen. He thought about calling her, but the more he replayed what she'd said, the more he felt the hard kernel of truth. He debated calling his grandfather, getting his nightmares out in the open once and for all. Dealing with his shit.

The noise...

That damn noise...

Fucking nightmares. He couldn't bring his parents back no matter how hard he tried, but could he salvage his relationship with Janie? He drew in a breath, determined to try.

His cell phone rang, and he was surprised to see Haylie's name on the screen.

After debating letting it go to voice mail, he worried something might have happened and answered. "Hey, sis."

"Tell me you are *not* turning down med school without letting Janie weigh in on the decision," Haylie snapped. "Boyd, haven't you learned anything?"

Apparently the Hudson grapevine was swift. He was going to kill Chet. "From what exactly?"

"From everything. From *life*. How many times have I told you to back off?"

Where was this venom spewing from Haylie's lips coming from? What the hell had he done to her? "How should I know?"

"Because I've been pounding it into your head since, oh, I don't know, the year after Mom and Dad died. You're the oldest, I get that. You wanted to protect us. You stepped in and made decisions you thought they'd expect of you. But you're so used to stepping in and deciding what's best for all of us that now you've done it to Janie. The one person who doesn't *need*, or *want*, you to."

"How would you know what Janie wants?"

Haylie huffed. "I spent the weekend with you guys, remember? I spent all day Friday getting to know her, and damn it, Boyd, I *like* her. I thought you'd finally found someone who *got* you, who could put up with your closed-off nature."

Closed-off nature?

"Someone you might open up to. But *no*. Instead you act like she's me or Chet. Like she needs you to make decisions for her." She sighed heavily.

"Tell me this, Haylie. What should I have done? Wouldn't it make me a bigger asshole to expect her to give up her life and move with me?"

"No, honey, it wouldn't. It would make you a guy who loves her too much to leave her behind. But it isn't about staying there or moving. It's about giving her a chance to weigh in on the decision."

His heart stilled. "You called me 'honey.'"

"Habit. Dad always called Mom 'honey.' Don't you remember?"

He shook his head. "No." *Apparently I've got a lot of ghosts to deal with.*

Haylie's tone softened. "You love her, don't you?"

"More than life itself."

"You're such an idiot, but I love you, and I hope you can get your head out of your butt long enough to fix this. True love always wins. At least that's what Janie wrote in her book."

Her book. Their bet. They'd come so far since then, and he'd managed to ruin it all with one phone call.

The alarm sounded as Boyd stepped from the cab at the firehouse. *Fucking hell.* He sprinted inside and raced to get into his gear, and then they were on the engine, his thoughts drowned out by the sirens. Adrenaline soared through him as he tried to make sense of what had gone wrong with Janie, but he couldn't concentrate. Not while Chief Weber was hollering about a fire at a five-story apartment complex.

The sirens were deafening, and he let himself get lost in their cadence, the way he would succumb to a lover. Needing to disappear into the sounds that had become his hiding place, the darkness he crawled into and found laser focus. Only there did he find solace.

At the scene of the fire he climbed from the engine, surveying the building. Flames shot out the windows of the top floor. Thick, black smoke plumed menacingly into the sky. Tommy did a quick 360 sweep of the exterior of the building while the roof crew sprang into action, ventilating the fire, working to contain it to the rooms it had already claimed.

"The building was supposed to be abandoned. Neighbors said kids are in and out all day long," Chief Weber yelled as they sprang into action. "Get in. Sweep it. Get out."

Boyd's father's demand from that desperate night so long ago crashed into his head—*Stay with them. Don't you leave them!* Fuck. He pushed past the command spoken so long ago, using it to fuel his determination. Fear and courage fought for balance, driving him forward. *Don't leave her.* His mind whirred—her? Janie? He wasn't leaving Janie. His father hadn't meant Janie. His father had meant Haylie—and Boyd had left her back in Virginia. Couldn't wait to get the hell away from the place his reality had become his nightmares.

Fear clawed at his gut.

Focus, Hudson.

Get in. Sweep it. Get out.

Cash grabbed his arm as they flew through the front doors, yanking him from the blinding confusion and bringing his job back into focus. Boyd sized up the scene. Smoke filled the lobby, billowed out from the open stairwell door. He tested the steps, then took the stairs two at a time with Cash on his heels, eighty pounds of equipment weighing them down—but not slowing them. Nothing ever slowed them down.

Until Janie.

Fuck. He forced himself to focus. Nothing would slow him down here, not now. Not when there were lives on the line.

Flames met them on the landing, pitch-black smoke stealing their sight. They hit the floor. Boyd pointed right, sending Cash to the left.

The roar of the fire filled his ears as he crawled with mastery and speed into the blinding smoke, searching with his hands as he called out, "Anyone here?"

Flames licked out from under a door on the far wall.

Crying. Faint, jagged breaths to his left. Boyd felt his way in the darkness. "Stay low. I'll find you." He moved faster, feeling the floor, and a whole lot of nothing.

A child's shrill voice cut through the flames. "He's dead."

Ice ran through Boyd's veins despite the blazing heat as his fingers met a limp leg. More crying, gasping for breath, sounded just ahead. Coughing, harsh wheezing. Boyd scooped the limp child into his arms as a small hand clutched his jacket. The whites of the crying boy's eyes were all he could see, big, round, terrified. He tucked the crying boy tightly between his arm and his side and scooped the limp boy into his arms. He had to get them out before the building flashed or collapsed. The crying boy fell quiet, his legs dangling behind them as Boyd cradled the other child against his chest. Keeping low, he moved swiftly toward the stairs with one goal in mind—getting them out and getting the boy breathing. Through smoke and heat he hit the stairs and flew out the front door. Outside the building the world blurred together—lights flashed, people shouted, instructions were hollered from all directions. Boyd leaned over the limp boy on the front lawn and began mouth-to-mouth, vaguely aware of an EMT taking the crying child from beneath his arm.

Breathe. Come on. Breathe. The boy couldn't have been older than ten or eleven. His chest was minuscule beneath Boyd's palms. Then the boy was coughing and the EMT, who had probably been crouched beside him the whole time, firmly gripped Boyd's arm, jerking him out of his tunnel vision to save the boy.

"We've got him, Hudson."

Boyd noted the medical team and headed back into the

blaze. His mind flashed to his father disappearing into the darkness that stole his life, to Janie's tortured face as she turned away, and finally, back to the belly of the beast in search of more unattended kids, or druggies, or anyone else who might need rescuing. As smoke consumed him, for the first time since the awful day when he'd lost his parents, he wished someone would rescue him from his own fucking head.

Chapter Thirty-Three

JANIE TRIED TO focus on work, but every breath felt like a gasp, every move a trudge through quicksand. Talking with Clay had been painful, but she'd made it through. How, she had no idea. By the time she left the office, she was barely holding it together. She didn't allow herself to shed a single tear, not one. She was strangely proud of that sick accomplishment. She'd just lost the man of her dreams, the man she wanted a future with, and she'd somehow kept it bottled up inside for eight straight hours.

I kept my love for him bottled up for weeks.

Her eyes went damp as she arrived at the clothing store where Kiki worked.

"Sweet Jesus, what happened?" Annabelle, one of Kiki's coworkers, rushed to Janie's side.

"Nothing." She sniffled. "I'm fine. Is Kiki still here?"

"Sweetheart you are really far from *fine*. Kiki's in the office. I'll take you back." Annabelle smelled like flowers, which only made Janie sadder, reminding her of the trip to Trick's she and Boyd had taken that morning.

Annabelle guided her through double doors, along a carpeted corridor that Janie knew well, and knocked on the office door.

"Come in," Kiki said from behind the closed door.

"Go on in," Annabelle whispered. "If you guys need me, I'll be out front. I hope you're okay."

"Thank you." She'd done it. She'd made it to the safety of Kiki's office without falling apart. Another accomplishment. *See? I'm still the independent, strong woman I've always been. Even if my heart is torn to pieces.*

She pushed the door open and heard Kiki gasp.

"Oh, shit. What happened?" Kiki's arms enveloped her, breaking the dam and setting free a rush of tears and incoherent explanations—*Broke up. Boyd. Lied. Unfair. Love him.*

"It's okay, Janie. I promise, we'll get through this. Just breathe, honey."

Janie shook her head. "Honey!" She sobbed.

"Sorry!" Kiki hugged her tighter. "Shh. It's okay. You're okay. I'm right here."

She cried a river, soaking Kiki's blouse regardless of how many tissues Kiki shoved in her hands. There weren't enough tissues in the world to soak up her despair. How could there be? She was probably drenching Kiki's shirt with blood, streaming up from her broken heart.

This couldn't be happening. Maybe this was a nightmare. The worst, most terrible nightmare ever. She sobbed and hiccupped and tried desperately to explain, but her chest ached. Apparently broken hearts could splinter and poke holes in a person's strength, turn them into a colander, and drain them, heart, soul, and energy. *Drip, drip, drip.* Her tears wouldn't stop. Kiki was talking, but nothing registered.

Sometime later—an hour, a day, a lifetime?—Kiki took her by the shoulders and in her strongest voice said, "Look at me."

It was a joke between them, and it usually made her laugh, but she didn't have enough energy to lift her head. Not even for Kiki. She wanted to stay there, with her heart seeping out her pores and Kiki holding her. Just until…maybe…forever?

A long while later they were still sitting on the couch in Kiki's office. Janie had no more tears to cry. She sucked in one uneven breath after another, trying to find her voice.

"Can you tell me what happened?" Kiki asked.

"He's turning down med school." She was wrong. She had plenty more tears to cry after all. They spilled down her cheeks like blood from a fresh wound. "Turning it down, Kiki!" Anger rose above the sadness. "Like it wasn't everything he'd ever worked toward."

"I'm confused. He broke up with you *and* turned down medical school? Why? He's so in love with you."

"*He* didn't break up with *me!*" Janie spat. "*I* broke up with *him.*"

Kiki went silent for a beat. "Why?"

"He said I could complete my year commitment at work and he'd try to get into school in New York. He lied to me. He told me he'd never treat me like I was different—"

"He never does, Janie. The man treats you like a queen. A stubborn, I-can-do-everything-myself queen."

That made her cry a little harder. "Yeah? Well, it was all a farce, because he's turning down medical school because I'm blind. He says it's best for me not to move." Janie lifted her chin, using her anger to try to regain control of her emotions.

"You have to kill him for me. You promised. And I can't do it, because I can't fucking see!" She fell forward, and Kiki caught her as she drowned in fresh tears.

"This is fucking great," Kiki said.

"I know. Right?" She sniffled. "If I could see I could kill him."

"Now I have to kill Boyd because he hurt you."

"Thank you." She felt herself smiling with their game. She needed something to pull her out of the deep, ugly, painful depression trying to drag her under.

"So I'll go to jail, and you'll be left without a best friend," Kiki said in a harsher tone.

"But I'll visit you and sneak in hot guys for conjugal visits. Maybe Sin and I can break you out of jail."

"You and Sin? A blindie and a loudmouth who doesn't ever do anything right? I'll be in jail forever, and all because you're too much of a dumbass to see that he was *trying* to do the right thing."

Janie pushed away. "What? Whose side are you on?"

"Yours, which is why I'm devising a plan to take the man's life, but for heaven's sake, Janie, can't you see?"

Janie raised her brows.

"Of course you can't see. You're *blind*. But I didn't realize you were emotionally blind, too." Kiki pushed to her feet, and Janie heard her pacing. Kiki only paced when she was *really* mad at her, and Janie could count the times that had happened on one hand.

"He's trying to make things easier on you, Janie. Can't you see that? Yes, he made a unilateral decision, but it sounds like he made it with the best of intentions."

"I can't believe you're taking his side on this when you *know* how important this is to me. I don't need another parent."

Kiki knelt before Janie and held her hands. "Listen to me, Janie Jansen. I love you like a sister—you know that. I'm always on your side. But I'm not going to let you throw the love of your life away because you're a stubborn, prideful woman. That's what Boyd fell in love with. *All of you.* Your determination, your drive, your ability to make things happen regardless of what roadblocks you face."

Tears slipped down her cheeks again with the truth of Kiki's declaration.

"Then why did he make the decision for me? Just this morning I told him I loved him." Sobs burst from her chest again. She swiped at them, but she was no match for the ocean of sadness consuming her. *Shouldn't he know I'm capable of making the right decisions for myself?*

Janie was confused, hurt, and so in love she didn't know which way was up. "I have to see him. Damn it, Kiki. You always warn me about things. You should have warned me that I'd have to get knocked on my ass to get swept off my feet." She rose to her feet, feeling guilty for blaming Kiki and anxious. "You know I don't blame you, right?"

"Of course I know, Janie."

"He hasn't called or texted. What if I've already lost him?"

"Then he wasn't worth having in the first place."

On her way out of the store, Janie's cell phone rang with Boyd's ringtone. She scrambled to answer it as she pushed through the doors to the sidewalk.

"Boyd?"

"Janie? It's Cash. Boyd's been hurt."

Janie's mind faded to black, his words barely filtering in. *Ceiling collapse. Doctors checking him out. Hospital.*

JANIE UNFURLED HER fingers from the door handle and

stepped from the cab on trembling legs.

"Oh, thank God." Siena's voice sounded seconds before her arms circled Janie.

"Boyd?" Janie barely managed as Siena guided her inside the hospital. The antiseptic smell brought memories of the last time she was there, drawing even more tears from her eyes. *Please let him be okay.*

"They just brought him back to his room. He's okay."

He's okay. He's okay.

Siena led her into the elevator. "He was lucky. Cash said it happened fast. Boyd was carrying a teenager out of the fire when the ceiling collapsed on them."

Ceiling. Collapsed. Oh God. Boyd.

"...broken leg."

Janie couldn't concentrate as Siena led her to Boyd's room, or when Cash's arms engulfed her.

"He's okay," Cash assured her. "He's groggy from pain meds. He has a broken leg, and they haven't ruled out a concussion, but he's okay."

She felt like she was floating through hell. Cash's hand left her back, and the hospital room door closed behind her. The first thing that registered was the cold, sterile feel of the room, then the heat of Boyd's eyes on her.

"Janie." His deep voice, full of relief and sorrow, pulled her forward.

She wanted to reach for him, but her arms wouldn't move. She ached to kiss him, to hold him, but she was still hovering in some strange state of shock and fear, underscored by hurt. Guilt wound around all those feelings like a noose, pulling tighter with each step. Boyd touched her hand, pulling her down onto the edge of his bed.

Hospital bed.

Reality hit her like a bullet train. She could have lost him today, and the last thing they would have had was their awful fight.

"Janie." His deep voice was filled with unspoken apologies and disbelief, which made it even more difficult for her to find her voice.

"I took a cab." *I took a cab?* He could have died, and that was the most important thing for him to hear? *I took a frigging cab?*

His fingertips touched hers. "You took a cab?"

"I didn't trust myself on the subway. I was too upset." Tears tumbled down her cheeks. "Boyd." She touched his face, feeling a bandage over a swollen lump below his cheekbone. Her chest constricted so tight she gasped.

"Can I—" She swallowed down threatening sobs and pushed the words from her lungs. "Can I hold you? Are you really okay? Cash said something about a concussion." She needed to *feel* that he was really okay. She had the scary feeling he might disappear again, and that made her feel sick and hurt and lonely.

"I'm so sorry, honey." His arms came around her and she leaned in to him, crying and touching and hoping he was *really* okay.

"Sorry?" she whispered through her tears.

"Janie," he said at the same time she said, "Boyd."

"You go first," he offered.

"I…" She touched his face, his hair, his shoulders, taking in everything and nothing at all. Her pulse was racing so fast she felt like she was hyperventilating. "I don't know where to start."

"I do," he reassured her. He was forever her anchor, and she hadn't even known she'd needed one.

"I've handled so many things wrong." He sounded so sad, so honest, so *real*. "Not just today but all along with you. And now you're here, and I thought I'd lost you for good. Honey, I never meant to hurt you, or to be closed off—"

"You're not closed off." Protective urges surged forward, despite the emotions warring inside her.

"I am."

She loved his honesty, even if it was hard to hear. The way he wore his emotions on his sleeve—even the ones he tried to hide. She thought of his nightmares. Was that why he said he was closed off? Because he was an open book emotionally. Even if he didn't want to talk about his nightmares, she knew how badly they tortured him. She remembered what he'd told Chet that morning. Hurt rolled in anew. The sinking feeling in the pit of her stomach returned. Anger and disbelief rose to the surface. A small voice in her head told her to be careful, but a louder voice quieted it. He didn't die. He was here, and he'd hurt her, and they had nothing if he kept pieces of himself locked away or if he wanted to control her.

ICY FEAR CIRCLED Boyd's heart as disquieting thoughts raced through his mind. Was this the end—or a chance at a new beginning? He knew what he had to do, but that didn't make it any easier to do it. He'd kept his fears bottled up for so many years he wasn't even sure how much of what he feared was real anymore. Janie was shaking, he was shaking, and he was sure it was for entirely different reasons. She thought he'd been hurt worse than a broken leg and possibly a mild concussion, while he'd thought he'd lost her forever.

She'd taken a fucking cab to see him. A cab. He couldn't even process that. She pushed herself through her worst fears *for him*. And he was too chickenshit to deal with his past.

She was watching him without seeing him, and he knew she felt everything he did, read his deepest fears. Knew he was struggling. She lifted her chin, struggling to keep her confidence where it needed to be. The last thing he ever wanted to do was hurt her, and knowing he had slayed him.

"I never should have excluded you from the decision about medical school. I *did* treat you differently. I did the one thing you begged me never to do, and I am so truly, deeply sorry, Janie. I wish I could take it back. But there's no going backward. We both know that all too well."

Her chin trembled, spearing his heart again.

"I had no right to make that decision for you. For us. But I honestly thought that asking you to choose to leave everything you have—your job, Kiki—and move away to a new town was unfair and selfish."

"You thought it was selfish to ask me to be part of your life? Unfair to want me as part of your future? My biggest fear is that you'll see me as a burden and that I'll hold you back. But I was able to push that aside and believe in your love for me. Why can't you believe in mine?"

"A burden? Janie, you're a gift to me. It wasn't that I didn't believe in your love for me. I believed in it *too* much. I know you'd give everything up to go with me, but you have so much here. How can I ignore that just to satisfy my own goals? I've lived a selfish life to attain my goals. Other than in my work, I've always put myself first. I haven't lied to you about that. It's been all about me, all the time. About me becoming a paramedic, a firefighter, going to medical school. Until I met you." Fresh tears filled her eyes. He lifted her hand and kissed it, hoping she knew he was being one hundred percent honest.

"I *love* you, Janie. But I don't want to ruin or rule your life."

She pushed back, her eyes serious, her beautiful mouth pinched tight. "Don't you see? That's exactly what you almost did. God, Boyd. I know you're hurt and you could have died, and this isn't the time to say it, but I have to or I'm going to explode."

Her words were fast and fierce, and he hated knowing he fueled the fire he saw in her eyes.

"When I told you I loved you, it was because I trusted you with that love. I trusted you with my heart and soul. I thought you understood exactly what you just said—that I didn't need to be told what to do. My parents do enough of that." She placed her hands on his cheeks and her voice softened. "If I choose to be with you, it's because I can handle it. I'm not afraid of much, but today scared the shit out of me."

"This morning scared the shit out of me," he admitted. "I don't ever want to make the same mistake again. I only wanted you to be happy. You were so thrilled about your promotion. I didn't want to take that away from you."

"You thought my promotion was more important than us?"

"No, honey. Not more important. Very important to you, which makes it very important to me." He took both her hands in his. "I messed up, baby. Can you ever forgive me?"

"You hurt me," she admitted. "Badly."

"I know, and I'll spend my life making it up to you."

"Maybe I was oversensitive. Kiki thinks I have a chip on my shoulder about being independent."

"And I think I have a thing about making decisions for the

people I love in an effort to protect them. But I forgot. You don't need protecting, except maybe from me and my stupidity. I'm so sorry, honey. How can I earn back your trust?"

"I might ask you the same thing. If I hadn't flown off the handle, we could have talked."

"No, I was late for my shift, remember?" He hoped and prayed she was really considering giving him another chance. "Give me another chance to do this right?"

"If you can give me the same chance. I said some horrid things to you about your nightmares, and—"

"And you were right." He fought against the urge to clam up, to bury his nightmares—that night—so deep inside it could only show its ugly head when he was asleep. Did he really want to do this? Could he do this, after all these years?

He fought the urge to put up the walls between his past and his future and focused on what he should have been focused on all along: giving the woman he loved all of himself, his good, his bad, his strengths, *and* as hard as it was to do, his weaknesses.

"In my nightmares, I hear a noise." His voice was scratchy, pained, the words burning as they left his lungs. The stench of smoke filled his senses. Fear clutched his chest, but he pushed through. Had to. For Janie. "I get out of bed and search the house for the cause, but I can never find it. I relive the night over and over again, running, chasing, struggling to breathe. Flames lick the floors, climb the walls, consume the house while I'm on an endless search for a noise that I should have investigated."

Her eyes teared up. "Oh, Boyd. I'm so sorry."

"I could have saved them that night. I heard a noise. I don't even know what it was. I remember waking up and thinking I should get up and see what it was, but I didn't. I don't even know *why* I didn't." He swallowed past the lump clogging his throat. "I could have saved them."

She touched his cheek, and he didn't even try to hide his tears.

"I want to find that fucking noise—to go back in time and give that night a different outcome. But there is no other outcome. There's only that terrible, awful night, and what came later."

She gathered him in her arms and held him as he cried. "You were just a child."

"It doesn't matter. I should have done something. I might never get past it, Janie. Don't you see that? It might haunt me forever. It might haunt us forever."

She wiped his tears as he kissed hers away. Logically he knew that he couldn't bring his parents back no matter how many times he relived the fire in his nightmares. And there was no going back with the things he'd said to Janie. He'd fucked up, but he hadn't fucked up like the night of the fire. He'd seen her face when she'd heard him on the phone, had heard her heart crack open, just like his. And he never wanted to see or hear that again.

"Baby, you're all I want. I can wait a lifetime for medical school, but I don't want to imagine a single day without you. I love you, wholly and completely. And if you can find it in your heart to forgive me, I promise I'll never make the same mistake again, and I'll try to deal with my nightmares. I'll see a therapist, talk to my family. Whatever it takes."

"We both made mistakes, and we'll make plenty more. Just promise to love me enough to trust me to make the right decisions *with* you."

"I do, baby. I will. Always."

She wound her arms around his neck and kissed him with the same warmth, and the same love, she always had.

"It's weird, isn't it?" He wiped her tears with the pad of his thumb and kissed her again. "We started right here in this hospital, with me taking care of you. Talking you down from the ledge. And here we are again, only this time I'm the one who needs help."

"You don't need help, Boyd. You just need faith." Janie's lips curved up in the smile he craved. "It's a scary thing, opening up the walls you've spent years building to let someone in. But if a gimpy girl who is blind can do it, so can a gimpy medical student."

"I haven't accepted the offer to attend UVA."

"Because you didn't know you should. I, on the other hand, turned down my promotion."

"No, baby. Please tell me that's not true."

"It's true. But not because of us, at least not completely. We *were* kind of broken up."

His heart ached again. Would it ever stop? Would he ever forgive himself for hurting her?

"When I told Clay I hoped to one day make a living writing fiction and wanted to take some time to put my efforts into finishing the story, he offered to let me telecommute. I can work from home as a technical writer up to thirty hours a week."

"What about the other promotion? The training position?"

"I turned that down completely. A wise man once told me that life was too short to do something I wasn't passionate about."

He felt like the luckiest guy in the world. "Janie—"

She placed her finger over his lips. "The only thing I want

to hear you say is that you're going to take that offer and we're going to move to Virginia. And maybe I can finally get a guide dog."

"I was going to say that I'm passionate about doing you." He pulled her into a sweet, delicious kiss. "What about Kiki?"

"You better not be passionate about doing Kiki!" She laughed with the tease. "She'll visit at least every six weeks. She can't keep her hands off my hair longer than that."

"You're really willing to give up everything for me to go to medical school? I can wait until I get into a school nearby."

"I'm not giving up anything. Haven't you heard a word I've said?"

"We're moving." He kissed her lips. "Getting a dog." He kissed her chin. "You're writing romance." He kissed the corner of her mouth. "And I'm passionately doing you."

Slanting his mouth over hers, Boyd knew the road ahead wouldn't be easy, but there was nothing he couldn't face, as long as Janie was by his side.

Epilogue

Six months later...

"ARE YOU READY, honey?" Boyd leaned against the door-frame of Janie's writing room in the cozy ranch-style home they'd rented in Meadowside, taking in the woman he adored. Janie's fingers flew over her braille device.

Friday—named for the night that changed Boyd and Janie's lives—barked at the disruption to his afternoon nap. Amber's mother had trained the lovable golden retriever as Janie's guide dog, and *then* she'd trained Janie. They were a perfect match. Friday loved to lie by Janie's feet while she wrote—which she had plenty of time to do now that Boyd was in medical school—and she seemed to love the company.

"One more sentence. Okay. Ready." Janie turned off her braille device and sank down to the floor to love up Friday. She'd finished *Sinful Fantasies* two weeks ago and immediately began writing *Decadent Fantasies*, the next book in what she hoped would be a series. She still worked for TEC in the mornings, and she even made time every few weeks to touch base with her parents. Sometimes she still had to draw that line in the sand, but her perspective was clearer now, and their overprotective questions no longer grated on her nerves.

She smiled up at him as Friday rose obediently beside her. They'd become a family, the three of them, and every morning when he woke up beside Janie he felt like one hell of a lucky man. She'd changed his world in so many ways. After they moved, he'd seen a therapist for three months, and he'd realized that he'd never heard a noise at all. His nightmares were his way of trying to shoulder the burden of the fire and trying to make that horrific night end differently. He rarely had nightmares anymore, but when he did, Janie was right there to listen as he talked through them.

His arm circled her waist as he kissed her cheek, his hand sliding down her sleek black costume. "You look gorgeous, Catwoman."

Boyd had kept his end of the bargain, agreeing to go to the romance festival next month, and Janie kept her end of the deal, too. They were on their way to Comic-Con, with Kiki, Sin, Cash, Siena, Haylie, and Chet.

"Oh, Batman," she said with a mischievous smile. "Is that a lightsaber, or are you just happy to see me?"

"I love when you mix up your heroes and talk dirty at the same time." He kissed her again, hearing Kiki's exasperated sigh as she entered the room. Friday wriggled with excitement beside Janie.

"Do you two ever stop?" Kiki teased. She'd even dressed for the occasion, as Lara Croft from *Tomb Raider*. "Come on. Sin's dressed as Thor and I'm having trouble keeping Haylie from drooling over him. Cash and Siena are making out in the kitchen, and if we don't get out of here, I'm likely to jump your brother."

"We're coming," Boyd said with a laugh. Not only had Janie's relationship with Kiki remained just as strong as always, but her circle of friends had grown like a warm embrace. She knew just about everyone in town and had begun running a monthly book club at Amber's bookstore.

"That's what I'm afraid of. Hurry up so we're not late." Kiki laughed all the way out the front door.

Boyd pulled Janie into his arms and kissed her deeply.

"Are you happy, baby?" His studies were time-consuming, but they still made plenty of time for each other. Their house was only half an hour from the university, and a seven-minute walk to town, perfect for their biweekly morning walks to the flower shop.

"How could I be anything but?" She kissed him with her sweet cupid's bow lips, the lips he dreamed of every day while he was at school, the lips that told him she loved him several times a day. The lips he had to kiss one more time.

Cash and Siena came out of the kitchen hand in hand. Siena was four months pregnant and barely showing in her little red Star Trek outfit.

"Ready, sexy sci-fi people?" Siena asked. She had introduced Janie to her brother Kurt, a bestselling thriller writer. Kurt had made a few phone calls and hooked Janie up with a literary agent. She had a long road ahead of her to get into the publishing game, but Boyd was thrilled she was following her dreams.

A horn sounded in the driveway.

"Can you tell Haylie we'll be right there?" Boyd winked, holding tightly to Janie, keeping her by his side and whispering, "I just want one minute alone with you before we're barraged with noise and geekdom. All those hot guys leering after my woman? I might get a little jealous."

She wrapped her arms around his neck. "You're the only man I ever want or need."

His heart swelled with love. "I hope so, but I think you should be properly accessorized *just in case.*"

Janie's brows drew together in confusion, her eyes widening with understanding as he dropped to one knee, holding her trembling hand in one hand and a ring in the other. Friday licked his cheek.

"Settle," he said to the pup, who obediently sat beside Janie as Boyd tried to quell the bees swarming inside him.

"Janie, I knew from the moment I saw you that you were special, and somehow, I also knew that I had to keep my distance from you, because you were the one person who could waylay my dreams. What I never realized was that you were the only person who could make them all come true. A life without you would have been simply a life I'd lived. A life with you is full and whole. It's intense and passionate and filled with never-ending hope for an even fuller future. I want that with you, Janie. I want to be the man who celebrates your successes and loves you through our hard times. I want babies and books and whatever else you want. I want you to wear my mother's ring, because I know my parents would have loved you as much as I do."

Tears streamed down her cheeks.

"Will you—"

She pushed her finger into the ring and pulled him up to his feet. An elated smile spread her beautiful lips and reached all the way to her eyes as she kissed him hard and fast and messily perfect.

"Yes. Yes. Yes."

With that one word, they succumbed to the heat between them. He sank deeper into the kiss, into her soft, supple body, into the essence of the woman he loved. Her right leg slid up his thigh, bringing them even closer together as the front door flew open and their friends charged in.

"Go play," he said to Friday, who immediately sought the ruckus of their cheering, laughing friends.

"They knew?" Janie asked against his lips.

"I couldn't let you get engaged without your entourage here to celebrate."

"What if I'd said no?" she teased as the girls pulled her into a hug and Chet slapped him on the back.

"That's what my entourage was for. To scrape me off the floor after you broke my heart."

As their friends congratulated them, Boyd never took his eyes off his future wife. She was smiling and laughing and showing off her ring. Janie lifted her eyes in his direction and as she mouthed, *I love you*, he knew she could see him better than anyone else ever had.

If this was your first Remington book, you have several more Remington love stories waiting for you, starting with Dex and Ellie's book, GAME OF LOVE (**free** in digital format at the time of this printing). Cash and Siena's story, FLAMES OF LOVE, is part of the Remingtons series. Kiki, Sin, and each of the Montgomerys will be getting their own books, starting with Grace Montgomery and Reed Cross in EMBRACING HER HEART, the first book in the Bradens & Montgomerys series.

Fall in love in Oak Falls

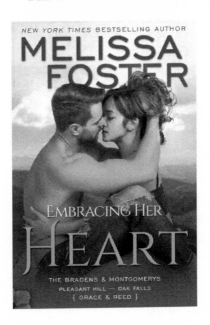

Chapter One

"OUCH!"

Brindle? Grace blinked awake at the sound of whispers in the dark room. It took her a moment to remember she was in her childhood bedroom at her parents' home in Oak Falls, Virginia, and not in her Manhattan loft. She narrowed her eyes, trying to decipher which of her five sisters were intent on waking her up at...She glanced at the clock. *Four thirty in the morning?*

"Shh. You're such a klutz."

Sable. Of course. Who else would think it was okay to wake her up at this hour besides Brindle, her youngest and most rebellious sister, and Sable, the night owl?

"I tripped over a suitcase," Brindle whispered. Something *thunked.* "Oh shit!" She tumbled onto the bed in a fit of laughter, bringing Sable down with her—right on top of Grace, who let out an "*Oomph!*" as her parents' cat, Clayton, leapt off the bed and tore out of the room.

"Shh! You'll wake Mom and Dad, or the dogs," Sable whispered between giggles.

"What are you doing?" Grace tried to sound stern, but her sisters' laughter was contagious. The last thing she needed was to be awake at this hour after a grueling week and a painfully long drive, but her sisters were excited about Grace coming home, and if Grace were honest with herself, despite the mounds of scripts she had to get through during her visit, she was excited to see them, too. Other than a quick trip for her friend Sophie's wedding, she hadn't been home since Christmas, and it was already May.

"Get up." Brindle tugged her off the bed and felt around on the floor. "We're going out, just like old times." She threw the slacks and blouse Grace had worn home the night before in Grace's face. "Get dressed."

"I'm not going—"

"Shut up and take this off." Sable pulled Grace's silk nighty over her head despite Grace's struggles to stop her. She knew it was a futile effort. What Sable wanted, Sable got. Even though she and her twin sister, Pepper, were a year younger than Grace, Sable had always been the pushiest of them all.

Grace reluctantly stepped into her slacks. "Where are we going?" She reached for her hairbrush as Brindle grabbed her hand and dragged her out the bedroom door. "Wait! My shoes!"'

"We'll grab Mom's boots from by the door," Sable said, flanking her other side as they hurried down the hall tripping over each other.

"I'm *not* wearing cowgirl boots." Grace had worked hard to shake the country-bumpkin habits that were as deeply ingrained as her love for her six siblings. Habits like hair twirling, saying *y'all*, and wearing cutoffs and cowgirl boots, the hallmarks of her youth. She stood on the sprawling front porch with her hands on her hips, staring at her sisters, who were waiting for her to put on her mother's boots.

"Step into them or I swear I'll make you climb that hill barefoot, and you know that's not fun," Sable said.

"God! You two are royal pains in the ass." Grace shoved her feet into the boots. *They're only boots. They don't erase all of my hard work.* Oak Falls might be where her roots had sprouted, but they'd since spread far and wide, and she was never—*ever*—going to be that small-town girl again.

The moon illuminated the path before them. The pungent scent of horses and hay lingered in the air as they crossed the grass toward the familiar hill. *Great.* They were taking her to *Hottie Hill.* Grace groaned, wondering why she hadn't tossed them out of her bedroom and locked the door instead of going along with their crazy like-old-times plan. Three weeks at home would be both a blessing and a curse. Grace loved her sisters, but she imagined three weeks of Sable playing her guitar until all hours of the night and her other younger sisters popping in and out with their dogs and their drama, all while their mother carefully threw out queries about their dating lives and their father tried not to growl at their responses.

Brindle strutted up the steep hill in her boots and barely there sundress, expertly avoiding the dips and ruts in the grass, while Grace hurried behind her, stumbling over each one as she tried to keep up.

Sable reached the peak of the hill first. She turned on her booted heels, placed her hands on her hips, and grinned like a fool. "Hurry up! You'll miss it!"

It was one thing to deal with family drama from afar, when all it took was a quick excuse to get off the phone, but *three weeks?* Grace couldn't even blame her decision on being drunk, since she had been stone-cold sober when her sister Amber had asked her to help bolster her bookstore's presence by hosting a playwriting course. *You made it, Gracie! You're such an inspiration to everyone here*, Amber had pleaded. *Besides, Brindle is leaving soon for Paris, and it's the last time we'll all be together for months. It'll be like old times.* Grace was living her dream, writing and producing off-Broadway plays, although lately, that's all the *living* she was doing, and the diva attitudes of the industry were grating on her last nerve. Besides, how could she say no to Amber, the sweetest sister of them all?

Grace slipped on the hill and caught herself seconds before face-planting in the grass. "Damn it! This is the last thing I want to be doing right now."

"Shh," Brindle chided as she reached for Grace's hand.

Sable ran down the hill annoyingly fast. Holding her black cowgirl hat in place atop her long dark hair with one hand, she reached for Grace with the other and said, "Get up, you big baby."

"I can't believe you dragged my ass out of bed for this. What are we? Twelve?" Grace asked in her own harsh whisper.

"Twelve-year-olds don't sneak out to watch the hottest men in Oak Falls break in horses," Brindle said as they reached the top of the hill.

"Liar. We've been doing it since you were twelve," Sable reminded her.

"I can't believe *they're* still doing this at this ungodly hour." *They* were the Jericho brothers, and they'd been breaking in horses before dawn since they were teenagers. They claimed it was the only time they had before the heat of the day hit, but Grace thought it had more to do with it feeling more exciting doing it in the dark.

The Jericho brothers were the hottest guys around. Well, at least since Reed Cross left town after high school graduation.

Grace tried to tamp down thoughts of the guy who had taken her—and given her *his*—virginity, and turned her heart inside out. The man she'd turned away in pursuit of her production career, and the person she'd compared every single man to ever since. She refused to let herself go down memory lane.

"I'm exhausted," Grace complained as they reached the peak of the hill overlooking the Jericho ranch. The Jerichos owned several hundred acres and were very active in the community, opening one of their barns once a month to the community for *jam sessions*, where anyone that played an instrument could take part. People of all ages came to enjoy the music, dance, and take part in various games like potato sack races, ring toss, and touch football. It was just another of the small-town events that Grace hadn't regretted leaving behind.

"It's not like I haven't seen these guys a million times," she pleaded. "Besides, Brindle, you've slept with Trace more times than you can probably count. It's not like you haven't seen him shirtless. Why are we even—"

"Shh!" Brindle and Sable said in unison as they pulled Grace down to her knees.

She followed their gazes to the illuminated riding ring below, where the four Jericho brothers, Trace, Justus, aka "JJ," Shane, and Jeb, and a handful of other shirtless, jeans-clad guys were milling about. They were *always* shirtless, because what men weren't when they were proving they were the manliest of the group?

"Trace and I are over," Brindle whispered. "For real this time." She and Trace had been in an on-again-off-again relationship forever. They were a hopeless case of rebellious guy and rebellious girl, up for anything risky. Two people who didn't have a chance in hell of ever settling down but seemed to fill a need in each other's lives—or at least in their beds.

"That's not what Morgyn said." Sable smirked. Morgyn was a year older than Brindle and just as outgoing.

"Why didn't you drag her out instead of me?" Grace complained.

"I would have, but she wasn't home," Brindle explained.

Grace and her sisters had spent many hours as teenagers lying on this same hill when they should have been sleeping, watching the Jericho brothers and other guys ride wild horses or rope cattle. Pepper and Amber had come with them only twice. Pepper had complained the whole time about it being a waste of brain power, and Amber had been more embarrassed than turned on by the shirtless cock-and-bull show. *If only I'd been born shy.*

She laughed to herself. *Shy? Right.* She'd blazed a path in a man's world. There was no room for *shy* in her repertoire. And there was no room for this nonsense anymore, either. She pushed up onto her knees. "Brindle, maybe at twenty-four this is still fun, but I'm twenty-eight. I've got work to do in the morning, and I'm so far past this it's not even funny."

"*God,* Grace! You've turned into a workaholic ice queen," Sable whispered as she yanked Grace back down to her stomach. "And I, your very loving sister who feels the need to keep you young, aim to fix that. Starting *now.*"

Grace rolled her eyes. "*Ice queen?* Just because I've grown up and don't find this type of thing fun anymore?" As she said the words the men below walked out of the ring and stood on the outside of the fence, their muscular arms hanging over the top rail.

"*Ice queen* because you think you're too good for—" Sable swallowed her words as Trace and JJ pushed open the enormous wooden barn doors and a wild horse blasted into the ring with a shirtless man on its back.

Their gazes snapped to the show below. It wasn't a Jericho on the back of this horse for its first ride, and despite her protests, Grace squinted into the night to get a better look at the virility before her.

"Damn," Brindle said in a husky voice.

"Holy shit, that's hot," Sable whispered. "See, Gracie? Totally worth it."

Grace took in the arch of the rider's shoulders as the horse bucked him forward and back, his thick arms holding tightly to the reins. His wavy brown hair and the square set of his chin sent a shudder of recognition through her.

"Ouch! Grace! You're digging your nails into me." Sable pried Grace's fingers off her forearm.

"Is that…?" Grace choked on the anger *and* arousal warring inside her. She'd recognize Reed Cross anywhere, even at a distance, after all these years of seeing him only in her dreams. She pushed to her feet, unable to make sense of seeing the forbidden lover she'd risked everything to have—and then cast aside—in Oak Falls, with the guys who'd once hated the sight of him. What the hell was he doing here? The last she'd heard, he'd moved to somewhere in the Midwest after high school.

"Reed…?" His name rolled off her tongue too easily, and she stumbled backward. Memories of being in his arms slammed into her, his gruff voice telling her he wanted her, he loved her. She didn't want to remember what they'd had, and as her sisters reached for her, trying to pull her back down to the grass, she took off running the way they'd come.

"Gracie, wait!" Sable shouted in a harsh whisper as she and Brindle ran after her.

Grace ran fast and hard, trying to outrun the memories, and knew it was a futile effort, which only pissed her off even more. She spun on her heels, anger and hurt burning through her. "You didn't think to *warn* me?"

"I knew you wouldn't come," Sable said.

"Damn right I wouldn't." She started down the hill again.

"Wait, Grace!" Brindle grabbed her hand and tried to slow her down, but Grace kept going, dragging her sister with her. "*What* is going on?" Brindle pleaded. "Why are you so mad?"

Grace slowed, realizing in that moment that Sable had kept her secret for the past decade. That was something she hadn't expected. Then again, she hadn't expected to have a visceral, titillating reaction to seeing Reed again, either. Hell, she hadn't expected to ever see him again. *Period.* He had been the quarterback at their rival high school. Small-town rivalries weren't taken lightly back then, and she and Reed had been careful never to be seen together for fear of Grace, a cheerleader, being ostracized by her friends. As graduation neared, they both knew Grace wanted to follow her dreams and write and produce plays in the Big Apple. They might have stayed together if Reed had told her that he would be willing to move away from the small town one day, but he'd been adamant about never leaving his family.

At least he had been until she'd ended their relationship to pursue her dreams.

Then he'd left town for good.

Or so she'd thought.

That still stung, even now, as his deep voice carried in the air, bringing with it memories of the secrets they'd shared and the stolen sensual nights they'd enjoyed.

"I thought you were over him," Sable accused.

"I am!" Grace huffed. She absently touched her lips, remembering the taste of spearmint and teenage lust mixed into one delicious kiss after another. Kisses that had never failed to leave her body humming with desire. *Great.* Now she couldn't *stop* thinking of him. This was bad. Very, very bad. She never should have allowed her sisters to drag her out and unearth memories she'd rather forget.

"Over *who*?" Brindle demanded as she traipsed through the grass beside Grace.

Grace ignored her question, unwilling to reveal her decade-old secret.

"Then what's the problem?" Sable snapped, also ignoring Brindle's question. She grabbed Grace's arm, stopping her in her tracks.

Unlike Grace, Sable had no qualms about one-night stands or taking what she wanted from a man. *Any* man, it seemed to Grace, as long as he struck her fancy for the moment. Even though Sable hid nothing when it came to her sexuality, she and Grace had a deep bond, and she was the only one of Grace's five sisters Grace had ever trusted with her sexual secrets. Sable *knew* how hard it had been for her to break up with Reed all those years ago. Grace's heart slammed against her chest as they stared each other down. She'd thought she was over Reed Cross. She *was* over him. She'd put him out of her mind. *Mostly.*

Sure, it was Reed's face she conjured up on lonely nights, and it was his lopsided grin and easy laugh she recalled to pull her through the toughest of productions. But that was *her* secret, not one she'd shared with Sable.

She should have stuck to weekend visits home, as she had for the past several years. Weekend visits were safe. *Fast.* Brindle never would have dragged her out if she'd be facing a long drive

Acknowledgments

I take an enormous amount of pride in bringing you Janie's story and owe heaps of gratitude to Mel Finefrock. *Touched by Love* was the most difficult book I've written to date. The initial inspiration for this story came from an accident Mel suffered. Mel and I met after she read HAVE NO SHAME, and we became instant sisters-by-heart. She was kind enough to let me grill her on everything related to not only being blind, but also cone-rod dystrophy, a degenerative eye disease. I have taken fictional liberties, so please note that any and all errors are my own and not a reflection of any of my resources. Thank you, Mel, for everything, and for reminding me that Janie needed to fall on her ass to get swept off her feet!

I also owe heaps of gratitude to Lieutenant Bruce J. Stark, Fairfax County Fire and Rescue, and paramedic and fire captain John Streeter, who patiently answered my never-ending questions. You guys are so fun to talk to and work with. Thank you for sharing your knowledge with me and please forgive my fictional liberties. I'd like to give a big shout-out to Tina Snook, a member of my fabulous Street Team, who was kind enough to refer John to me. Thanks, Tina!

My good friend Bonnie Trachtenberg always has my back when it comes to getting around New York City. Thanks for your thoughts on locations and help with navigating the Big Apple, Bon.

When I started on this journey, I expected the writing process to be challenging in many ways. I had to remove what most of us romance authors rely on—visual stimulus. Because of that, I had to find other ways to evoke the emotions that visual stimulus does so well, and I tried to do that without too much repetition. I hope I have done a solid job of it. It was also very important to me to convey the wonderful life Janie had, and her fierce independence, along with all that she faced and would continue to face, without inciting pity. Janie would definitely not be happy with pity. I hope I have done a commendable job at that, too. There are so many more things that were important to me with this story, like bringing a voice and love story to a heroine who was blind and hope my sighted readers could relate well enough and enjoy the story.

And then there was Boyd. He stole my heart from page one. I adore his big heart, his stubborn nature, and even his desire to push through life without slowing down. Hearts are the most interesting things, aren't they? I'm so happy he slowed down enough to make his whole. You'll be happy to know that Boyd's sister and brother, Haylie and Chet, as well as Janie's friends Kiki and Sin, will be appearing in future books, including the upcoming Montgomery series.

I'd like to give a special shout-out to all my fans and readers for sharing my books with your friends, chatting with me on social media, and sending me emails. You inspire me on a daily basis, and I can't imagine writing without our interactions. Some of you have even had characters named after you, which is always so much fun for me. Thank you for sharing yourselves with me.

If you don't yet follow me on Facebook, please do! We have

such fun chatting about our lovable heroes and sassy heroines, and I always try to keep fans abreast of what's going on in our fictional boyfriends' worlds.
facebook.com/MelissaFosterAuthor

Remember to sign up for my newsletter to keep up to date with new releases and special promotions and events and to receive an exclusive short story that was written just for my newsletter fans about Jack Remington and Savannah Braden.
www.MelissaFoster.com/Newsletter

For a family tree, publication schedules, series checklists, and more, please visit the special Reader Goodies page that I've set up for you!
www.MelissaFoster.com/Reader-Goodies

As always, heaps of gratitude to my amazing team of editors and proofreaders: Kristen Weber, Penina Lopez, Jenna Bagnini, Juliette Hill, Marlene Engel, Lynn Mullan, and Justinn Harrison.

~Meet Melissa~

www.MelissaFoster.com

Melissa Foster is a *New York Times* and *USA Today* bestselling and award-winning author. Her books have been recommended by *USA Today's* book blog, *Hagerstown* magazine, *The Patriot*, and several other print venues. Melissa has painted and donated several murals to the Hospital for Sick Children in Washington, DC.

Visit Melissa on her website or chat with her on social media. Melissa enjoys discussing her books with book clubs and reader groups and welcomes an invitation to your event. Melissa's books are available through most online retailers in paperback, digital, and audio formats.